## Praise for *The Lies I Tell*

"Julie Clark has done it again! In her latest riveting domestic thriller, Clark takes you straight into the collision course of two dynamic, complicated women—who will go to any length to fix their past and find their way to a different future. *The Lies I Tell* is a winner!"

—Laura Dave, #1 *New York Times* bestselling
author of *The Last Thing He Told Me*

"*The Lies I Tell* is a meticulously plotted mind bender, with a last page I can only describe as a triumph. Do not miss it."

—Jessica Knoll, *New York Times* bestselling
author of *Luckiest Girl Alive*

"Another terrific nail-biter by Julie Clark. *The Lies I Tell* weaves together the stories of two strong, complicated women - a brilliant con artist, and the journalist determined to unmask her. Fast-paced and beautifully plotted."

—Sarah Pekkanen, coauthor of *The Golden Couple*

"*The Lies I Tell* is a knockout. Smart, savvy, and so duplicitous with a propulsive storyline and two of the most beguiling female characters I've ever met. Julie Clark does it again!"

—Mary Kubica, *New York Times* bestselling
author of *Local Woman Missing*

"Clark knocks it out of the park with *The Lies I Tell*. A modern-day Robin Hood with a feminist twist. This is one of the best books you'll read this year. Unputdownable!"

—Liv Constantine, international bestselling
author of *The Last Mrs. Parrish*

"*The Lies I Tell* is a uniquely riveting cat-and-mouse game with two artfully nuanced female protagonists that is at once a razor-sharp, page-turning mystery and a brilliant, thought-provoking exploration of what it truly means to do good in the world."

—Kimberly McCreight, *New York Times* bestselling author of *A Good Marriage* and *Friends Like These*

## Praise for *The Last Flight*

"*The Last Flight* is thoroughly absorbing—not only because of its tantalizing plot and deft pacing, but also because of its unexpected poignancy and its satisfying, if bittersweet, resolution. The characters get under your skin."

—*New York Times Book Review*

"A premise that sounds highly thrilling takes its share of poignant turns too."

—*Entertainment Weekly*

"There are lots of twists and turns. It will keep you guessing. You won't be able to put it down."

—*People*

"The moral dilemmas that the multifaceted, realistic characters face in their quest for survival lend weight to this pulse-pounding tale of suspense. Clark is definitely a writer to watch."

—*Publishers Weekly*, Starred Review

"A tense and engaging woman-centric thriller."

—*Kirkus Reviews*, Starred Review

"Clark is an exceptional writer... Highly recommended for fans of thrillers, mysteries, and crime fiction."

—*Library Journal*, Starred Review

"A delicious thrill ride of a read...a suspenseful, timely tale about smart, strong women who support one another in their determination to not just survive, but also thrive, uncertainty and risk be damned."

—*BookPage*, Starred Review

"*The Last Flight* is a wild ride: One part *Strangers on a Train*, one part *Breaking Bad*, with more twists than an amusement park roller coaster! Julie Clark is a devilishly inventive storyteller."

—Janelle Brown, *New York Times* bestselling author of *Watch Me Disappear*

"*The Last Flight* is everything you want in a book: a gripping story of suspense; haunting, vulnerable characters; and a chilling and surprising ending that stays with you long after the last page."

—Aimee Molloy, *New York Times* bestselling author of *The Perfect Mother*

"I'm a sucker for suspense stories crafted around an airplane crash, and Julie Clark's *The Last Flight* lived up to the hype and then some. Clark starts with a bang, then keeps the pace at full throttle, deftly weaving two seemingly separate stories into one wild and entertaining ride. The perfect combination of beautiful prose and high suspense, and an ending that I guarantee will catch you off guard."

—Kimberly Belle, international bestselling author of *Dear Wife* and *The Marriage Lie*

"Strong women take center stage in this *Breaking Bad* meets *Sleeping with the Enemy* thriller. *The Last Flight* has it all—original characters, fast pacing, and clever twists, all in one explosive package!"

—Wendy Walker, nationally bestselling author of *The Night Before*

"*The Last Flight* sweeps you into a thrilling story of two desperate women who will do anything to escape their lives. Both poignant and addictive, you'll race through the pages to the novel's chilling end. A must read of the summer!"

—Kaira Rouda, international bestselling author of *Best Day Ever* and *The Favorite Daughter*

"Julie Clark's *The Last Flight* is a stunner: both a compelling, intricately woven tale of suspense and a thoughtful, nuanced portrayal of two very different women, each at a dangerous crossroads in her life. I couldn't turn the pages fast enough!"

—Kathleen Barber, author of *Truth Be Told* and *Follow Me*

"*The Last Flight* will propel you headfirst into the frantic lives of two women, both determined to escape their current reality. Julie Clark weaves their stories effortlessly, delivering a pitch-perfect suspense novel that absolutely lives up to its hype. Do yourself a favor and pick this one up!"

—Liz Fenton and Lisa Steinke, authors of *The Two Lila Bennetts*

"Get ready to hold on to the edge of your seat. This is a fantastic thriller about real people facing tremendous challenges. Exciting, touching, haunting, *The Last Flight* will stay with you long after you turn the final page. Julie Clark has written a bang of a novel."

—Rene Denfeld, international bestselling author of *The Child Finder* and *The Butterfly Girl*

# ALSO BY JULIE CLARK

*The Last Flight*

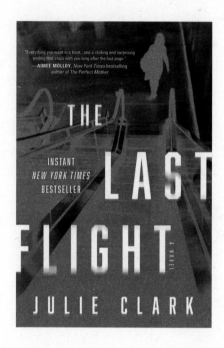

# The Lies I Tell

# THE LIES I TELL

*A Novel*

## JULIE CLARK

Published by Sourcebooks Landmark, an imprint of Sourcebooks
P.O. Box 4410, Naperville, Illinois 60567-4410
(630) 961-3900
sourcebooks.com

Library of Congress Cataloging-in-Publication Data

Names: Clark, Julie, author.
Title: The lies I tell / Julie Clark.
Description: Naperville, Illinois : Sourcebooks Landmark, [2022]
Identifiers: LCCN 2022002257 (print) | LCCN 2022002258 (ebook) |
    (hardcover) | (epub)
Subjects: LCGFT: Novels.
Classification: LCC PS3603.L36467 L54 2022  (print) | LCC PS3603.L36467
    (ebook) | DDC 813/.6--dc23
LC record available at https://lccn.loc.gov/2022002257
LC ebook record available at https://lccn.loc.gov/2022002258

Printed and bound in the United States of America.
WOZ 10 9 8 7 6 5 4 3 2 1

*For Pap-Pap, who told me I could.*
*For Mom, who showed me I could.*

# KAT

Present–June

She stands across the room from me, in a small cluster of donors, talking and laughing. A jazz quartet plays in a corner, the bouncing, slipping notes dancing around us, a low undertone of class and money. *Meg Williams.* I take a sip of wine, savoring the expensive vintage, the weight of the crystal glass, and I watch her. There are few photographs of her in existence—a grainy senior portrait from an old high school yearbook, and another image pulled from a 2009 YMCA staff directory—but I recognized her immediately. My first thought: *She's back.* Followed closely by my second: *Finally.*

As soon as I saw her, I tucked my press credentials into my purse and kept to the perimeter of the room. I've been to all of Ron Ashton's campaign events in the past three months, watching and waiting for Meg to make her appearance—called there by a Google Alert I set ten years ago. After a decade of silence, it pinged in April, with the creation of a new website. *Meg Williams, Real Estate Agent.* I always knew she'd return. That she'd done so under her real name told me she wasn't planning to hide.

And yet, when she entered, smiling as she handed over her coat at the door, my sense of equilibrium shifted, launching me into a moment I wasn't sure would ever arrive. You can prepare yourself for something, imagine it a hundred different ways, and still find yourself breathless when it actually happens.

I spoke to her once, ten years ago, though she wouldn't have known I was the one who'd answered the phone that day. It was a thirty-second call that changed the trajectory of my life, and to say I hold Meg partially responsible would be an understatement.

Scott, my fiancé, will surely argue that the cost—both financially and emotionally—will be too great. That we can't afford for me to step away from paying jobs to chase a story that might never happen. That immersing myself in that time, in those events, and in those people, might undo all the work I've put into healing. What he doesn't understand is that this is the story that will finally set me free—not just from the fluff pieces I'm paid pennies per word to write, but from the bigger demons that Meg sent me toward so long ago.

I attach myself to a larger circle of people, and I nod along with their conversation, all the while keeping an eye on her. Watching her mingle and circulate. Watching her watch him. I've spent hundreds of hours deconstructing her last few years in Los Angeles, and no matter which way I look at it, Ron Ashton stands at the center. While I don't know her heart—not yet at least—I do know she isn't the kind of woman to pass up an opportunity to balance the scales.

She tosses her head back and laughs at something someone says, and as Ron approaches her from behind, I marvel that I get to be here to see this moment. That I'm the only person in the room who knows what's about to happen.

Well, not the only person. She knows.

I turn slightly so I appear to be looking out a large window, at the sweeping views from downtown to the ocean, and I watch as introductions are made. Witty banter, some laughter. He bends down so he can hear her better, and I wonder how she does it. How she can trick people into believing she is who she says she is, into handing over their deepest desires, opening themselves up to her manipulation and trickery. Offering themselves willingly to her deception.

I watch as a business card is passed and pocketed before looking away, my mind latching on to her entry point. Which will now become mine.

# MEG

It starts how it always starts.

With me, quietly slipping alongside you—no sudden moves, no loud fanfare. As if I've always been there. Always belonged.

This time, it's a $10,000-a-plate fundraiser. After nearly ten years, I feel right at home among the extravagant trappings of the rich— the original artwork on the walls, the antiques that cost more than most people make in a year, and the hired help I pretend not to notice, quietly moving through homes like this one, perched high on a hill with all of Los Angeles glittering below us.

If you're one of my targets, know that I've chosen you carefully. It's likely you're in the midst of a major life change—a lost job, a divorce, the death of a close family member. Or a heated run for elected office that you're on the verge of losing. Emotional people take risks. They don't think clearly, and they're eager to believe whatever fantasy I feed them.

Social media has become my primary research tool, with its check-ins, geo-tags, and shameless self-promotion. And those quizzes some of your friends take and share? Dogs or cats? Number of brothers and sisters? Most of the questions seem harmless, but the next time you see one, take a closer look. Name five places you've lived or Four names you go by—both of which allow me to approach you. *John? It's me, Meg! From Boise, remember? I knew your sister.*

It's so easy, it's criminal.

I spend hundreds of hours on observation and research. Profiling the different people in your life, finding the one I can befriend, the one who will lead me to you. When I'm done, I know everything I possibly can about you, and most of the people around you. By the time you're saying *nice to meet you*, I've already known you for months.

Does this worry you? It should.

———————————

"Have you tried the crab cakes?" Veronica appears at my elbow, a cocktail napkin in hand. We've become close in the six months I've been back in Los Angeles, having met in a yoga class in Santa Monica, our mats positioned next to each other in the back. What started as a friendly greeting with a stranger at the beginning of class was a budding friendship by the end. It's amazing how easy Instagram stories make it to put yourself in the right place at the right time, next to the right person.

"I haven't," I tell her. "I heard they're serving filet mignon for dinner, so I'm saving myself for that."

There's a heat inside my chest, the slow burn of excitement I always get when I start a new job. I enjoy this part the most I think, the setting of the hook. Savoring the delicious anticipation of what's about to happen. No matter how many times I do this, I never tire of the thrill this moment always brings.

Veronica crumples her napkin. "You're missing out, Meg."

It's still a shock to hear people use my real name. I've gone by many over the years, mostly variations of my own—Margaret, Melody, Maggie. Backstories that range from college student to freelance photographer and most recently interior decorator and life coach to celebrities, all of them elaborate fabrications. Roles I played to near perfection. But tonight, I'm here as myself, someone I haven't been for a very long time.

I'd had no choice in the matter. My entry into this job required me to get my real estate license, and there was no getting around the social security number and fingerprinting. But that's okay, because this time I want my name to be known. For Ron Ashton—developer, local politician, and candidate for state senator—to know it was me who took everything from him. Not just his money, but the reputation he's spent years cultivating.

I see him across the room, his broad shoulders a few inches above everyone else's, his gray hair neatly combed, talking to Veronica's husband, his campaign manager.

Veronica follows my gaze and says, "David says the election is going to be close. That Ron can't afford a single misstep in these last few months."

"What's he like?" I ask. "Between us."

Veronica thinks for a moment and says, "Your typical politician. Closet womanizer. Fancies himself to be Reagan reincarnated. David says he's obsessed with him. 'He won't shut up about fucking Reagan.'" She gives a small laugh and shakes her head.

"But what do *you* think?"

She looks at me with an amused expression. "I think he's like every other politician out there—pathologically ambitious. But he pays David well, and the fringe benefits are great." Then she nudges my shoulder.

"I'm glad you could come. I think there'll be quite a few people here who will be good for you to meet. Possibly some new clients."

I take another sip of wine. My whole reason for being here tonight is to snag one client in particular. "I could use the business," I say. "It's been hard starting over."

"You'll get there. You've got years of experience in Michigan behind you. I mean, the way you handled our purchase of the Eightieth Street property. I still don't know how you got the sellers to drop their price like that."

I suppress a smile. Shortly after we'd met, Veronica had mentioned over post-yoga sushi that they were looking for an investment property, but the agent they were using wasn't finding them anything in their price range.

"Did she show you that property on Kelton?" I had riffed, knowing exactly what they were hoping to find. "The one-story traditional that was on the market for $1.7 million?"

Veronica's eyes had widened. "No, and that would have been perfect. I should ask her about it."

"It sold in multiples the day it hit the market, so it's too late," I said. "Your agent works out of Apex Realty in Brentwood, right? We're always getting internal email alerts announcing her deals—ten million, twenty million." I took a piece of sushi and held it between my chopsticks. "I can tell you, managing escrows at that price point can be consuming."

My story was that I'd moved home to Los Angeles after a successful career selling real estate in Ann Arbor. My new website links to another one in Michigan, featuring listings pilfered from Zillow and Redfin.

Veronica had set her chopsticks down and said, "She was great when we purchased the Malibu house, but maybe this price point is beneath her." I took a sip of my lemon water and let Veronica spin this out in her mind. Finally, she'd said, "I'd love to throw you the business. Maybe you can put your feelers out, see what you can find."

7

I'd found them something almost immediately. A single-story traditional in Westchester on a tree-lined street. Hardwood floors, a bay window, and a fully remodeled kitchen. When I handed Veronica the listing setup, outlining the house's features and price, she'd balked. "This is nearly $500,000 above our maximum budget."

In another lifetime, I'd once taken classes toward a digital design degree. I still have the certificate of completion tucked in a box, somewhere in storage. Granted, it's a forgery, but I'd learned enough to get by in the beginning, and even more in the years since.

"I think I can get them down significantly. Let's just take a look and see what we think. It's on lockbox, so we can go now if we want."

The listing I'd handed her was mostly accurate—bedrooms, square footage, HVAC; I'd only inflated the price. From there, I'd proceeded to "negotiate down" to just over $200,000 above the actual list price.

This only worked because apps like Zillow and Redfin don't exist for people like Veronica and David. In their tax bracket, no one does anything that can be outsourced. Accountants and bookkeepers who pay their bills. Maids and housekeepers to do their grocery shopping and cook their meals. And a trusted real estate agent to do the searches, coordinate with the listing agent to preview properties, set up private showings, and manage the transaction for them.

David and Veronica signed paperwork when I asked them to, wired the funds where I told them to, and if they ever noticed they'd never met the listing agent or sellers, it was a fleeting thought and then it was gone again.

In the end, David had proclaimed it the easiest transaction he'd ever done. Why wouldn't it be, when everyone got exactly what they wanted? The sellers got $200,000 over the real asking price. Veronica and David felt like they got the deal of the century, thanks to the one I'd fabricated. And I got a shiny—and ironclad—reputation within their circle of friends.

The main element of a good con is a strong thread of legitimacy. Of *almost* being who you say you are. Just like on a movie set, I'm real. My actions are real. It's only the background that's fake.

David joins us now, wrapping his arm around Veronica's waist. "Meg, you look gorgeous," he says. "I hope my wife hasn't been boring you with details of the remodel?"

I force a smile. "Not at all," I say. "We were actually just talking about Ron. I hear the election is going to be close?"

David nods. "Our internal polls show them nearly tied. Tonight's fundraising will go a long way toward our final push."

"You must be exhausted," I say. "Veronica tells me you're never home."

David winks at Veronica. "Sounds like the two of you have been getting into some good trouble in my absence. Thanks for keeping her busy."

"It's been my pleasure."

When the conversation turns toward their annual winter vacation to the Caribbean, I tune them out and watch the crowd of people mingle and mix, small clusters forming and then re-forming into new configurations as the quartet in the corner launches into a new rhythm. Los Angeles is so different from Pennsylvania, where I'd been last. I've had to make a steep adjustment, softening my approach, making sure all my edges match who I say I am. Here, people are naturally wary, looking for the angle, the hitch, the trick. It's expected that no one you meet is exactly who they say they are.

I work hard to embed myself into other people's circle of friends, so that no one notices that I don't have any of my own. I haven't had a true friend in years, not since before I left Los Angeles. I try not to think of Cal, or wonder where he is, whether he's still with Robert. I have very few regrets in my life, but how things ended with Cal is one of them.

A tendril of anxiety winds its way through me as I think through my timeline once more. Unlike my past jobs, this one has an expiration date—fourteen days before Election Day. Which leaves me twenty weeks. One hundred forty days. It sounds like a lot, but there will be very little room for mistakes or delays. There are specific benchmarks I'll need to meet along the way in order for everything to work. The first of which is an introduction to Ron, and that has to happen tonight.

As part of my background research, I've dipped into Ron's real estate portfolio, searching public records to get a feel for how much he's got in equity and how much he's leveraged. Thanks to his run for office, I've been able to look through his taxes as well. One thing that stood out was how many financial risks he's taken and how many of them played out to his advantage. I think back to how he tricked my mother, robbed us both of what was rightfully ours, and I wonder how many others Ron has used and then discarded on his path to state senator.

"Meg, help us out. Saint John or Saint Croix?" Veronica's eyes are pleading.

I know she's been angling for Saint Croix, so I say, "The last time I was in Saint John was about three years ago." I shake my head as if saddened by the memory. "As much as I love that island, I was really disappointed. You stay at the Villas, right?"

David nods. "They've always taken really good care of us."

I wrinkle my nose in distaste. "I think they've unionized. Definitely not the experience I was hoping for."

"Jesus," he says. "Saint Croix it is then."

Veronica gives a tiny clap and says, "I don't know why you never listen to me."

A voice from behind cuts into our conversation. "I hope you three are discussing my victory party." I turn and find myself face-to-face with Ron Ashton, the man who tore my life apart, sending my mother into a downward spiral she never recovered from and leaving me to live alone in a car for my final year of high school and beyond.

I smile. "The man of the hour," I say, holding out my hand. "Meg

Williams." A small part of me thrills, knowing that what I'm offering him is the absolute truth. I've spent years imagining this moment, wondering if he'd recognize me or my last name. See the shadow of my mother's features in mine. Wondering if I'd have to pivot and turn our meeting into a happy reunion, a coincidence of naivete and sexual innuendo. Enough to glide over the bump of our prior connection and convince him I knew nothing then, and know even less now. But his expression is blank, and I'm relieved to remain anonymous.

His grip is warm and firm, and I hold it just a fraction of a second longer than is typical, until I see a flash of interest behind his eyes. He will remember this moment. Come back to it again in his mind, and ask himself if he could have made a different decision. My job is to make sure the answer to that question is *no*.

"Meg has just moved to Los Angeles from Michigan," Veronica offers. "She was the one who got us that stellar deal on the Westchester property."

Ron's interest deepens, as I knew it would. According to Ron's social media accounts, he's been working with the same real estate agent for nearly fifteen years. A man who had two complaints for sexual harassment to the California Realtors board. It had been easy enough to become his third and final one, leaving Ron Ashton without representation for nearly four months now. For a developer, that's a problem.

"Real estate," he says. "What's your sales record like?"

"In Michigan, I was in the top one percent for the last ten years," I tell him. "But here in Los Angeles? It's slow going." It's always good to infuse a shade of humility. People appreciate knowing they're better than you.

"Do you have a card?" he asks. "I might give you a call."

I pull one out of my clutch and hand it to him. "Check out my website. Even though I'm newly arrived in town, I'm not new to the business, and I know Los Angeles well. I'd be happy to chat if you're interested." Then I turn to Veronica and say, "In Saint Croix, you absolutely need to eat at The Riverhead."

As Veronica begins to outline their itinerary, I feel it, a tingle on the back of my neck that I learned long ago never to ignore. I take a small step backward and look down to my left, as if I'm trying to make sure I don't misstep. When I look up, I sweep my gaze across the room searching for someone who might be watching me, but all I see is a room full of people talking and laughing, drinking and celebrating a man they're hoping to send to Sacramento.

I smile and nod at Veronica, but I'm no longer listening. I'm running through my arrival, the people I spoke to—the valet, the campaign staff covering the front entry, various donors. Harmless small talk necessary for a new-to-town real estate agent trying to build her client base. All of them are accounted for, all of them are occupied. Perhaps it's just the familiarity of being back in Los Angeles. The air here is unique, a blend of grass and car exhaust, and sometimes, if you're close enough, the smell of salt on an ocean breeze. I'm far away from where I grew up, but beneath all the layers—all the identities I've held, the years that have passed—I'm still the person I was when I left. A woman on the run, flush with the power of knowing I could become anyone. Do anything. All I had to do was tell a man what he wanted to hear.

# TEN YEARS AGO

Venice, California

# MEG

I was born to be a grifter, though I didn't see it until after I'd been one for some time. I'd just thought of what I did as *getting by*—a date, a free meal, a doggie bag with the remains of my food and sometimes his too. I tried not to think what my mother would say—almost four years gone—if she knew this was where I'd landed. Evaluating men on whether they might be the type to use fabric softener on their bedsheets, or keep toiletries—shampoo, soap, toothpaste—under the bathroom sink where I could swipe them. But in October 2009, I had to accept that living this way wasn't working anymore.

Rain battered the windows of the internet café where I sat, nursing a mug of hot chocolate—more filling than coffee—and scrolled through my dating profile on Circle of Love. I glanced toward the street where my mother's old minivan was parked and tried to calculate how much time I had left on my meter. My feet ached from a long day standing behind the counter at the Y, where I checked people in for their daily workout, handed them a towel, and pretended I wasn't dying inside.

It was a job I couldn't afford to lose. It was where I showered every day, where I kept my clothes, and where I could toss in a load of laundry alongside the towels I was tasked with washing. It paid for gas, which kept the car where I slept in operation. I made just enough money every week to cover my personal expenses plus the interest payment on my mother's funeral costs, several thousand dollars of debt she never intended for me to carry. There was no room for error. I couldn't afford to get a parking ticket, or a cavity, or even a cold sore. I was one UTI away from the homeless shelter.

But last night had scared me. I'd parked on a quiet, tree-lined street in Mar Vista, one of many I rotated through over the course of a month. It was one of my favorites—not a lot of foot traffic and few streetlights.

I'd burrowed into my nest of blankets, tucked behind tinted glass, the sunroof open just a crack to keep my windows from steaming up. Someone in the neighborhood was listening to Sting's "Fields of Gold," which my mother had loved. The music floated over me as I fell asleep, my muscles releasing, my mind easing into darkness.

I'd been yanked awake by the sound of someone trying to pop the lock on the passenger side door. Through the window I could see a huge, shadowy figure in dark clothing, a hood over his head, just a thin piece of glass separating the two of us. I'd acted on instinct, leaping from the backseat, grabbing my keys, and leaning on the horn as I jammed them into the ignition, peeling away from the curb and nearly hitting another parked car in my panic to get away.

It took an hour of driving aimlessly before my hands stopped shaking, before my heart stopped pounding, and I shuddered to think what would have happened if he'd gotten in. I kept imagining scenarios, each one more horrific than the last. A hand over my mouth. Being driven to a deserted location. Being dragged into a ditch.

My eyes were gritty from lack of sleep as I reread my dating profile, where only my name and age were true. Meg Williams, age 21. Profession:

Marketing. Likes: live music, dining out, travel. I love to laugh and am always looking for adventure! Age range: 18–35. Looking for fun, not marriage. That last part was the line that kept me fed. I managed to get at least three dates a week, and I pushed hard for dinner and not coffee. When you live in a car, the last thing you need is more liquid. I said yes to every invitation, and I became a master of flirty online banter, giving the illusion that good things might happen after a sit-down dinner that included cloth napkins, appetizers, and a dessert menu.

A minimum of three dates a week saved me at least $50, money I'd hoped would grow until I had enough to afford a place to live. But something always set me back. Car registration. Rising gas prices. A parking ticket.

And so, on that rainy October afternoon, I finally gave up and admitted to myself I needed more than just a one-night reprieve every few days. I needed a safe place to live, and someone willing to give it to me. I wouldn't find that from the men on my screen, all of whom were in their twenties and thirties. They were interested in casual dates. Hookups with no strings. Not an instant, live-in girlfriend.

I was going to have to go older.

I clicked over to my settings and slid the age range from thirty-five to forty. Would that be old enough? Forty-year-old women were over the hill, but men had longer shelf life.

"Fuck it," I muttered under my breath and slid it up to fifty-five.

I thought back to my mother, a beautiful woman who had insisted on doing everything for herself, making my childhood ten times harder than it needed to be. She never accepted help when it was offered, and because there always seemed to be some poor fool in love with her, it was offered frequently. She said no when one of them wanted to buy me new shoes or to pay for a week at summer camp. She declined offers of a place to live when we needed one. Car repairs. An occasional meal at a nice restaurant or a day at Disneyland. It wasn't like I wanted her to sell herself. Just agree every now and then to things that would have made our lives a little better.

But she believed women should stand on their own. She wanted to find a true partner, not a handout. She thought she'd found that partnership with Ron Ashton, never seeing the rotten core of him until it was too late.

A new page began to load profiles of men two or three times my age, many of them completely gray, and my breath hitched as I imagined sitting across a table from one of them, faking an attraction I was never going to feel.

I clicked through profiles, one by one. Too old. Too creepy. Usually, when I hit on a potential date, I'd try to find something we had in common, and if I couldn't, I'd make it up. I love Steely Dan! A quick Google search would bring up their concert schedule. I even went to Vegas to catch their show last August. Epic! At the end of the night, if the guy seemed nice enough, it didn't matter what the truth was.

But the men on my screen now were from another generation altogether. Any personal connection with them would likely involve Barry Manilow and a deep affection for Tom Brokaw.

I took a sip from my hot chocolate, flipped to the next profile, and nearly choked when I saw the face on the screen. "Oh my god."

Cory Dempsey. Mr. Dempsey, math teacher at my former high school. His blue eyes were just as vibrant on the screen as I remembered them, with that same unruly brown hair curling around his ears. The girls loved him, and the boys wanted to be him. His profile listed his age as forty-eight, but he'd always seemed younger—more like the students than the other teachers. Engaging and energetic, always voted the most popular teacher by the senior class, including mine.

But great teaching wasn't why people whispered about him. In the girls' bathroom, in the corners of the cafeteria, on the bleachers at the football game.

*Mr. Dempsey is so hot.*

*After math class, Mr. Dempsey was totally flirting with me. I bet I could have made a move.*

*Ohmygod, please. You're not special, he flirts with everyone.*

I read through his profile again. Cory Dempsey. Profession: High School Principal.

Status: Single, never been married.

Likes: Basketball, fantasy football, surfing, inspiring the youth of today to become their very best selves.

Of course, Kristen came to mind immediately. We weren't exactly friends—she was popular, and I was just the nobody who sat next to her in English class. But she'd always included me in group projects, and made sure to say hi in the hallways while everyone else's eyes slid right over me, as if I were invisible.

To them, I'd been *The Bag Lady* because of the reusable grocery bag I used to carry my books, never able to justify the cost of a backpack. But Kristen had always defended me. "Don't be an asshole," she said once to Robbie Maxon. "Last week I saw you pick your nose in chem lab."

She'd pulled the conversation away from me, directed it so masterfully that no one noticed me slip away, my heavy grocery bag cutting into my shoulder, grateful for her kindness.

"Why are you so nice to me?" I'd asked her once. We'd been alone in the bathroom, shoulder to shoulder at the sinks, me washing my hands while she applied lip gloss. Her eyes met mine in the mirror and she said, "It's the girl code. We have to look out for each other because no one else will."

And then, midyear, Kristen had simply vanished. One day she was in the seat next to mine, cracking jokes with her best friend, Laura Lazar, and the next, she was gone. At first, I figured she was just sick. But after a couple weeks it became clear she wasn't coming back. No one seemed to know where she'd gone, or why.

Of course, people had their theories.

*She went to boarding school in Switzerland.*

*She got a spot at Ms. Porter's.*

*Her grandma was sick, so the family moved to Florida.*

*She got pregnant and went to one of those homes for unwed girls.*

Laura Lazar had refused to talk about it, claiming she didn't know. But I could tell she was lying. Laura knew why Kristen had left, and I thought I did too.

By high school, I'd mastered the art of blending in. Of finding corners where people wouldn't notice the frayed edges of my thrift store clothes, or the fact that my hair was usually one day past needing a wash. And I saw things other people didn't.

Like Kristen, slipping out of Mr. Dempsey's classroom at lunchtime, cheeks flushed and hair slightly mussed, tugging at the hem of her skirt. Or the afternoon I saw her glance over her shoulder before sliding into the passenger seat of his car.

Nothing obvious, but enough to make me notice how subdued she'd become. How much harder her friends had to work to get her to join in their conversations.

Whatever might have happened between Mr. Dempsey and Kristen, it was none of my business. And after a while, I assumed what everyone else had—that Kristen had moved away and that was the end of it.

———————

I wasn't that invisible girl, hiding in corners, anymore. In the three years since high school, I'd learned how to mold myself into a woman who knew how to enter a room in an outfit designed to draw attention. How to order wine at an expensive restaurant and what the tiny fork was for. I knew how to apply makeup with a light touch and how to keep lipstick off my teeth. If I were to pass Mr. Dempsey on the street, I was the kind of woman he'd notice, but never recognize.

Did Mr. Dempsey have something to do with Kristen's abrupt departure? Possibly. Could I exploit that? Definitely.

I imagined sending him a message. Hey there, Mr. Dempsey! My name is Meg Williams, Wolverine class of 2006! Rawr!

The gamer next to me pounded away on his mouse, earning himself a dirty look from the guy working the counter. I looked back at my screen, imagining a first date with Mr. Dempsey and the typical questions people always asked—where I grew up, my family, what I was doing with my life. I was raised by my single mother, until she'd died of cancer due to a lack of access to quality medical care. I'm currently living in my car, just south of the poverty line. I love Bruce Springsteen and the Dodgers.

I couldn't simply message him and hope for the best. If he said no, that would be the end of it. I first needed to learn everything I could about him—what he believed in. What repulsed him. What he cared about above all else, so that I could mirror that back to him.

Outside, the rain slashed against the windows, and I thought about the sound it would make on the top of the car that night as I tried to sleep, my nerves still a tangle. Then I imagined what it would be like to have a home with locks on the doors and windows. To listen to the rain on the roof of a house instead of a car. To have a television to watch and another human to talk to.

I logged out, navigating back to the Circle of Love home page, and clicked on the *New Account* button.

―――――――

The first fake profile I created—Deirdre, age forty-three, perhaps a little new age, definitely in denial about growing older—didn't work. Her message—You seem like the kind of guy I'd like to get to know better— didn't even get a response, so two days later, I was back at the internet café to try again.

Sandy. Age 32. Status: Never been married. Occupation: Server. Likes: sunrise in the mountains, vodka tonics at 5:00 p.m., road trips to Mammoth. Sandy's message to Mr. Dempsey: You're hot. Sandy wanted sex.

Within minutes, the icon beneath Sandy's message flipped from Sent to Read. I leaned forward, three dots showing that Mr. Dempsey was responding.

One minute. Two minutes. I imagined what he might be writing— something flirty, complimentary perhaps. It didn't matter that I looked nothing like Sandy. I only needed her for a short while.

Finally, his message appeared. Thanks, but I'm looking for something a little more committed. I wish you luck!

I stared at the screen, parsing his words, my mind turning over my next move. I thought back again to Kristen, who'd only been seventeen. If I'd made Sandy a decade younger, would his answer have been different?

Another image search, another photo. A blond, caught midlaugh, the sun setting behind her. I was like Goldilocks, if Goldilocks were a twenty-one-year-old homeless woman with a passion for indoor plumbing and a willingness to sleep with a man to get it.

Amelia. Age: 21. Status: Never been married. Occupation: Student (majoring in early education), currently on hiatus and hoping to get back on track. Likes: Surfing. Romance. Looking for a serious relationship.

My message to Mr. Dempsey read, Maybe we could catch some waves? I hit Send and logged off, knowing this would have to be my last attempt on Mr. Dempsey for a while. A small part of me wondered what kind of high school principal had a dating profile where any of his students might see it.

The answer came almost immediately. *One who didn't care. Who might even welcome it.*

---

That night I parked in a well-lit parking lot to sleep, though I probably didn't clock more than three or four hours total. Every sound—a car door slamming, a siren, footsteps—jerked me awake, and it was a relief to pull into the gym parking lot early the next morning. I always worked the opening shift, turning on the lights, pulling the towels out of the dryer and folding them. It got me off the street before anyone could call in a complaint about someone sleeping in their car. Aside from the time for a shower and throwing in a load of laundry, I also loved the quiet. No obnoxious membership sales staff, no kids club chaos or the yoga-mommy brigade with their enormous jogging strollers and BPA-free water bottles. Just the early morning gym rats, who were still half asleep when they swiped their cards through the reader and grabbed one of my towels.

I stared at the plate glass windows in front of me, the dark street reflecting my image back. My wet hair was pulled into a neat ponytail. The white polo shirt with the Y logo on the front was bright, though my features were blurry around the edges, which was how I felt most of the time. As if I were slowly seeping into the space around me, and pretty soon the only things left would be my car keys and a pile of unfolded towels.

I turned on the computer and logged on to the dating website, not expecting anything. But in addition to the Read icon, there was a response.

Where do you like to surf?

I looked over my shoulder, as if someone might come up behind me and see what I was doing. Beyond the cluster of dark offices came the faint thrum of the treadmills, the clang of weights, but all was silent up front. A pulse of energy zipped through me.

I did a quick Google search for *best surfing spots in Los Angeles* and tried to think about the kind of person Amelia might be. What she might care about and who she might dream of becoming. Then I started to flesh out her backstory. Amelia Morgan, born and raised in Encino. Maybe she did a few semesters at Cal State Northridge, before having to drop out. The kind of person Mr. Dempsey might think he could help.

The curser blinked inside the blank message space, and I felt the weight of it, the importance of drafting the perfect response. Zuma, I typed back. A beach near the northern edge of LA County would make the most sense for a girl who grew up in the valley. It was also unlikely that Mr. Dempsey—Cory—would be a regular there. Best waves in Malibu! I added.

I hit Send and felt a rush of nerves. I was no stranger to lost opportunity. One moment, you might be on the verge of an entire life, the next you're feeding quarters into a do-it-yourself car wash once a week so that your minivan wouldn't look like someone was living in it.

I looked at his profile picture again. A slightly crooked tooth offered a bit of character to a megawatt smile. Athletic shoulders honed from years of surfing. So much better than any of my other options.

---

"Hey, kiddo," my best friend, Cal, said when he arrived at 8:30. "Robert and I went to go see *Ricochet* last night and, oh my god, you have to see it. Maybe we could catch a matinee this weekend."

I glanced over my shoulder, where Johnny, our manager, sat, lips pursed like a Sunday school teacher, tapping away on his computer.

"I'm scheduled all weekend," I told him.

"Too bad. Want to do lunch today?"

"That'll work."

Cal rapped the counter with his knuckles and said, "Stay gold, Ponyboy."

At least a decade older than I was—*a person of a certain era never reveals their true age*—Cal was the only one who knew I lived in my car.

He found small ways to help, without making me feel self-conscious about it. When he and his boyfriend, Robert, traveled, they always asked me to house-sit, even though they had no plants to water or pets to feed. He also took me out to lunch at least once a week, supposedly to thank me for pushing new members into signing up for training sessions with him. He always ordered too much, then gave me the leftovers. Cal started at the Y like I did, working the front desk while he went to school at night to get his trainer certification. He was always on me to take classes. *Community college was invented for people like us.* I supposed I could, I just wouldn't know what to take. How did a person better themselves if the image of their future was a blank page? What would I even take? Accounting? Beauty classes? Welding?

"Meg," Johnny called from his office. "Remember to fold the towels in thirds first, then in half."

----

All morning, I kept the Circle of Love website pulled up on the computer in front of me, hidden behind a few other windows. Around eleven, I toggled back to it and reread Cory's latest message. You are the best kind of distraction, but I almost missed a parent meeting.

Amelia and Cory had been going back and forth all morning, starting out with a flirty one from him. I can't believe I've been surfing LA beaches forever and never run into you. But in the hours since that first message, he'd also revealed a lot about himself, and I was gathering the information, trying to draw out more.

I started with a simple question. What matters the most to you?

His response was predictably sappy. My family. Above personal success or wealth, above health, everything.

His greatest regret was about not making amends with his grandfather before he died. It was painful, but I learned a lot from it. Who are we if we're not constantly learning and growing? I think it's the difficult lessons that teach us the most.

When I asked about his job, he wrote, Engaging young minds is both a thrill and a privilege.

I also learned smaller details, things that would cement a connection. He was allergic to cats. He didn't understand hockey but pretended to. He despised anything with ginger in it and loved black coffee. He called himself a conscious optimist.

Don't feel bad, I had to Google it too.

Amelia shared as well, telling Cory how she dropped out of college her sophomore year to help her parents care for her younger brother who got sick with leukemia (*he was fine now but the path back to college was hard!*). How she lost her serving job because she reported a coworker who was stealing food, not realizing the coworker was her manager's girlfriend.

It astonished me how easily the stories came. They arrived, fully formed, and all I had to do was retell them. I can't believe how effortless it is to talk to you, I typed now. Most guys on here ask three superficial questions and then go straight for the hookup.

I liked being Amelia. To be able to shed my problems and become a different person was liberating. Amelia had options where I had none, and with a few keystrokes, she could have even more. Today she might be out of work, but tomorrow she could find an even better job, simply because I said so.

"What are you doing?" Johnny's voice, just over my shoulder, made me jump. I toggled away from the dating site, but he'd already seen it. "No personal business on the computer. If I catch you again, I'll have to write you up."

"I'm sorry," I said. "It won't happen again." I hated myself for groveling, but I needed this job.

I closed the tab and resumed staring out the window, and when

Johnny dumped a new batch of freshly laundered towels on the counter in front of me, I offered him a bright smile and started folding.

———————

After work, I drove to the public library in Santa Monica, not wanting to splurge on another session at an internet café. If I wanted to eat this weekend, I needed to set up at least one date. I entered the large space with its oversize book return bins and the circulation desk that spanned an entire wall, and let my memory travel backward. Libraries had always been my refuge. My mother used to take me every weekend, and we'd spend hours reading in a corner, insulated from the outside world. She'd fill her biggest purse with snacks—granola bars, small bags of chips and cookies—and we'd settle in as soon as the library opened, staking out the best chairs on the second floor that overlooked the street below. We'd take turns looking for books, surreptitiously eating and reading the day away, only leaving when the lights flashed and the closing announcement was made.

I approached the librarian working the information desk and showed her my library card. She pointed to the bank of computers and said, "Take your pick."

There were only two other people online—an older man who may or may not have been homeless, and a teenager who should have been in school. I picked a machine near the end of the row and logged in to Amelia's account.

There were no new messages from Cory, and I was surprised by the flash of disappointment that passed through me. How quickly I'd become addicted to the thrill of a new message from him.

Then I logged in to my account. There were three guys I was messaging with, each of them a slightly different version of the same person. Jason, the venture capitalist who seemed to start every sentence with the word *I*. Sean, a mortgage broker in Manhattan Beach. And Dylan, the party promoter.

Up until now, my criteria had been pretty simple: they had to have a job, they had to ask me at least three questions about myself, and they couldn't look like the Unabomber. I always made sure I met them in a public place, and I never went home with anyone who felt unsafe. But sometimes, I couldn't tell until it was too late. Fingers running through my hair that tugged too hard. Hands that gripped too tight. Bruises in places easily hidden. It didn't happen often, but when it did, I'd learned how to compartmentalize. To turn off my thoughts and go somewhere else in my mind until it was over.

I stared at Jason's last message, an invitation to a restaurant that just opened in Venice, imagining an interminable evening stroking his ego, before closing it without responding.

Then I toggled over to the community college website, just so I could tell Cal that I looked. *Accounting. Art History. Business Administration.* The words began to blur until my eyes snagged on Digital Art Certificate. This six-month course will take you through the basics of HTML code, web design, and Adobe Photoshop. Students will gain skills valuable to any existing business, or allow them to work for themselves as a freelancer. I studied the sample images that went alongside the Photoshop course. A picture of a family portrait taken at a park with several people in the background. The second image was the same photo, this time with everyone behind them edited out, as if no one had ever been there.

I clicked on the tuition button and blew out hard. Including registration fees, it would be nearly $200 to complete the coursework and get the certificate. More, if the class had any required materials to buy. And then there was the equipment I'd need once I'd finished—a computer. Software. For someone who made less than $150 a week after taxes—most of it already spent the moment it hit my account—$200 might as well have been $2 million. I closed the window, feeling the pinch of regret I always felt whenever a door closed.

I logged out and gave the librarian a wave. I had about four more hours of daylight to find a place to park for the night.

---

Instead, I made a detour through Brentwood, the streets as familiar to me as an old friend. The Brentwood Country Mart where my mom used to buy me ice cream and, if I was lucky, a book from the bookstore there. The corner where I fell off my bike and skinned my knee. The large stump of a tree that came down in a storm when I was seven, cutting off traffic on San Vicente for an entire day.

I turned left onto Canyon Drive and navigated as if on autopilot. The houses there were on large lots, set far back from the street, some behind tall gates you could barely see through. I wound my way slowly, as if pulled by some magnetic force, back to the place where it all started.

I parked just south of the house, a spot that gave me the best vantage point from which to study it. To follow the familiar contours of the dark wood and white stucco. The round tower that housed the circular staircase that led to a tiny third-floor study. The large windows of the living room, where my mother said her grandfather would spend his days, smoking a pipe and worrying about his son—her father—who spent more time in rehab than out of it.

"The front door is made of oak, milled from a forest in Virginia," I recited into the silent car. "A tree that probably greeted the colonists of Jamestown before arriving here to keep us safe." The start of my mother's monologue, the one she'd use to help me sleep at night. Like a bedtime story, she'd walk us through the home we both yearned to return to. Always, I'd picture it behind my eyes. The plastered walls that still held the tray marks of the artisans who smoothed them. The wide, wooden beams that spanned the width of the ceiling in the great room. The fourth stair that always creaked if you stepped on it near the banister. The closet with the trapdoor that led to the attic, and the wall that measured not only my mother's height, but a few months of my own heights as well.

My mother, Rosie, had been born right before her parents had graduated high school. Her mother had disappeared early on, and her father had descended into drugs and alcohol use, leaving Rosie in the care of her grandparents—my great-grandparents—whom we both called Nana and Pop, the only stable influences she ever had.

It was Nana and Pop who went to her school open houses. Who taught her how to ride a bike. Who waited up for her when she went on dates in high school, raising her as if she were their own.

My mother fell in love only twice in her life. The first time was with a college hockey player who'd gone to Europe and never returned. That relationship had given her me and the set of rules that dictated my entire childhood:

*Convenience and comfort aren't worth settling for. We can earn what we need; we don't need a man to hand it to us.*

*If money is tight, we work harder.*

*Two women working together are a force to be reckoned with.*

She managed to make ends meet by working multiple jobs, renting studio apartments when we could afford the security deposit, and staying with Nana and Pop when we couldn't. I marked the periods of time we spent with them as some of the happiest I'd ever known. Nana taught me how to bake chocolate chip cookies from scratch. She showed me how to start a vegetable garden. Pop taught me how to play cribbage and poker.

The second—and last—time my mother fell in love was a few years after Nana and Pop were gone. His name was Ron Ashton.

Across the street, automatic gates swung open, and a woman exited on foot. A maid, carrying a plastic bag of rags and cleaning supplies. She eyed me suspiciously, and I could see her wondering whether she should go back and tell her employers about the woman sitting in front of the neighbor's house, staring at it. I gave her a smile and lifted my cell phone to my ear, as if I'd pulled over to take a call, then turned my attention back to the house. The one that should have stayed in our family. The one that Ron Ashton stole from us.

———————

Cory's message arrived the following morning shortly after eight. I want to meet you. How about today at four? Rocketman Coffee on Main Street?

The dryers tumbled behind me, my fingers hesitating over the keyboard. Like a song I was just beginning to learn, I let my instincts guide me. And they were telling me to take a breath. To not give him a response within seconds. Sometimes, doing nothing was the most powerful move.

I waited until almost noon. Today at four works for me! I'm looking forward to it. A flash of excitement passed through me, knowing that I'd have the advantage firmly in my pocket from the moment I entered the coffee shop.

When my shift was over, I took a shower and put on a pair of jeans that hugged my curves in all the right places. I slipped on a form-fitting tank top that lowered into a V-neck and layered a soft wrap sweater on top of it. Amelia was a surfer and a student who had fallen on hard times. I wanted to make sure I could slide into the spot she left when she didn't show up.

———————

I parked a few blocks away from Rocketman Coffee and waited in my car, giving Cory time to get there and get settled. Pulling my phone from my purse, I flipped it open and dialed Cal.

He answered on the second ring. "Hey there."

"Can you do me a favor?"

"Always," he said.

"In about a half hour, can you call my cell? I don't need you to say anything or to stay on the line. I just need the phone to ring."

He laughed. "Got a date you're thinking of ditching?"

I watched a woman maneuver a fancy stroller down the front steps of her apartment, her toddler strapped in safely. "Something like that," I told him. "Can you do it?"

"Sure. I'll set an alarm so I don't forget."

"Thanks."

I disconnected the call and locked the car, my heart pounding. If this didn't work, I'd be back at the internet café, sorting through a list of men old enough to be my father. I'd be back in the minivan, driving through dark neighborhoods looking for a safe place to park at night. I took a jittery breath and let it out slowly.

I entered the coffee shop and spotted him at a back table, a large mug in front of him, already knowing what was in it. *Black coffee.*

I felt a surge of power, as if I was the director of a play, calling the shots, controlling the pace. I was a stranger to him, and yet I knew what he liked and didn't like. I knew what he wanted and what he cared about.

There was a small possibility he'd remember my face from the halls of Northside High. If he did, I planned to lean into it. Confess a crush. *So embarrassing!*

I ordered my own cup of black coffee and carried it toward him, plastering a hopeful expression on my face as I neared his table.

"Roger?" I said, and held my breath, waiting for a flash of recognition in his eyes.

But there was none. "Sorry, no," he said with a kind smile. Up close, the golden hazel of his eyes was framed by thick eyelashes, a faint tan line of a wetsuit around his neck.

I sank into a seat at the table next to him. "That's embarrassing. Blind date," I explained.

He smiled. "Same."

"It never gets any easier, does it?"

He offered a noncommittal shrug and I let it sit, sipping my coffee, biding my time.

After about twenty minutes, he began checking his phone more frequently, looking for a missed call or text. I mirrored him, glancing between the door and my own phone on the table in front of me. At one point, I offered him an awkward smile, which he returned. I grew tense, wondering if he'd leave before Cal's call, and tried to think of a way to keep him there. I was about to turn toward him with a comment about the weather when my phone rang.

"Hello?" I said.

"Here's the call I promised you. I've got to run, but fill me in tomorrow."

Cal disconnected, but I kept talking. "Oh. I see." I closed my eyes, as if I were fighting off a crushing disappointment, letting my shoulders drop. "I understand. No really, it's fine." I let my voice wobble on the word *fine*, and out of the corner of my eye, I could tell Cory was listening. "Well, congratulations, I guess." Another pause. "Yeah, thanks."

I disconnected the call and stared down at my cold coffee, as if I didn't know what to do next. Finally, I looked up, embarrassed and hurt. "He got back together with his girlfriend," I said.

Cory gestured toward my phone. "At least you got the courtesy of a call."

"Meeting someone in Los Angeles is impossible," I said, echoing a thread from one of Cory's messages to Amelia yesterday.

"Tell me about it. It's like trying to find a winning lottery ticket."

"Playing the lottery is fun," I said. "Dating…not so much."

Cory laughed. "Let me buy you another coffee. Maybe we can salvage the day after all."

Good fortune and second chances. Everyone wants to believe those are real.

---

We walked down Main Street, our shoulders brushing, as Cory told me about his job as a high school principal. "The kids have an energy that you can't find in any other field," he said. "It's intoxicating. Their passion. Their potential."

I thought back to how he spoke of his job to Amelia. "What a privilege to be able to have such a positive influence on young lives," I said, wondering if he would recognize his own words being spoken back to him. Intentionally spoon-fed in small bites, building a connection he'd feel rather than see.

He looked at me, his expression fiery. "Exactly."

I was astonished at how easy it was. It was as if he wrote the script and all I had to do was read my lines. I toyed with the lid of my coffee cup as we waited for the light to turn green. When it did, I said, "I used to want to be a teacher. Elementary school."

We stepped off the curb, making our way toward the boardwalk and the beach beyond. "What happened?" he asked.

I shrugged. The best lies were the ones planted in truth. "My senior year of high school, my mother got sick. I didn't have time to apply to colleges. I was just trying to stay afloat with my classes and taking care of her."

We passed a trash can, where we both tossed our empty cups. At the edge of the bike path, we waited for a stream of cyclists to pass. Cory took my hand, and we jogged across and settled on a bench overlooking the vast expanse of sand that led down to the water. "Did she get better?"

"No." I let the word hang there, the weight of it heavy in the air. "It was an incredibly hard chapter in my life. But it was also a gift."

Cory looked intrigued. "In what way?"

I pretended to think about my answer, but the words were ready, a shimmering facsimile of what he told Amelia yesterday. "I learned that the worst can happen and I'll still be okay. Life is filled with lessons. We can either choose to suffer from them, or learn from them."

I could tell I hit my mark by the way he leaned forward, the way his eyes flashed with a mixture of surprise and admiration. "Not many people your age would have that kind of wisdom," he said.

I shrugged, as if his opinion was one I'd heard before. "Optimism is a choice."

"That's what I always say!" His delight was palpable. "I didn't learn that until I was much older though."

I gave him a skeptical look. "You're not that old."

He grimaced. "Forty-eight."

I bumped my shoulder against his. "I like older men."

He chuckled. "Good to know." We were quiet for a moment. "Where did you grow up?" he asked.

"Grass Valley. A tiny town in the Sierras," I told him. "You've probably never heard of it. Population twelve thousand. Everyone knows everyone else. After my mother died, I couldn't get out of there fast enough." I studied his face, looking for any trace of skepticism, but it was open and trusting. *He believes me.*

"What brought you to Los Angeles?"

"A boyfriend," I admitted. "Oldest story in the book. But I'm happy here. I'm at the city college in Santa Monica, doing a digital design degree. I'm living in student housing right now, but as soon as I'm done, I hope to get a place and start my own design business."

He looked into my eyes and asked, "Do you believe in fate?"

I believed in making your own opportunities. I believed in taking what you wanted from life, and if you had to hurt someone in the process, it had better be for a good reason, because I also believed in karma. "I do today," I said.

He leaned forward and kissed me. His lips were soft against mine, and I closed my eyes to the laugh lines around his eyes, the gray peppering his hairline.

"When can I see you again?" he whispered.

A woman on Rollerblades whizzed past us on the bike path, the beat from her headphones a whisper in the air around us. I looked toward the ocean, where the sun was sinking below the horizon. Stepping into this role felt as easy as sliding on an old coat, contouring my body as if I'd been wearing it for years. "How about Thursday?"

# KAT

I'd been working at the *LA Times* when the story of Cory Dempsey had broken. I was lucky to have the job. My mother had cashed in a favor with a friend of hers, landing me as a junior reporter under the famed investigative journalist Frank Durham. It was my first big story, and I was eager to prove myself, accompanying him as he made the rounds to press conferences, to the police station, and to meet with sources close to the investigation. I was even present when Frank met with Cory's family, a rare interview granted with the very strictest of parameters.

That was where I'd first heard Meg Williams's name. Not in the course of the interview itself—two parents working hard to stay on the right side of public perception, deflecting blame away from themselves for what their son had done to those girls.

But in the corner, where I sat taking my own notes, I heard different things from the cousins who'd driven Mr. and Mrs. Dempsey up from San Diego. Bits and pieces of a whispered conversation I wasn't supposed to overhear. As far as they knew, I was just a young, female assistant with headphones shoved in her ears, waiting for her boss to finish his interview so she could type up his notes.

"Supposedly, this all happened while Cory was living with his girl-friend. Right under her nose." A male cousin in his late twenties.

"God, can you imagine finding out your boyfriend did something like that to a young girl?" His female counterpart.

I held my eyes on my notebook, writing the words *live-in girlfriend* and circling them. And then I kept listening, bobbing my head to a beat that wasn't there.

"If he was Cory? Yes."

"Who told you he had a girlfriend?"

The male cousin grimaced. "Nate."

Nate Burgess, Cory's closest friend. Frank had included his contact information in the legend he'd given me. I added Nate's name to the web I'd started sketching out in my notes.

"What else did Nate say?"

"Not much about the high school girls. Claimed he had no idea."

The woman gave a derisive laugh. "Right."

Out of the corner of my eye, I saw the man's gaze cut to me, and he lowered his voice. "He said something interesting though. About the girlfriend, Meg."

I added the name *Meg* to the page and held my breath.

"Nate says she came out of nowhere seven months ago, infiltrated Cory's life, and conned him into giving her access to everything."

"Let me guess, she was young and hot."

"Probably, but here's the thing—Nate claims everything Meg told Cory about herself was a lie. That she targeted him from the beginning and used what he was doing to his students as cover to empty his bank account and disappear."

"That doesn't make her a con artist; that makes her a hero."

Back in the car with Frank, I brought it up. "One of the cousins brought up the possibility that Cory's girlfriend, Meg, was conning him. That she set all of this up."

I looked at Frank across the center console, his white hair erupting out of his head in a way that had earned him the nickname *Einstein* among the other reporters. He was a legend, and I was lucky to be able to learn from him. But it wasn't easy, having to constantly fight for the real assignments, not the public records searches and lunch orders my male colleagues kept trying to stick me with.

He grunted and said, "While that may be, the story we're going to write is the one about a predatory high school principal."

"But they think Meg might have been the one who put it all in motion. A female con artist could be an interesting angle."

Frank shook his head. "It's important that you learn early on that not every great story will be told," he said. "Newspapers are a dying business, and our job is to write stories that will sell papers. Sex and scandal sell. That's what we're writing."

I didn't agree with him, but I wasn't going to argue. I also wasn't going to let it go. My mother had warned me: *As a woman in the news industry, you're going to have to work harder, be smarter, take bigger risks to prove you're just as good as the men.*

When we got back to the *Times* offices, I waited until Frank went out to get a cup of coffee, then dug around in his notes until I found the number for Cory's parents.

"Good evening, Mrs. Dempsey, this is Kat Roberts from the *LA Times*. I met you earlier today with Frank? As we were going through his notes, we realized we didn't have the full name of the woman who'd been living with Cory at the time of his arrest."

"We never met her, but her name was Meg Williams," Cory's mother said. "I'm not sure if Meg is short for something, or if that's her real name at all. She took off shortly before everything broke open. In fact, if you find her, could you let us know?"

"Absolutely," I said. "We'll be in touch."

Frank returned, coffee in hand, and said, "What are you going to tackle first?"

I closed my notebook. "I'm going to get started fact-checking some of the statements from your interview today."

He nodded and settled in to write what would become a four-part series on public schools and the structure that allowed a man like Cory Dempsey to do what he did.

And that was the night I started my search for Meg Williams, the woman who had exploded Cory Dempsey's life and then disappeared. The woman who would soon destroy mine as well.

# MEG

Right away I could tell Cory was a man for whom the anticipation of sex was as exciting as the act itself. I played into that dynamic, sharing early on—and with a fair amount of self-consciousness—that I'd only been with one other person, the boyfriend I'd followed to LA, and that it had been over a year since we'd broken up.

"I hope it's okay that I don't have a lot of experience," I'd said. We were on the couch, Cory's shirt in a puddle on the floor where it had been dropped a few seconds before I'd abruptly pulled back. "I feel things for you that I've never felt before, but I need to go slow. This is new for me."

"Of course," he'd said. "I like that you don't have a lot of experience." He traced the outline of my jaw with his finger, trailing it down my neck. "That way I can show you the way I like to do things."

I gave him an incredulous look, as if I couldn't believe my good fortune. "Seriously?"

He tipped my chin up and brushed a kiss across my lips. "Seriously."

If I hadn't been looking for it, I would have missed the spark of hunger for a young girl, inexperienced and nervous. I knew then that the power was mine, for as long as I could manage to hang on to it.

---

By the third week of our relationship, I'd started my classes and was spending at least four nights a week at Cory's house, a small bungalow in Venice. I inhabited all corners of my role, pretending to have problems so Cory could be the one to help me solve them: *Your mistake was not reading the parking signs posted.* Getting advice I didn't need: *Introduce yourself to your professor right away. They'll grade you more favorably if they can picture your face.*

On the surface, Cory was attentive and caring, but his affection was laced with control, needing to know my work and class schedule, who I spent time with on my breaks, or who I hung out with on the nights I didn't spend with him.

I kept most of the details about my life as close to the truth as possible, though it was a tricky dance, trying to grow closer to him while at the same time keeping him from knowing that the nights we weren't together, I was sleeping in my car parked on various streets on the Westside.

But I wasn't doing all of this so I could still live in a car three nights out of seven. I needed Cory to want me with him all the time.

So, I invented a neurotic roommate named Sylvie who loved to get high. "It's disgusting there," I told him. "I can't believe you don't smell the pot on my clothes."

I complained about Sylvie constantly and made sure she caused problems for Cory as well. I'd be too tired to go out to dinner because, the night before, Sylvie had had people over until two in the morning. I was late to meet him for lunch because Sylvie had locked me out of our room. Waiting for him to offer another solution: *Move in with me.*

But Cory wasn't biting. Instead, he'd tell me stories about his college roommate, Nate, who'd once had a girl in their room for over twenty-four hours, forcing Cory to sleep in the common room. Or the time Nate accidentally set fire to a plant that had died on their windowsill.

The nights in my car became almost intolerable as I tossed and turned, my blankets too scratchy compared to the high-thread-count sheets at Cory's. Trying to sleep in the chilly fall weather, having to wait until daylight to find a bathroom.

Which is why, on a Tuesday night in mid-November, I showed up at his apartment carrying a large duffel bag filled with my clothes, my hair messy and my eyes red.

"What's this?" he asked as I dropped my bag on the floor by the front door.

"I got kicked out of the dorm," I told him, letting my voice wobble.

"What? What happened?"

"Fucking Sylvie happened."

He guided me into the living room, sat me on the couch, and poured me a glass of wine. I gave him a grateful look and took a sip. "Someone said they smelled marijuana coming from our room. The RA came and did a search and found a stash of pot in our fridge. Sylvie swore up and down it wasn't hers. Obviously, I said the same." I closed my eyes and tried to imagine the scene. How desperate I must have been to be believed. How much that would derail the plans I'd made for myself, if any of them had been true. "We were lucky we didn't get kicked out of school. But we're both out of the dorm. Sylvie will just move back home with her parents, but I'll have to figure something else out. And fast, if I don't want to live in my car."

As soon as I said the words, I regretted them. *Too close.*

Cory pulled me into a hug and I let myself rest against him, counting the beats of his heart, waiting.

"Move in here," he said.

I pulled back, wide-eyed. "No way," I said. "It's too soon."

"You practically live here already," he argued. "It's just a few more clothes and a key on your key ring."

Relief unfurled in my chest, but I shook my head, my tone firm. "My mother taught me to earn what I need, not take it from a man willing to trade sex for convenience," I told him.

He looked hurt. "Is that how you see me?"

"Of course not," I told him. "But favors create expectations, which create resentment. What we have is still new. I don't want to ruin it."

"You know it wouldn't be like that."

I let the silence drag out, pretending to be considering his offer, and thought about the one time my mother said yes. Ron Ashton had been the man she'd been waiting for. *He's different*, she'd told me. *A healthy relationship isn't just about love. Each person brings something to the table, creating a partnership. A committed collaboration.*

My mother brought a property worth millions. Ron brought lies.

"I insist on paying rent," I finally said.

"I don't want your money." Cory slid his hands around my waist, his fingers lifting the bottom edge of my shirt, thumbs brushing against bare skin. "It'll be good for our relationship to have you here all the time. We can start to build some trust. Break down some of those walls."

I'd been holding out for almost a month. Dancing up to the edge of intimacy and then away again. But the time had come to cash in. This was what I needed—security. Stability. Everything had a price.

I blew out hard, considering. "Okay."

———

I waited until he was asleep that night to sneak out of the bedroom—*our* bedroom—and over to his computer, logging in to my Circle of Love account. I bypassed new messages from several men interested in meeting and clicked on Account Settings in the upper right-hand corner. Then I scrolled down to the bottom and hovered my cursor over the Suspend Account button before jumping over and clicking Delete Account.

Then I deleted Amelia's account as well.

The silence of the house felt like a prayer as I absorbed the significance of this moment. No more forced smiles, flirty banter I never felt, or faked enthusiasm. As I sat in front of Cory's computer, I promised myself I'd never sleep in a car again.

Then I went back to bed.

---

"Wear the black skirt and the red boots I bought you."

Cory and I were meeting Nate for drinks.

I looked down at the outfit I'd chosen, a nice pair of dark jeans and a wrap top, and swallowed a sigh. The black skirt cut into my waist; the boots pinched my toes. But I smiled. Small concessions fed his belief that I was a pliable young mind in need of guidance. "Sure. Give me a second."

"Be quick," he said. "I don't want to be late."

The bar was one I'd been to several times, on dates with men from Circle of Love. That night, it was packed with the after-work crowd—men in dress shirts with ties loosened around their necks. Women in slightly rumpled business attire, tossing back shots at the bar.

We found Nate at a corner table beneath a large-screen television that was playing a silent 49ers game. He stood and shook my hand. "The infamous Meg."

"I could say the same about you," I said.

Nate's eyes traveled up, down, then up again—before releasing my hand.

"Two beers," Cory said to a server passing by our table.

"I'd prefer a glass of wine," I said.

Cory draped his arm across the back of the booth. "You can't drink wine in a sports bar. She'll have a beer," he repeated, dismissing the server.

Nate lifted his half-empty pint in a silent salute.

I crossed my legs, catching the way Nate eyed my skirt as it slid up to midthigh. Cheers erupted around us as the 49ers scored a touchdown.

"Tell me, Meg," Nate said. "What do you do?"

"She's a student," Cory answered for me.

Nate raised his eyebrows and said, "Living the fantasy, huh?"

Cory laughed and clarified. "College student, you ass. She's at the city college."

"Studying digital design," I offered.

"Cory says you've moved in." His tone was light, but I felt the weight of his stare, silently questioning my motives.

I shrugged, trying to downplay it. "I got kicked out of the dorms. We figured since I was spending most of my time there anyway, it made sense."

"I didn't realize the city college had dorms."

While Cory's attention shifted to the game on TV, I held Nate's eyes. "Housing on the Westside is expensive. Where else are students supposed to live?"

He took a sip of beer and gestured toward Cory. "Regardless, congratulations on snagging this one," he said. "He's a hard one to pin down, though you're exactly his type."

"Lucky me."

Cory turned back to us, and soon the two of them were deep in conversation about work, mutual friends, and Nate's many dating conquests.

Throughout the evening I caught Nate staring at me, as if he were trying to unwrap me. But I gave him nothing to latch on to. I smiled, drank my beer, and mostly kept my mouth shut.

---

It takes time to grow roots in someone else's life. You have to establish routines—brunch on Sundays, a favorite restaurant for special occasions. Rituals that bind you to another person. Life with Cory was 80 percent routine, and if he noticed the only friends we socialized with were his friends, he never said anything.

But Nate noticed. "Where are your friends, Meg?" he asked one night. "Why don't they ever come out with us?"

"And have them suffer through an evening with you?" I shot back.

His stare was hard and steady. "I just think it's strange. A girl your age, with no girl posse. Where's your posse, Meg?"

"You're showing your age, Nate. It's 'woman,' not 'girl.'"

Cory laughed, and Nate did too. But Nate held my gaze a fraction of a second too long, and I knew I needed to watch him.

---

Most men are generous, simple creatures. You just have to know what they care about, and then give it to them. To figure that out, I started looking through Cory's things when he wasn't home, searching for the parts of himself he kept hidden. The engraved pocketknife from his grandfather, tucked inside his underwear drawer. An undated birthday card from his mother that read, *We'd love to see you at Dad's 70th. He may not come out and say so, but I know he's forgiven you.*

I'd been working slowly, one drawer at a time, waiting to see if he'd notice that his things were slightly shifted inside their spaces, jumbled in a different way. Every now and then I took something, just to see what would happen. A couple twenties from cash he had hidden under his clean socks. Bigger things too, like the spare car key I found in a kitchen drawer, the black fob fitting snugly in my palm. But he never noticed a thing. I spent the cash, but kept the car key in the outer pocket of my purse, a reminder that my time here had a purpose.

I had the contents of Cory's nightstand drawer emptied on the bed when my cell phone rang, startling me. "Hey, babe," I said. "I was just getting out of the shower."

"I'm glad I caught you," Cory said. "I left the budget binder on my desk and I need it for an afternoon meeting. Can you bring it on your way to class?"

I began putting things back in the drawer, approximating their original placement as best I could. "Sure. I just need to put on some clothes and dry my hair. Twenty minutes?"

"It'll be lunch by then and I might be hard to find, so just drop it in the office."

"You got it."

---

I parked at a meter on a side street and walked the short block to the high school. Kids flowed through the gates, opened for the lunch hour. I signed my name on a clipboard and attached the visitor's badge to my shirt, turning away from the main office and instead making my way toward the north quad.

As I rounded the corner of the history building, I slowed to a halt and stood there, taking in the scene. The area was packed with students, backpacks flung onto the ground next to them. Even though this wasn't my high school, the snatches of conversations took me back to my time at Northside High, maneuvering my way to a quiet corner to eat my sandwich and study.

Also familiar was the cluster of girls who surrounded Cory when I finally spotted him. Flipping their hair, edging closer as they spoke, a dark-haired girl placing a hand on his forearm to make a point. I waited for him to take a step back. To maintain a professional distance. To say something reassuring and then continue his rounds of the quad. Instead, he leaned into the attention. Ate it up.

I wondered if any of those girls had fantasies about sneaking out of Cory's office, her clothes in disarray. Slipping into the passenger seat of his car.

I plastered a smile on my face and approached them. When he saw me, he looked surprised, finally taking that step back. "Meg," he said.

I handed him the binder and said, "Budget report, as requested."

"Aw, that's so cute," one of the girls said. "She's bringing him his homework."

Cory's eyes shot toward her and then back to me. "I thought I told you to drop it in the office."

"I didn't want to come all this way and not see you." I stepped closer, as if leaning in for a kiss, but he took another step back. The girl who'd had her hand on his arm just moments before shot me a triumphant look.

Finally, I said, "Well, I'll get back to it. See you at home?"

Cory gave me a relieved smile. "Sure."

I turned and made my way back through the campus, my mind turning over the scene, filing away impressions. Ideas. Suspicions. Then figuring out how I wanted to respond.

---

I thought an argument would be best. "It was insulting, the way you dismissed me," I said after dinner.

"You're blowing this out of proportion." Cory shot back. "I'm an authority figure. I can't be seen kissing my girlfriend in the middle of the quad at lunchtime."

"It was like you were embarrassed." I remembered how close he stood to the girls, feeding their desire in a subtle yet clear way. "It's like you didn't want them to even know I was your girlfriend."

"It's none of their business who you are to me," he said, swiping a hand through his hair. "But regardless, I'm not going to justify my actions to you or explain myself. You should have done what I asked and dropped the binder at the office."

Cory had shifted to the offensive, which told me it was time to acquiesce. I'd registered my jealousy. That was enough.

I turned away from him that night in bed though, and he huffed in frustration, but didn't press it. I stared at the wall, listening to his breathing slow as he fell into sleep, a satisfied smile playing at the edges of my mouth. Everyone wants someone who will fight for them.

---

By the time I got around to Cory's desk, I'd become a master at passing through a drawer undetected. Looking through all the bits and pieces tucked into corners, evaluating their worth to me, then moving on.

I learned that he'd paid $900,000 for his tiny two-bedroom house. He had three separate bank accounts at Chase Bank—savings, checking, and a household account with about $30,000 in it.

I learned that his computer didn't need a password to access it and that his personal email inbox was mostly a flood of forwarded jokes and crass sexual innuendos from Nate.

Also interesting was what was missing. Cory had very few photographs of his family, whom he supposedly loved, according to his Circle of Love profile, and very few email exchanges with them. The ones he did have were invitations to family functions that Cory always declined, making me wonder about the obvious distance between them, and what might have caused it.

I was just finishing up with his bottom filing drawer, my mind barely registering what I was seeing—car insurance documents, homeowner's insurance—when I saw it. *Northside*. The label was written in faded pencil, as if he'd been hoping the word would disappear altogether.

Inside were the papers outlining the terms of an agreement Cory had made with Northside and the district.

It took me a few minutes to get the hang of the legal jargon, but the date on the cover page placed the agreement six months after Kristen had left school. I'd never asked Cory much about his transition from teaching to administration, assuming it must have been a typical promotion. But as I read, a different picture began to unfurl—of a man who'd abused his position as a teacher, a young girl traumatized by it, and a district desperate to cover it up.

The agreement itself was cold and detached. Facts only. But the last page was a victim statement, which shattered my whitewashed assumptions of what had happened to Kristen. Yes, it had been consensual at the beginning. But just because she wasn't being forced into that car or dragged into that classroom didn't mean she wanted to stay there.

My mind flew back to the girls in the north quad the other day, testing the power of their youth and beauty, no clue how quickly that power could be snatched away and held in a vise, out of reach.

I flipped back to the agreement page and read it with fresh eyes. In exchange for his participation in mandatory therapy and a quiet exit, Cory would get a letter of recommendation for an administrative position at a different high school and no formal charges.

This was what a young girl's life was worth. Some sessions with a counselor and a promotion.

# KAT

Frank dropped a stack of yearbooks on my desk in the newsroom and said, "Look through these for background—quotes about Cory Dempsey, awards he won, clubs he sponsored. Don't skim, be thorough. I want eyes on every page."

I grabbed the one on top and stared at the cover. *Northside High 2005–2006* and a student-rendered illustration of a breaking wave and a sunset. I sighed and thought back to my own high school years, my own senior yearbook only four years older than this one. I flipped open the cover and started paging through candid shots of kids who looked exactly like the ones I went to school with. People who knew how to have fun while I became consumed with living up to my mother's unfulfilled potential. Trying—and failing—to make up for the opportunity stolen from her by a positive pregnancy test two years into her career at the *Washington Post*.

I'd poured myself into the task. Not just writing for the school newspaper, but becoming the editor of it. Attending football games with a notebook instead of a water bottle filled with vodka, waiting outside the locker room looking for a quote instead of a hookup.

My true passion had been fiction—filling pages with short stories and bits of dialogue that popped into my head at odd times. I fantasized about book tours and being short-listed for prizes—possibly even winning one of them. My favorite college professor had written me a letter of recommendation that had landed me a coveted spot in the Iowa Writers' Workshop for grad school, but my mother had said no, convincing me that journalism was the more distinguished field. *Fiction is for teenagers and bored housewives.* I'd ended up at Northwestern's journalism school instead. Over $200,000 in student loans and two years of my life for the privilege of looking through yearbooks for Frank Durham.

I flipped through the senior portraits, skimming names and faces—tuxedo bow ties, pearls and off-the-shoulder formal wear—pausing when I reached Kristen's. It would have been taken at the beginning of the year, fresh off summer vacation. I imagined her spending her days at the beach, the center of a large group of laughing girls, flirting with surfers and lifeguards.

I stared at her smiling face, the way her hair swept back across her shoulders. Her senior quote was one by Charlotte Brontë. *I try to avoid looking forward or backward, and try to keep looking upward.* I wondered why she chose it and whether it might mean something different to her now.

On an adjacent page was a candid of her, arm in arm with another girl. The caption read *Kristen Gentry and Laura Lazar*. I jotted Laura's name in my notes and kept flipping. Page after page of seniors, each one the same as the last. Until I saw a name I wasn't looking for. *Meg Williams.* There she was, staring into the camera, a half smile playing across her lips. She looked unremarkable, someone you'd see and then promptly forget.

I glanced around the newsroom, everyone consumed with their own work—talking on the phone, fingers flying across a keyboard, leaning on a doorjamb chatting up Marty at the Metro desk. Then I thought about my team—three men, plus me—all of us hungry to contribute something relevant. To see our own name at the bottom of one of Frank's stories. *Additional reporting by Kat Roberts.*

I turned to my computer and logged in to one of the search engines we used to track down sources and entered Laura Lazar's information. In seconds I had a current phone number and address.

---

We met during her lunch break. She worked as a temp in a tall office building in Westwood. "I only have forty-five minutes for lunch," she said on the phone, "so it's going to have to be salads from the café in the lobby. Hope that's okay."

We sat across from each other at a rickety metal table on the sidewalk in front of her building, cars on Wilshire zooming past. Laura was taller than I'd expected, dressed in what was probably one of her interview suits. We peeled the plastic lids off our prepackaged salads and started eating. "You went to UCLA?" I asked.

"Just graduated with a degree in communications." She rolled her eyes. "I should have gone to grad school. The job market is shit."

"I know I told you I wanted to talk with former students about Cory Dempsey, but I was hoping you could give me a little background on a side project I'm working on."

She looked up from her food, wary. "I'm not going to talk about Kristen," she said.

"Actually, I want to ask about a different classmate of yours. Meg Williams."

Laura looked relieved and poked at a piece of cucumber with her fork. "Wow, I haven't thought about her for a long time. What do you want to know?"

"Some people think she was the one who exposed Cory Dempsey."

Laura stopped chewing, her fork suspended in the air, a smile playing across her face. "You're kidding me. How'd she do that? And why?"

"I was hoping you could tell me. People close to him think she targeted him. That it was deliberate."

She set her fork down and gave a loose laugh. "To be honest, I didn't know her well. Meg was a loner, always lurking around on the edges of things. Kristen was friendly with her, but Kristen was friendly with everyone. *Girl code*, she used to call it."

"Do you think Meg was also a victim of Cory's?"

Laura shook her head. "I doubt it. She was a mousy thing, not at all his type. He liked fire. Personality. He mostly ignored girls like Meg."

"Do you think Kristen would have confided in her?"

"If she did, she never said anything about it to me."

"What would Kristen have told her about Cory?"

Laura gave me a shrewd look and took a sip of her soda. "I told you I'm not talking about Kristen."

I turned off my recorder and capped my pen. "I don't want to write about Kristen. In fact, we can put this whole conversation off the record. That means I can't quote you or paraphrase you. I won't even tell anyone other than my editor that we've talked. But whatever happened to Kristen, I think Meg knew about it, and that's why she did what she did. It might explain why she put herself in Cory's home, under his influence."

I waited, letting Laura think. I'd already decided I wasn't going to push it. Forcing a woman to talk about sexual assault—even if it wasn't hers—wasn't a line I was willing to cross. "The court documents that have been released don't include any details about what he did to her," I said. "Secondhand accounts are my best bet. If it was revenge, I'd like a clearer picture. Revenge for what?"

"Off the record?"

"Off the record," I confirmed.

Laura dropped her plastic fork on top of her half-eaten salad and pushed the container away. "It started in September," she said. "Little things at first. Extra help during lunch. Then small gifts—a braided bracelet, a cute necklace—nothing expensive, but not exactly appropriate either." Laura played with the straw in her soda, poking it down into the ice, and continued. "There were privileges. Inside jokes. I think she was flattered by the attention. Mr. Dempsey was handsome, and he'd picked her. What high school girl doesn't love to feel chosen? Soon she started making up excuses to stay after school. He'd text her, and suddenly she'd remember a study group she needed to go to." The wind kicked up and Laura's napkin flew off the table and into the busy street. We both watched as it skittered across four lanes of traffic before getting flattened by a bus. "I told her it was creepy," she said. "We fought about it a couple times, so I stopped bringing it up and hoped she'd move on. But in October she broke up with her boyfriend. She stopped eating lunch with us, wouldn't go to football games. It was senior year and she just vanished. I mean, she was there, but she wasn't, you know?"

"Did she ever tell you the specifics of what was happening?"

"Not until afterward." She crossed her arms over her chest, her eyes on the passing cars, remembering. "What he did to her was sick. Oral sex in his office. In his car. He told her he wanted to teach her how to do it right, that it was a skill many women never learn to master." Laura's eyes cut to mine, her expression dead. "They'd drive up the coast after school, to deserted beach parking lots. Have sex in his backseat. She'd lie to her parents, telling them she was sleeping over at my house, but she was staying over at his instead."

"They never caught her?"

Laura gave a sharp laugh. "Her parents were…" She trailed off, as if searching for the right words. "Absent. Her dad was some executive—I don't know where exactly—but he made enough money so her mom could go shopping and have lunch at the beach club every day. Neither of them cared what she was doing so long as she played the part of perfect daughter. Don't ask, don't tell, you know?"

"How did their relationship get discovered? Did Kristen tell someone?"

"She called me, out of the blue, in November. Crying. Begged me to sneak out and meet her. I'd assumed the relationship had ended badly. Maybe he dumped her or came to his senses." Laura swiped a strand of hair off her forehead and tucked it behind her ear. "But she was pregnant, and the baby was Mr. Dempsey's."

I sat back in my chair, imagining a seventeen-year-old girl caught in an illicit relationship with her teacher, pregnant with his baby, and what that must have felt like. The shock and fear of discovery, the irrevocable consequences that a girl as smart as Kristen would have understood immediately.

Laura sighed, her expression distant. "I sat with her when she told her parents." She looked back at me. "You want to know what they said? 'You should have known better.' As if Kristen had been caught cheating on an exam or ditching school."

"Then what?"

"They pulled her out. Kristen's dad was a powerful guy, and I was sure his attorneys would have a field day. I kept waiting for Mr. Dempsey to lose his job, or for them to put him on administrative leave. Something. But when he showed up after winter break cracking jokes, eyes sliding over Kristen's empty seat like it was nothing..." She shrugged. "What more could I do? At that point, I just wanted to get the hell out of that school and away from all of it."

"How is she now? Did she have the baby? Graduate high school?"

"They moved away. Sorry, but off the record or not, I'm not telling you where. She had an abortion. Got her GED. I don't really talk to her anymore, and she's not on social media." Laura looked sad. "She was brilliant. She wanted to be a doctor, and Mr. Dempsey stole that from her. It sounds like he tried to do it again."

"Yes, but Meg stopped him."

Laura shook her head and gave a hollow laugh. "I never would have guessed the Bag Lady had it in her." She looked sad, still haunted by what had happened to her friend. "I should've done more—spoken out. I didn't even tell my parents until last month when the news broke about Mr. Dempsey."

"You were young," I said. "You trusted the adults in the room to take care of it. To do the right thing. That they didn't is on them, not you."

"I'm glad Meg did what she did, but it should have been me."

"Next time," I said. Our eyes met and held across the table, a sad acknowledgment passing between us. Because we both knew there were plenty of men still out there like Cory Dempsey.

# MEG

I went into the bedroom and began pulling clothes from drawers and the closet, shoving them into a duffel bag. I had two hours until Cory would be home, and I planned to be gone by then.

In the living room, I gathered my school notebooks from the dining room table and took a quick glance around, trying to think of what I might be forgetting. I loaded a shopping bag with a couple of rolls of toilet paper from the hall closet, loaf of bread and peanut butter from the pantry, then grabbed a butter knife from the drawer.

Through the window, I saw my car parked in the driveway, could already feel the cold seeping into my bones, the tension in my shoulders as I hunched into myself to stay warm.

Once again, I was being chased from my home. Five years ago, it was Ron Ashton who came in with promises that ended up being lies. *This is just how financing works.*

And now it was happening again. Another man taking what he wanted while the rest of us scrambled to accommodate him. I remembered what Ron had said to my mother when she'd confronted him. When she realized she had no legal recourse to fix it. *There are winners and losers in life, Rosie. You're the loser here. Take the loss and be smarter next time.*

Then I saw Kristen's eyes meeting mine in the mirror. *It's the Girl Code. We have to look out for each other because no one else will.*

Slowly, I retraced my steps, putting things back where they'd been. My notebooks back onto the table, my clothes back into their drawers, the food back into the pantry.

Thanks to Kristen's *girl code*, I was going to have to stick around and make Cory pay.

---

You might think it would have been impossible to stay after discovering what Cory had done. I admit, the first week was hard. But every time I thought about leaving, every time I suppressed a grimace when he reached out for me, I kept my mind far into the future, on what the landscape of his life would look like when I was done.

After a while, it got easier. I played the role he wanted me to play. Reminded myself I'd done harder things. I can admit now, I was good at it. The pretending and manipulation slipped over me like a second skin. Maybe you judge me for staying. For holding him close instead of casting him out. But if you take a look at where Cory is now, I think it's pretty obvious that holding your enemy close makes it much easier to slip the knife into their back.

---

It's amazing how much heavy lifting a printed Craigslist ad can do, if you leave it in the right place. For sale—2006 MacBook Pro—$500 obo.

"What's this?" Cory asked, carrying it into the kitchen, where I'd been cooking dinner, nursing a glass of wine, waiting for him.

I flipped the pork chops in the pan and said, "I can't work in the computer lab indefinitely. I'm going to need my own machine."

Cory set the ad on the counter and said, "But a used one? What you'll save in the short term will cost you more in the long run. Invest in a good machine now and it'll last for years."

I gave him an exasperated look. "Wouldn't it be nice if I had a spare $3,000 sitting around?" I said. "This is how people in the real world get the things they need." When he didn't answer, I said, "I suppose my friend Liam could probably find one for me off the market."

"I'm assuming that means stolen."

I shrugged and took another sip of wine.

"I'm not going to let you do that," he said.

"*Let* me?" I set my glass down. "I appreciate your advice, but I've been on my own for a long time. I don't need you telling me what to do."

I left the room before any more solutions could be suggested, leaving *used* and *stolen* as the only options in play. Over the last two months, I'd discovered that Cory craved being the problem solver. The wise sage who fixed the messes I often created for that purpose—the overdrawn bank account, a snafu with the city college admissions office, a grade dispute with an unreasonable professor—his tone always slightly condescending and smug. Satisfied that I was exactly who he believed me to be—young, naive, and wholly dependent on him. Cory loved being the hero. All I had to do was give him the space to be one.

---

Three days later, Cory came home with a brand-new MacBook Pro. "You shouldn't have done this," I said, admiring the box. The delight on my face was entirely legitimate, mostly because of how easy it was to get there.

Cory slid another bag toward me and said, "And a case to put it in. Consider it an early holiday gift."

I pulled out a padded leather case with a long strap that could be worn across the body and a zippered pouch for the cord.

I looked up at him, tears in my eyes. "My whole life, I've had to scrounge and piece together the basics. And now…" I trailed off, absorbing the possibilities ahead of me. "You've given me my future." It wasn't a lie.

He tilted my chin up so he was gazing into my eyes. "I'm sure you can think of a way to thank me."

He was reaching for his belt buckle when the doorbell rang. "Damn. I forgot, Nate and I made plans tonight." He adjusted himself and crossed the room to open the door.

"Bottomless pitcher over at Flynn's," Nate said as he entered. To me he said, "Grab your fake ID and join us, Meg."

I ignored him and kept my eyes on my new computer.

"How'd you afford that?" Nate asked.

"Cory bought it for me."

Nate raised his eyebrows and said, "Really?"

Cory grabbed his keys and dropped a kiss on the top of my head, whispering, "Wait up, and wear the black nightie I bought you."

I slipped off the couch and followed them to the door. As I was closing it, I heard Nate say, "That's a pretty expensive gift for someone you barely know."

I hesitated, straining to hear Cory's response. "I wouldn't say that. We've been together a couple months now."

"But what do you really know about her? She just appeared out of nowhere, at a coffee shop."

Cory laughed. "With Meg, what you see is what you get," he said. "Small-town girl, small-town sensibilities."

I pushed the door closed quietly, flipping the bolt, and made my way back to my new computer, humming quietly to myself.

———

My English teacher in high school once brought in a novelist to talk to us about the creative process. She told us she always knew how her books were going to end, but didn't always know how she would get there. That part of the art—and part of the fun—was figuring it out.

I enjoyed living inside that same type of ambiguity. Having the outline of a plan, waiting for opportunities to arise. I learned to pay close attention, seeing things through the lens of how to exploit them, looking and waiting for my openings. And I was good at it—the planning. Setting traps and walking away, trusting Cory would fall into them.

Not everything I tried worked. When I told Cory about a fundraiser to help a *family friend* rebuild after a fire, he declined. Another time, I used a wrench to crack one of the bolts on the lid of the toilet, having found a video on YouTube that would show me how to fix it for about $2. When I told Cory I'd scheduled a plumber to come, and that he should leave $200 to cover the bill, Cory fixed it himself.

But I learned something from every attempt. I learned how to see the holes in a plan, how to anticipate when an answer might be no, and then take that option away. I got better. I got smarter. The loop I'd cast around Cory was growing tighter.

———

I found the photos right after the new year. I'd been late for class, hurrying to get ready, and as I flipped the light switch in the closet, the bulb buzzed and then popped, casting everything into darkness. "Shit," I said.

Cory kept the light bulbs in the cupboard above the fridge, but they were back farther than I could reach. I pulled over a chair and stood on it, shifting aside an old roasting pan and some cans of ginger ale. That was when I saw it, a small, white envelope tucked behind an air popper we never used. I dislodged it and turned it over, the glue on the flap just starting to yellow.

Inside were five photographs, a series of bedroom shots, taken of Kristen and Cory. Black and white, both of them in stages of undress. I lowered myself to sitting, flipping through the shots, one by one, studying them.

She looked younger than I remembered, her smile hollow and fragile. Had she realized yet how out of control things had gotten? I tried to imagine what she must have been thinking the moment the shutter clicked, perhaps worrying where these photographs would end up. Knowing that refusing was not an option for her.

I pushed down the rage tumbling around inside of me—of what this meant, of how she must have suffered. Emotion wasn't going to be useful, but these photographs would be.

I returned them to their envelope and replaced it behind the air popper, then sat back down, imagining what I could do with them.

In my pocket, my phone buzzed with a text. When I pulled it out, I found a message from Cal.

I never see you anymore. I miss our lunches.

I still worked the early morning shift at the Y, that money going toward slowly chipping away at my mother's funeral debt, though my schedule barely overlapped with Cal's now that I was taking classes. But I'd also been avoiding him, unwilling to bring Cal too far into my life with Cory, for fear Cal would say something that would expose me.

Busy with classes, I typed. Let's catch up soon.

But I knew, with a flash of clarity, that we wouldn't. That I would continue to keep a safe distance from my only friend and would end up losing him in the process.

I think that was the first time it really hit me. In order to do what I needed to do, I would have to cut myself off from anything real. Everything true.

Cory insisted on paying for everything—the household bills, groceries, nights out. Every now and then I'd offer to pitch in—no more than temperature-taking, looking for cracks in his generosity. But the reality was that it was easier for him to control me if he controlled the money.

I needed to flip that narrative.

We were at yet another bar with Nate when I saw an opportunity. We'd been there for several hours when Cory signaled he was finally ready to go home. He pulled his card from his wallet and handed it to me. "Pay while I use the restroom. Sign my name and tip $10."

The mirror behind the bar was edged with Valentine's Day hearts. In it, I watched Nate lean closer to a woman seated to my right, reaching out to twirl a piece of her hair.

"I have a boyfriend," she said, pulling away.

"Let me get you another drink," he said. "Just as friends." He signaled the bartender for another round.

As the bartender passed me, I handed him Cory's card. "Close it out for us please?" I asked.

I stared at the doorway leading to the men's room, silently urging the bartender to hurry. When he returned, he placed two beers in front of Nate and his friend, then handed me Cory's card and receipt.

I signed with a flourish and fit the card in my palm, waiting.

"I'm not going to drink that," the woman next to me said.

"I'll bet I can change your mind," Nate responded.

"No means no," I muttered under my breath, leaning my forearms on the bar and positioning my elbow a few inches away from her full beer.

When I saw Cory approaching, I let my elbow kick out as I turned to greet him, knocking the full glass over and spilling beer down the woman's back, using the chaos to slide the card into my back pocket.

"I'm so sorry," I said to her, reaching for some napkins.

"Jesus, Meg." Cory snatched them out of my hand and quickly mopped up the mess, people shuffling their stools away from the large puddle now dripping onto the floor.

I slipped into my coat as the bartender took over, wiping the rest of the beer up with a bar towel.

"Let me drive you home," Nate said to the woman.

"That's okay," she said, holding her arms stiffly at her sides. "I've got my car."

"I'm really sorry," I said again to her, then offered Nate a tiny shrug. *Tough luck.*

As we walked toward the door, Nate called after us, "Don't forget to give Cory his card back, Meg."

I glanced over my shoulder. Nate stared back at me, his eyes narrowed, waiting.

I reached into my pocket and handed the card back to Cory as cold air from outside blasted into my face. Through the window I could see Nate, alone at the bar, a fresh drink in front of him.

That plan was bound to fail—if not in the moment, then in the days following. Cory would have asked for his card back eventually, and I would have had to give it to him. But the night was still a success because it showed me that I couldn't steal what I wanted. Like the laptop, I needed to figure out a way for Cory to give it to me willingly.

———————

The next morning Cory announced he was making a grocery run after his staff meeting that afternoon, and asked me to put a list together and text it to him by the end of the day. When he arrived home that night, he was short-tempered and exhausted. "The market was a mess," he said, putting the bags on the counter.

I kissed his cheek and said, "Take a hot shower and change your clothes. I can deal with the groceries."

"The staff meeting was a shit show," he continued, as if I hadn't spoken. "My math department chair is completely useless, and we lost out on a major grant opportunity because he forgot to submit the paperwork."

I pulled a cold beer out of the fridge and handed it to him, "Go. Relax. Dinner will be ready in thirty minutes."

As I put the groceries away—fair trade organic coffee, grass-fed organic milk, and two filet mignon steaks that cost $12 each—my mind tallied up what this midweek trip must have cost. Two hundred dollars perhaps? That was about what my mother and I would have spent on food in a month.

I seasoned the steaks and popped them into the broiler. Then I threw together some romaine lettuce, a couple red peppers, carrots, and cucumbers—all organic, of course—for a salad while the steaks cooked. By the time Cory returned in sweatpants and wet hair from the shower, I'd set the table, lit the candles the way he liked, and poured the wine.

We settled across from each other, and I let him go into the details of his day, making sympathetic noises about the difficulties of running a public high school. Funding shortages, staffing problems, troubled students who might not graduate.

"You have so much on your plate," I told him. "You do so much for so many people. Including me."

He nodded and picked up his knife and fork.

"Let me help," I continued. "I feel like all I do is take. I live here for free, I eat for free, you buy me expensive computers and love me…let me do something for you."

"You do plenty for me," he said, giving me a wink.

I pulled myself straight in my chair and said, "To be honest, it's start-ing to make me uncomfortable. I've always been independent. Paid my own way and taken care of myself." I crossed my arms and looked into the living room. "I know you mean well, and I appreciate everything you give me, but this isn't how I was raised." I looked back at him, my expression serious. "It makes me feel cheap."

"Don't be ridiculous," he said.

"I need to feel like an equal partner here. I know you think I'm young and naive." He started to speak, but I kept talking. "I hear how you and Nate talk about me. And it's fine, you're not wrong. I don't have as much experience in the world as you do; I don't make as much money, but I can afford to contribute something. I can make life easier for you if you'll let me."

He thought for a moment. Finally, he said, "What did you have in mind?"

"Let me buy the groceries. Imagine how nice it'll be to have that errand done for you. To come home to a hot meal." Under the table I tugged the hem of my shirt so the V of my top would sink lower. "Maybe I'll wear an apron."

I could see him imagining it—me in something skimpy, serving him. "I suppose we can give that a try."

I smiled and leaned over the table to kiss him.

––––––––

The following week, I made a big show of assembling a list and checking for staples that needed to be replenished. "By the time you get home, the cupboards will be filled and dinner will be ready." I grabbed Cory around the waist and hugged him. "This feels good," I whispered into his ear. "Thank you."

He slid his hands under my shirt and caressed my stomach. "I'll be home at seven."

———————

I'd given myself a $100 budget for the weekly groceries, but I wasn't going to spend it at Cory's high-end designer market. Instead, I headed for the major retailer with plenty of coupons. This time when I unloaded groceries, they were items from my childhood. Campbell's soup. Velveeta cheese. Cheap white bread and instant coffee. A large log of ground beef and a $7 bottle of wine. Nothing organic, everything generic.

I threw some ground beef into a pot, dumped a jar of sauce over it, and set it to simmer. Then I got another pot of water boiling for the pasta and waited for Cory to get home.

I met him at the door with a glass of wine. He took a sip and grimaced. "What's this?" he asked.

"It was on sale," I said, looking proud.

He took another exploratory sip and handed the glass back to me. "You'd have been better off tossing that money into the trash. I'll have water."

"Dinner in five," I said. "Go get changed."

I'd assembled two large bowls of spaghetti with meat sauce, and a plate of flimsy white bread buttered, salted, and broiled to a crispy brown. When he arrived at the table, he took in the twist-top wine bottle and the steaming bowls of pasta. Then he picked up his fork and took a tiny bite, chewing carefully.

I watched with an expression of anxious anticipation, until he said, "It's different."

"Different good?"

He took a large gulp of water and said, "I wouldn't go that far."

"I'll get better," I assured him. "I'll look up recipes. Maybe watch a few of those cooking shows on TV." I smiled at the idea and dug in to my meal, wondering how many weeks of generic groceries Cory could handle.

———————

Three weeks. Three weeks of hot dogs, tomato soup, and grilled Velveeta cheese sandwiches. Three weeks of Folgers ground coffee from a giant red can. Three weeks until he finally spoke up. "Meg," he said. "No offense, but I can't keep eating this shit. My sodium is probably through the roof, and your pants are looking a little snug." He pinched my waist hard.

I covered my eyes, embarrassed. "I know what you're going to say," I started. "I went to your market, you know. Parked the minivan next to the Teslas and Audis. I walked around, dodging Lululemon ladies and hipsters, filling my cart with all the things you love. The fresh pressed juice, the organic veggies and meat." I looked up at him, letting my eyes water a little bit. "I didn't have enough money," I whispered. "So I went back to what I know—coupons and bargain baskets. But it's awful." I gave a short laugh. "I really wanted to do this for you. I love taking care of you. Feeding you." I knew he loved it too. I'd overheard him bragging to Nate about how well my *training* was going. *Seven o'clock on the dot. I come home now and she's got food and sex ready. Every night.* An exaggeration for sure, but he'd grown attached to the idea of it, which was all I needed.

"Why don't we compromise," he said. "You continue to shop for the food, but let me pay."

I shook my head and pulled back. "But that's the whole point," I argued. "I want to contribute."

He gave me a patronizing smile and said, "Don't make it about the money; make it about the act. Taking on a chore that's a huge hassle for me matters more than who ends up paying for it." He reached into his pocket and pulled out his wallet, and I had to work hard to keep my face neutral as he handed me the ATM card. "You're now in charge of all things house related. Groceries, hardware store, all of it. It's a big responsibility," he lectured. "I'm going to need you to be reliable. When I tell you something needs doing, you need to do it."

I took the card and traced my finger across his name embossed on the surface. "Will they let me use a card that doesn't belong to me?" I asked.

"The PIN is 5427. And Cory could be a woman's name. I don't think you'll have any problems."

I shook my head and handed it back. "I'd feel better if you'd call the bank to authorize me," I said. "One time, when I was a kid, my mother gave me her credit card to buy new shoes, and the store clerk called security on me. I had to wait in this tiny, windowless room while they tracked her down so she could confirm I had her permission. Apparently, she should have written me a note or something."

"How about I do both," he said. "I'll call the bank tomorrow, put your name down as an authorized user, *and* I'll write you a note."

I hooked my finger through his belt loop and gave it a playful tug. "Are you teasing me?"

"You make it so easy."

I took the card back and tucked it into my pocket, feeling the thrill that came along with a plan well executed.

––––––––––

I let another two weeks pass—filled with high-quality produce, grass-fed meat, organic everything—before pushing forward again. This year, Cory's high school was hosting the county's annual robotics tournament, and in the weeks leading up to it, there had been many late nights and weekends spent preparing. I waited until the day of the tournament to act, knowing Cory would be distracted, knowing he would be grateful for my help.

"The card won't work," I said when I called him, just past

lunchtime. I'd spent the morning at Home Depot, buying several hundred dollars' worth of potted plants for the backyard, which now sat in the driveway.

In the background I could hear announcements over the loud-speaker and the dull roar of voices. "Hold on," he said. "Let me go somewhere a little quieter." The sounds receded a little bit. "Okay, what did you say?"

"The bank card," I repeated. "It won't work."

Irritation flooded his voice. "Can you wait to use it?"

"I had a cart full of groceries and an angry line of people behind me while the checker voided my entire order." I lowered my voice, concerned. "If something is going on with your account, you don't want to ignore it. A lot of damage can be done in a few hours. This happened to me one time and it turned out a guy in Florida had my account infor-mation and he was buying sex toys off the internet with it. It was a night-mare to unravel."

"Jesus. I can't deal with this right now."

"I came home and tried calling the bank myself, but they won't let me do anything without a password."

"Okay," he said, lowering his voice. "It's Shazaam. Capital S. Two A's."

"It'll be sorted by the time you get home."

I went into Cory's office and sat at his desk, the bank's website already pulled up on the computer. In thirty seconds, I was in.

I spent a few minutes looking around. The mortgage posted yester-day, with a few more automatic payments to the utility company and cable. I navigated over to Daily Cash Withdrawal Limit and saw it set at $500. I clicked on the field and entered the maximum, $2,500.

Later that night, after he'd finished telling me about the success of the tournament, we circled back to the bank issue. "What was the problem?" he asked.

"Too many charges posted on the same day," I told him. I handed him a piece of paper with notes I'd created. "After I got the plants for the backyard, I was too close to the daily limit to cover the groceries. I spoke to someone named Amanda and wrote down her employee number so you can speak to her yourself if you want. She said you needed to increase your limit to avoid this happening in the future, which we did." I shook my head. "I spent about an hour on hold waiting to speak to someone. The problem itself only took ten minutes to actually fix."

"I saw the email. Thanks for taking care of it."

"If you had a smartphone, you could have done it yourself in about five minutes."

"That would have been five minutes I didn't have to spare. Besides," he said, "I don't want to be tied to my email twenty-four hours a day."

I poured more wine into his nearly empty glass and smiled at him. "Amen to that."

---

On a Saturday morning a few weeks later, while Cory was out for his morning run, I returned to the Chase website and finished up. I logged in quickly, toggled over to the notifications page, and changed his notifications from email to text. Then I entered my cell number. I saved the changes and logged out.

Cory's email pinged with an email alerting him of the changes to his account. I moved it to the trash and then deleted it from there, removing all traces of it. The entire process took less than a minute.

I went into the kitchen, poured myself a cup of coffee, and stared out the window. Dew still covered the grass in a silvery layer, the sun just beginning to peek over the top of the houses across the street. One of my mother's rules popped into my head: *Two women working together are a force to be reckoned with.*

I wasn't exactly working with Kristen, but I was certainly here because of her, finishing what she started. Making sure the end of her story with Cory was a good one.

# KAT

The phone call came through to my desk while Frank was at lunch.

"I need to speak to the reporter working on the Cory Dempsey story." It was a woman.

"He's at lunch, but I'm happy to help."

She hesitated, as if she wasn't sure she wanted to continue, so I said, "I can assure you, what you tell me will stay confidential."

"You need to talk to Cory Dempsey's best friend, Nate Burgess."

I recognized the name, and I knew that, so far, he'd been stonewalling Frank's attempts to interview him. "Why? What is it you think he can tell us?"

"All the questions people have—how many girls there were, how often, where Cory found them—Nate knows all of it."

"Have you told the police?" I asked.

"I'm telling you. Talk to Nate, and he'll be able to fill in all the gaps."

"How did you come to have this information?"

"Let's just say that for the past seven months, I've had a front row seat to how Cory and Nate work."

It was that statement that caught my attention. I reached for my notes and flipped through the pages until I found the conversation between Cory Dempsey's cousins. *He said she came out of nowhere seven months ago, infiltrated his life, and conned Cory into giving her access to everything.*

"And what makes you think Nate will talk to us?" I asked.

"He won't if he thinks you're a reporter. But you can find him eating lunch every day at Millie's Tap Room on Culver Boulevard. He's always there by one and sits at the bar. Right under the television. He talks a big game after a couple drinks."

Her meaning was clear—Nate would be more forthcoming if he believed I was just an attractive woman in a bar. Perhaps someone sympathetic to his friend's plight, who might believe that seventeen was just a few months shy of legal and not a horrific abuse of power.

I glanced around, the newsroom mostly empty during the lunch hour. Those who were there weren't paying any attention to me. They had no idea I had Meg Williams on the phone—the woman who'd lit the fuse and then disappeared. Why had she done it? Had she really targeted Cory, or was there another reason, one I didn't yet understand? I had a choice—I could wait and pass the message on to Frank, let him decide what—if anything—he wanted to do with Meg's information, or I could take advantage of the opportunity in front of me. "We can look into Nate Burgess, but Ms. Williams, I'd love to talk to you. Name the place and I'll be there."

At the mention of her name, she hung up.

I lowered the phone slowly, thinking. This could be a big score for me—the interview with Nate Burgess that had been eluding Frank. I could deliver new and shocking revelations about other victims. Provide details about how Cory found them. And maybe, while I was there, I could get Nate to tell me something about Meg, flesh her out enough so that I could pitch that story again and get a different answer.

Ten minutes later, Frank returned from lunch. "Any calls?"

"Nope," I said.

---

My mother was always telling me to *think like a man. Grab opportunities like a man.* Which was why, three days later, I entered Millie's Tap Room and sat where Meg told me to, a copy of the *LA Times* opened to another story about Cory Dempsey.

The dim lighting, sticky floor, and neon beer signs on the wall contrasted with the high-end beer on tap and top-shelf liquor. A late lunch crowd dotted the place, and my knee jiggled as I checked my watch. In less than two hours, Frank wanted me over at the high school to follow up with the teacher who'd mentored Cory. I'd be out of a job if I couldn't get Nate to tell me something that would justify my presence here.

But Nate entered right on schedule, sliding onto the stool next to mine. Up close, I was struck by his fading good looks—reddish-brown hair flecked with gray and a rakish smile that appeared to be professionally whitened. His gaze slid over the paper I'd positioned on the bar, snagging for just a fraction of a second on Cory's name.

"The usual," he said to the bartender, who nodded and put in his order with the cook before pouring him a tumbler of whiskey.

"What's good here?" I asked.

He turned, taking in the different parts of me like a buffet. "Depends on what you're in the mood for."

I pointed to his whiskey and said to the bartender, "I'll take one of those please. And a plate of fries."

"I would have gone with the onion rings, but you do you."

I gave him a flirty smile, reveling in the fun of it all. The chase, the contact. The fact that he didn't know who I was or what I wanted from him.

He gestured toward the paper, a small thumbnail photo of Cory next to the headline "High School Principal Pleads Not Guilty," Frank's latest piece. "Some light lunchtime reading?"

I looked embarrassed, as if I'd been caught. "True confession, I'm kind of obsessed with this story. I've read every newspaper article and blog about it."

"Yeah, well. The media loves a circus, and people love to read about it."

"I keep imagining it. One moment he's going to faculty meetings and supervising the dismissal gate. The next, he's in handcuffs." I paused and shook my head, as if I couldn't believe it. "I mean, who hasn't had a crush on the hot teacher? How many of us wouldn't have acted on it if given the chance? Van Halen even wrote a song about it."

"No way," Nate said. "She has to be eighteen, or I walk away. No exceptions."

"All I'm saying," I said, trying to backtrack, "is that if either of those girls had been a few months older, this story wouldn't be happening. A man's life wouldn't have been destroyed simply because he fell in love with the wrong person at the wrong time." I turned my glass of whiskey in small circles, hoping I sounded convincing.

Nate looked at me, as if weighing his words. "Believe it or not, I actually know the guy."

I widened my eyes. "No way."

He took a sip of whiskey and said, "We went to college together."

I leaned forward. "Are you still friends?"

Nate gave a short laugh. "We were for a long time. I probably know him better than anyone else. But no, we're not friends anymore."

"And you never knew?" I pressed. "In all those years, not even a hint? A sideways comment about a beautiful student, or a hypothetical fantasy about one of them?"

Nate shook his head, the corners of his mouth lifting in a smile. "Never," he said.

"Come on," I said. "I find that hard to believe."

"Believe it."

"My guess is that there were more than two girls," I said. "I mean, look at him. Maybe they weren't always his students—I'm sure there are a lot of places he could have found underage girls willing to date him. The beach, or maybe they worked at a restaurant he frequented regularly."

"I wouldn't know," Nate said.

Our food had arrived, and I picked up a french fry and took a bite, trying to think about what to ask next. I didn't have a lot of time, and he seemed pretty committed to keeping his distance from Cory.

Nate gestured toward the newspaper. "I will tell you, there's more to it than what you've read."

"There usually is." I lifted my glass to my lips, the whiskey burning as it went down, and pivoted. "I read somewhere that there's a girlfriend they want to talk to, but they can't find her."

"Meg," Nate muttered. "God, she was a piece of work. She lied about everything and had no friends as far as I could tell. She just snuck into Cory's life and appropriated his, convincing him to give her a free place to live. He bought her clothes, helped pay her bills. She even conned him into giving her access to his bank account, which she then emptied."

"Where'd he meet her?"

"In a coffee shop. They both got stood up by their respective blind dates." He shook his head. "It was a little too coincidental."

I ate another fry, though I was too jumpy to have much of an appetite. "You don't think it's possible that there might be two people in a coffee shop, each of them meeting a blind date?" I asked. "Or that they'd both been stood up?"

"I'm saying that Meg's likes and beliefs aligned just a little too easily with Cory's."

"But why target him?"

"Why wouldn't she? Meg was working the front desk at the Y. For a girl like that, Cory would be a catch."

I gave him a playful glance. "*A girl like that?*"

Nate held up his hands, grinning. "What I meant is that Meg wasn't exactly flush with opportunities. Community college was a stretch for her."

"And yet you claim she orchestrated a huge con on your friend," I reminded him.

"Former friend," he corrected. "And yes. I think she saw an opening to live in a nice house, to have a boyfriend who would buy her nice things."

"That's not a con," I argued. "That's just taking advantage of someone. She was the one who reported him. Why would she do that if she'd been in the middle of some big scam?"

Nate swirled the last inch of whiskey in his glass and then tossed it back, signaling the bartender for another one. "I made some calls. Nothing official like a private investigator could do, but Meg's story was that she'd grown up in Grass Valley and moved to LA with a boyfriend a couple years ago." He shook his head. "No one up there has ever heard of her."

"Did you tell Cory that?"

"I tried. He didn't want to hear it."

I took another sip of my drink, mindful that I needed to stay sharp. "Wouldn't it have been obvious what she was doing?" Just then my cell phone rang. It was Frank. I held it up and said, "I'm sorry, but I have to take this."

I stepped outside, the bright sunlight making my eyes water. "Have you gotten to the high school yet?" he asked. "I want you to stop by the main office and see if you can get the office manager to confirm the date Cory started working there. I'm not getting anywhere with district HR."

I checked my watch. It was nearing 2:15. I was going to have to wrap this up quickly if I wanted to get to Northside by the dismissal bell. "I'm on my way now," I lied.

"I need this information, Kat, or the whole story gets pushed back and we risk someone else running it first."

"I understand."

I entered the bar and took my seat, checking the time again.

"Somewhere you need to be?" Nate asked.

"Work," I told him. "I should be getting back."

"But you've barely eaten anything," he said. Then he pushed my glass toward me and said, "Finish your drink and I'll lay it all out for you. Tell you exactly how I think Meg conned Cory."

I checked the time again, my nerves tightening, trying to think what my male colleagues might do. The ones who never seemed to worry about being a little late, who wouldn't think twice about being somewhere they weren't supposed to be, if it meant getting an important lead on a story. I could be across town by three. Chances were, that teacher would still be sitting in his classroom, grading papers by the time I got there, and office managers usually worked until five.

I grabbed the glass and tossed the rest of it back, cringing as it went down.

And that's the last thing I remember before I blacked out.

---

I woke with a pounding headache in a room I didn't recognize. Early morning light had only begun to filter in through the drawn shades. In the bed next to me, Nate was asleep.

I sat up, the room spinning precariously, no clue how I got there or what had happened. A T-shirt I didn't recognize covered my top, but I was naked from the waist down. "Jesus," I said, and a swirl of nausea passed through me.

I managed to make it to the toilet in time. Sour brown liquid landed in the water, the stench of alcohol clouding the air around me. My hands shook as I flushed the toilet and splashed cold water on my face. My makeup was smeared, and I stared at myself in the mirror, searching my memory for something—anything—that would explain how I'd gone from a few sips of whiskey at two in the afternoon to Nate's apartment the next morning. I remembered Frank's call. Leaving the bar to take it so Nate wouldn't overhear our conversation. And then…nothing.

When I entered the bedroom again, Nate was sitting up. He smiled. "Hey. You feeling okay?"

"What did you do to me?" I asked, my voice raw and scratchy in my throat.

He held up his hands. "Hey now," he said. "We had a couple drinks. You told me your boss was going to be livid you missed some important meeting, but that you didn't care." His voice grew softer. "I was just trying to be a good friend. It seems like you've got some issues with your mother you need to resolve. I just let you talk."

"Did we…?" I trailed off, looking around at the evidence that we had. My clothes in a pile on the floor. An open condom wrapper on the nightstand.

"I asked, and you said yes," Nate said. "I always ask."

"I don't even remember leaving the bar," I said. "How can I remember saying yes to you?" I shook my head and instantly regretted it, feeling like a sack of hammers was tumbling around in there.

"I guess you'll have to take my word for it," Nate said.

"I need to get home."

"I can give you a ride to your car if you want."

"No thanks," I said, grabbing my clothes and heading back to the bathroom. "I'll call a cab."

"Suit yourself," Nate said.

---

I managed to hold myself together on the ride back to the bar, my car the only one left in the lot. I swiped my credit card to pay for the cab, my hands still shaking. When I was safe behind the wheel, I let the tears come. In the span of a few hours, I'd become a different person. A rape victim. I was now one of those stories people read about, the ones where they'd shake their heads and say, *How could she not have known that might happen?*

I checked my voicemail. Four messages from Frank. Three from my mother. I knew I should drive straight to the nearest police station and report Nate. But as I pulled onto the empty road, I thought about the questions I'd have to answer. The paperwork I'd have to fill out, followed by a trip to the hospital for a rape kit. It would eat up my entire day, and what I needed to do was get to Northside and catch that teacher on his way into school. That way I could still get Frank what he needed. Make up some kind of a story about why it was late, so that I wouldn't have to explain that I hadn't been where I was supposed to be. That I'd withheld Meg's tip from Frank, hoping to keep it for myself.

*Think like a man. Grab opportunities like a man.* I made a U-turn and headed toward Northside High.

# MEG

The first few weeks with Cory's card in my wallet, I worked hard to stay transparent.

About to use the card at CVS, I'd text. Then afterward $37.43 for shampoo plus new razors for you. That night I'd leave the paper receipt on his computer keyboard, where he'd be sure to see it.

But Cory quickly grew impatient with this routine. "Jesus, Meg," he said one night, crumpling the receipts I'd left for him and tossing them in the trash. "This plus the constant texting is driving me crazy." His voice rose a couple octaves, as if imitating mine. "'I used the card for a parking meter on Seventh Street—$2 for two hours.' I don't need a play-by-play."

"I just want to be open about what I'm spending," I said. "It's your money, after all."

"Just do what you said you'd do. Buy the groceries and shut up about it."

Okay, then.

————————

As I got closer to my goal, I began to realize I was going to have to sell my car. The minivan that had once been my mother's, my last remaining connection to her. That car had saved my life. It was my home, my escape hatch. It allowed me to live on my terms. But it also had a limited range, and I needed something that could take me across the country if necessary.

I spent several days thinking and rethinking my approach. If it failed, I'd be stuck with no transportation at all. No way to disappear when the time came.

I posted a listing on Craigslist: 1996 Honda Odyssey for sale. One owner. $6000 obo. and then my number.

I ended up selling it to a single mother with three kids. There was a kind of symmetry to that, of passing the car on to someone I knew my mother would approve of.

I signed the title over to her, filed the paperwork online with the DMV, and she was kind enough to drive me to the bank where I deposited $5,500 into my own bank account, and another $500 into Cory's household account.

Then I took the bus home.

---

"You're here," Cory said when he entered the house later that night. "Where's your car?"

I sighed hard and said, "Gone. Broke down on the side of the road. I called a tow truck and they took it to a mechanic. It would have cost $8,000 for a new transmission, another $5,000 for a new fuel system. More than the car was worth. I was lucky they were willing to give me $500 for it. I deposited it into the household account. Might as well contribute something."

"You should have called me," Cory said.

I shook my head. "It's fine. It's done."

"You need a car to get to school every day. To get to your shift at work."

I shrugged. "I can take the bus."

There were two kinds of people in the world—those who viewed public transportation as a blessing and those who viewed it as a curse. Cory was the latter. "That's going to tack hours onto your day," he finally said.

"I don't have much choice."

Cory shook his head. "And how are you supposed to run all the errands? Get the groceries?"

"I'll figure it out," I told him. "I can wait until you get home from work and borrow your car in the evenings. Or take it on Saturdays and do everything at once." I slipped my arms around his waist. "Plenty of households make one car work for them."

He disengaged, irritated. "I can't just sit around all weekend, waiting to use my own damn car."

I raised my voice, frustrated. "Then I guess it'll be the bus. And you can go back to hitting the grocery store after work." As soon as I said the words, I knew I had him.

Over the last month, I'd made sure Cory had grown very comfortable being taken care of. He had zero responsibilities, everything magically appearing before he realized he needed or wanted it. Folded laundry that smelled like expensive dryer sheets. His favorite beer in the fridge. A new bar of soap in the shower, well before the old one was used up.

"That won't work either."

My voice grew thoughtful, as if an idea was just occurring to me. "I could always rent a car to run the errands."

Cory gave a derisive laugh. "That may be your dumbest idea yet. It's no wonder you can't save any money, the way you're so eager to throw it away." He sighed hard. "I guess this weekend we're shopping for a new car."

"No," I said, keeping my voice firm. "You've given me enough. You are not buying me a car."

"That minivan was a piece of shit. It was only a matter of time before it died."

"You're not listening to me," I told him. "I don't want to take any more from you."

"For god's sake, Meg," he said, sounding exhausted. "Everything is always an argument with you. Just take the damn car."

———————

That weekend, we test drove four cars, finally landing on an eight-year-old Honda Accord being sold for $9,000 by a pregnant couple—Ted and Sheila—who needed to upgrade. I accompanied Cory to the bank to get the cashier's check, and I studied it on the way back to Tom and Sheila's, running my finger along the edges, mapping out my strategy.

"Excited?" he asked.

"It's so much money," I said. "I still think we could have figured out a way to share yours."

"I've seen you drive. There's no way I'm letting you behind the wheel of this car."

I shrugged and looked out the window, slipping the check between the seat and the center console, with just the top edge peeking out.

When we arrived at Ted and Sheila's, I wandered over to the Honda and admired its shiny black paint. The gray leather interior with a back seat that would never be used for sleeping.

Inside, Ted had everything ready. "Should take about twenty minutes," he told us.

My eyes swept around the space, taking in the warm colors, the soft chairs flanking the bay window, and imagined myself living in a house like that someday.

"Ted tells me you're a high school principal," Sheila said to Cory. That was enough to pull him away from Ted and launch into his monologue about the *energy of young minds.*

I stepped closer to Ted, pretending to look at the photos on the wall above him while tracking his movements, my nerves tight.

The timing had to be flawless. Up until now, everything I'd done was open-ended, allowing Cory the space to act or not. Today, I couldn't afford to give him that leeway. I needed to get Cory out of the room while Ted filled in the title, because I had to be sure it was my name that went onto it.

I watched as Ted pulled it from his stack of papers, and when he reached for his pen, I said, "Oh jeez, Cory, I left the cashier's check in the car. Can you go get it?"

"I'm in the middle of a conversation," he said, before turning back to Sheila.

My heart rate ratcheted up, knowing we were seconds away from Ted asking whose name should go on the title. Time seemed to slow, my eyes tracking Ted as he filled in the date and then back to Cory, before remembering Cory's spare car key I'd taken all those months ago, still tucked in my purse. My hand slipped inside, and I felt around until I found it, my thumb pressing the panic button.

The car alarm began to blare, making us all jump. I quickly stepped toward the window and peered out. "I think I saw someone trying to get into your car," I said to Cory.

In two steps, he was out the door to investigate.

"Maybe it was just a cat," I said to Ted, a sheepish expression on my face.

Ted resumed filling in the form. "Whose name should I put here?"

I took a step closer and said, "Meg Williams." I spelled out my last name for him and watched him ink it in.

He pulled his laptop forward and was copying the information from the title into the DMV website when Cory came back inside. "I didn't see anyone," he said.

"Thank goodness." Then I said, "What about the check?"

He shot me an annoyed look, but this time he went. And by the time he returned, the forms had been submitted.

"The check was practically under the front seat," he said to me. "What were you trying to do, hide it?"

I gave him a dubious shrug.

As he handed the check to Ted, his eyes flicked downward toward the title and caught my name there. "Wait. That's not..." He trailed off and looked up at me, confused.

I looked back, widening my eyes in alarm. "Oh my god. I thought when you said..." I covered my face with my hands. "This is why I didn't want to do this," I moaned.

"Is there a problem?" Ted asked.

The silence was thick and heavy, and I savored it. "No problem," Cory finally told him.

"I'll take care of it," I said, looking at Cory. "I'll do it immediately. As soon as the new title is issued, I'll transfer the ownership over to you. You won't have to do a thing."

Cory nodded, his expression stiff, and I wondered if I'd reached the outer boundary of what was possible.

---

At Cory's car, I folded myself into his arms and said, "I can't believe I misunderstood." I pulled back and looked into his eyes. "I swear I'll fix it."

I saw something flash across his face—there and then gone again. Doubt? Suspicion? But he only said, "Why don't you take it for a drive. I'll see you at home."

I waited for Cory to leave before unlocking the car and inserting the key into the ignition. The engine turned over easily, nearly silent compared to the rattle of the minivan. When I reached the corner, instead of turning right toward home, I was tempted to go left. To just keep driving. But I knew it wasn't time yet.

I'd hoped Cory would brush the mistake off. Say *No big deal, the car is yours.* But he hadn't. There were limits on his generosity, and if I was going to finish things off, I'd need to stay inside of them.

---

First thing Monday, I was set up at Cory's desk, the DMV website pulled up on his computer, my laptop open to a scanned image of a blank car registration form. I was slowly building a duplicate, making sure the font matched, making sure the text landed in the right place on the line—not too high, not too low. In my mind, I was already formulating what I'd say to Cory this evening when he got home. *I left work early to get to the DMV before they opened, and there were already fifty people in line! It took three hours, but it's done.* And then I would hand him the forms, with his name as the new registered owner and my signature on the bottom. Proof I'd done what I said I'd do. *Six to eight weeks for the title to come in the mail,* I'd tell him. I'd be long gone by the time he realized it was never going to arrive.

I was nudging his name slightly lower in the text box when Cory's computer pinged with an incoming message. Curious, I toggled over to his inbox, but there weren't any new messages.

I clicked on his icon in the upper right-hand corner and found a second linked account I'd never seen before—*SurfGuyLA.*

There were only three pages of messages, all of them from someone named *StacyB01.* I clicked through until I got to the very first email exchange, then scrolled down to the bottom to read Cory's initial email.

Hi, Stacy, Mr. Dempsey here. I hope it's okay that I reach out to you about what happened at school today. I didn't want to write from my school account since I wanted to be able to speak freely. Despite what was said in today's meeting with Dr. Michaelson, I will be personally monitoring the situation from here on out. Please feel free to email me on this account any time you need to talk. I'm here, and I'm always listening.

Stacy's response had been effusive. Thank you so much, Mr. Dempsey. It means a lot to me, and I feel so lucky to have your support. Everyone always says that you're the best principal we've ever had, and I agree.

The email in and of itself wasn't alarming, other than the fact that Cory felt the need to move it off the school server. I closed the message and opened another one from a month later.

Congratulations on your truly remarkable performance in Sound of Music, Cory had written. I remembered the play; Cory had gone to every show, claiming the principal had to be there. I'd declined, not wanting to sit through off-key renditions of "My Favorite Things" and "Do-Re-Mi." Cory hadn't pushed, and now I understood why. If I could have, I would have brought you roses to commemorate it, but it would have looked odd for the principal to be bringing flowers to only one cast member, no matter how talented and beautiful she is.

Stacy's reply arrived within minutes. Thank you, Mr. Dempsey, that means a lot coming from you. I could feel your eyes on me the whole time. Oh my god, I can't believe I'm typing that to my principal. But to me you're more than that. You're a friend as well.

His response was time-stamped at two in the morning, and I imagined myself, asleep in the next room as Cory corresponded with a student in the middle of the night. I'm glad you feel as I do. True friends are hard to come by in life, and I definitely count you as one.

More recent emails turned up pictures. Selfies Cory had snapped at the beach, his hair glistening from the ocean, his chest bare. And Stacy, in a bikini, lounging by a pool somewhere. Perfection, Cory had written back.

I recognized her immediately. The girl from the north quad. The one who'd stood the closest, whose hand had rested possessively on his arm, whose eyes had glittered with jealousy.

If I was looking for a sign that it was time to finish up and go, this was it.

I printed several copies of the most incriminating messages, slipping them all into a large envelope that I shoved in my purse. Then I forced myself to get back to work finishing up the car registration.

I was just printing that out when the doorbell rang. I crept from the office into the living room, glancing out the window, hoping it was a solicitor I could ignore. But it was Nate. He pounded on the door. "I know you're there, Meg. Open up."

I swung the door open. "Cory's at work."

Nate stepped past me and into the living room. "I'm here to see you."

My eyes followed him. "Make yourself at home," I finally said.

He turned to face me and said, "We need to talk."

I tilted my head to the side, looking confused, though my palms were growing sweaty. "About what?"

"The truth about who you are."

"What are you talking about?" I asked, my mind scrambling to find a foothold.

"I made some calls," Nate said. "Paid $30 for an old yearbook from the high school in Grass Valley. Found some alumni online. None of them have ever heard of you."

I glanced toward the street and saw old Mrs. Trout, our neighbor who lived on the corner, locking her front door, her ancient basset hound, Dashiell, waiting patiently.

"So then I started thinking about how you and Cory met," Nate continued, pulling my attention back to him. "Talk about being at the right place at the right time," he mused. "What a coincidence."

"Get to the point, Nate. Whatever fantasy you're spinning, please finish it. I have to get to class."

"You don't have class today," Nate said.

I took a step back. "Have you been following me?"

Nate's voice was low and angry. "For some time now. Because you don't add up, Meg. Not on paper, not in real life. Everything you've told Cory is a lie, isn't it?"

"I need you to leave," I said.

Nate shook his head. "You're pretty comfortable here, aren't you?"

I thought about the emails I'd just discovered and wondered what Nate would say about them. Whether I could justify what I was doing by throwing something even more appalling in his face. But Nate was a man who forced women in bars to accept his unwanted drinks and advances. Whatever Cory was doing, Nate wouldn't care at all.

My plan had been to use the next four weeks to empty Cory's account in $2,500 chunks. To be gone before he noticed his most recent bank statement never arrived. Before he started asking where the car title was. But Nate's accusation changed everything. I was going to have to leave now. Today. I'd be able to do one withdrawal, but I wouldn't have time for more. I scrambled to think about what I did have. The car—still registered in my name, the forged registration paperwork sitting on the desk in Cory's office—and my laptop. *Not enough.*

A fiery rage rose up inside of me. Why should men like this always be the ones who won? The ones who disregarded the rules and did whatever they wanted? I glanced out the window again, Mrs. Trout now standing across the street, waiting for poor Dashiell as he sniffed around the base of a tree.

Then I let out a blood-curdling scream.

Nate leapt away from me, his eyes wide. "What the fuck?" he hissed.

I took a deep breath and let out another one. Then I flung the door open and charged out of the house. "Help me!"

Mrs. Trout's gaze shot up, her expression stunned to see me running toward her, my feet bare, glancing over my shoulder. Nate stood in the doorway of the house, color drained from his face.

"He attacked me," I cried, cowering behind Mrs. Trout.

Nate pushed himself through the doorway and approached us. "She's lying."

"Stay away from me," I said, forcing my voice to wobble. To Mrs. Trout, I said, "He shoved me against the wall, tried to kiss me, then reached up my shirt..." I trailed off, as if I couldn't continue.

Mrs. Trout took me by the arm and said, "We can call the police from my house."

Nate looked incredulous. "You're fucking crazy, Meg."

"What I am is traumatized," I shot back.

Nate glanced between me and Mrs. Trout, then back at the house, the front door still standing open. He held up his hands. "Fine," he said, heading to his car.

When he was gone, Mrs. Trout came inside and sat with me as I called Cory. Demanded he come straight home.

---

At first, Cory didn't want to believe me. "Nate's been my best friend since college. He would never do anything like that."

But Mrs. Trout corroborated my story. "She came tearing out of the house like a cat on fire," she told him, her eyes wide behind her thick glasses. "Nearly gave me a heart attack."

An hour later, as Cory stood on the sidewalk and watched to make sure Mrs. Trout and Dashiell got back to their house okay, I did some quick math. Twenty-five hundred dollars a day for twelve days would get me $30,000.

Cory returned and sat next to me, taking my hand. "I can't believe this," he said. "Nate's made some questionable decisions in the past, but I never thought he'd do something like this to me."

I forced myself to count to three before pulling away. "He told me if I didn't sleep with him, he was going to convince you I'd targeted you somehow. He even told me he would tell you that I'd lied about my background. That no one in Grass Valley knew who I was. He's insanely jealous of you." I could practically feel the satisfied vibration passing through Cory. "Nate wants what you have," I went on. "He wants the house, the success, the relationship. He's always wanted to be you."

Later that night, I listened in on Cory's side of the conversation. Whatever Nate was telling him, it wasn't working. "She told me you'd say that. That you'd try to convince me she was a fraud." I held my breath, hoping that I'd fed Cory just enough of Nate's story to convince him that I was the one telling the truth. Finally, Cory said, "We've been friends a long time. You've always been there for me. But this crosses a line. I need you to stay away from Meg. Stay away from the house." Another pause, as Nate most likely tried to plead his case. "I mean it, Nate. Next time, we're filing a police report."

That night, when Cory reached for me in bed, I pulled away. "I can't," I said. "I can still feel his hands on me, grabbing me." I turned my back and pulled myself into a tight ball.

Finally, he said, "You're safe, Meg. He won't come back."

I nodded and pressed my lips together. *Twelve days*, I reminded myself.

––––––––––––

Time seemed to slow down. Over the next twelve days, I woke before Cory and stayed awake long after he'd gone to sleep. I stopped going to work and class, claiming I was afraid to leave the house, worried Nate would follow me. Cory suggested a restraining order, and I told him I'd think about it. But the minute he left for the day, I got to work.

I began every day with a trip to the ATM, withdrawing the maximum amount per day. By the time I left town, the household account would be nearly empty, and I'd have a large amount of cash, a new car, a laptop, and some very marketable web design skills, according to the community college website.

I submitted a change of address to the DMV, requesting a copy of the title be sent to the new PO box I'd set up. And always, I kept an eye out for Nate. Checking the street before I left, looking in parked cars, making sure he wasn't waiting to confront me again. It was exhausting, and I fell into bed every night, fatigued from holding myself together all day.

I spent a hurried hour in the college computer lab, scanning the photos of Cory and Kristen, checking over my shoulder as I printed three copies of each and put them into three separate envelopes along with the emails between Cory and Stacy I'd printed. I kept everything hidden in my computer bag, which I took with me everywhere.

Multiple calls from Cal went unanswered. Then the texts started. Why aren't you showing up for your shifts? You need to answer your phone.

A few days before my departure, I hid in the bathroom, sitting on the lid of the toilet, my hands shaking as I typed my response.

You need to stop calling me.

As expected, my phone rang again.

I blew the hair from my forehead before I picked up. "You don't follow directions very well, do you?"

Cal's voice was laced with concern, nearly breaking my resolve. "Are you okay? What's going on?"

I thought of all I'd lost. My mother. My home. Why couldn't I keep this one thing?

"I think our friendship has run its course," I finally said. "I need a fresh start. A new beginning."

"I never thought you'd be the kind of person who dumped her friends the minute she got a boyfriend."

My finger traced the edges of the white tiles surrounding the tub. Cal should know by now that I was the kind of person who did whatever she had to do to save herself. "Please don't call me again."

I had no idea where I would go, but I thought it best to leave California. Maybe Arizona or Nevada. Or maybe I'd keep driving east until I found a place where I felt like I could rewrite who I was and what I'd done to get there.

I bought a large metal toolbox with a padlock and kept it in my trunk. Every day, I put another $2,500 in it. The last thing I did was make copies of Kristen's settlement agreement, including her victim statement, and slid those into the three envelopes as well before addressing one to the school board president, one to the *Los Angeles Times*, and a third one with the name of the math department chair—Cory's nemesis, Dr. Craig Michaelson. I hid the original photos of Cory and Kristen in the back of his desk drawer, knowing Cory was unlikely to notice them but that, eventually, the police would.

And when the twelve days were up, I was ready. I waited for a Saturday, when Cory liked to go into school and catch up on paperwork, and invited myself along. "I won't get in the way," I told him. "I just want to be near you."

Even though it was early May, the mornings were still chilly. I put on a pair of running tights and a large coat with deep inner pockets. Into one of them, I tucked the envelope for Dr. Michaelson.

When we arrived, I waited while Cory unlocked the administration building and punched his code into the alarm. "Is the bathroom open?" I asked.

"Yep. Just down that hall," he said, flipping on the lights. I looked to where he pointed, past a long counter, behind which were a cluster of desks. Along the far wall were the teacher mailboxes.

"Thanks," I said.

I headed into the bathroom and stood at the sink, counting to thirty, waiting for Cory to get settled with whatever task he'd left for himself.

Then I slipped out and over to the mailboxes, searching the names until I found the one I was looking for. *Craig Michaelson, Math Chair.* I pushed the envelope toward the back of the box and counted the hours until Monday when he'd open it.

The president of the school board and the *LA Times* might not get the ones I'd dropped in the mail yesterday until Tuesday or Wednesday. But by my estimate, no later than Friday, Cory's entire life would explode.

———————

On Sunday, I fabricated several errands I needed to run—a fictional meeting with some classmates about a project, followed by lunch. "You're right," I told Cory. "I have to stop living in fear. Go back to work. Go back to class. Not let a guy like Nate scare me." While he'd showered, I'd packed my bag and put it in the trunk of my car, alongside the locked box full of cash.

I had a plan for Nate too. Once the story broke, I'd make a phone call to whichever reporter had the privilege of writing about Cory. A tip about Nate, directing attention onto him as well. Maybe even an anonymous call to the police. It wouldn't matter that none of it was true.

As Cory watched a basketball game, I walked through the house one final time, checking to make sure I hadn't missed anything. In the kitchen, I returned his spare car key to the drawer before wandering into the office, where I'd made sure to leave papers scattered across my desk—half-finished projects, notes from class that I no longer needed. I wanted to be out of California before Cory realized I was gone.

Back in the living room, I grabbed my coat, keys, and purse. "I'll be going," I said.

"Bring home some pizza for dinner, will you?" he said.

I smiled as I opened the door, perhaps my first genuine one in weeks. There wasn't enough money in the account to cover a napkin, let alone a pizza. "Home by seven," I said.

My plan was to get on the freeway and drive. In nine hours, I'd be in Las Vegas, and from there, I could go anywhere. But instead, I found myself again on Canyon Drive, parked outside my old house, Ron Ashton's Porsche 911 in the driveway.

It was midmorning, and there were several people out walking dogs or going for a run. In my newer Honda, I didn't stick out the way I had in the minivan. People glanced at me and then away again, a nice-looking young woman in a new-enough car. But I pulled my cell phone up to my ear anyway, pretending to be on a call as I stared at the house one last time. The blinds were open, revealing a shadow passing through the living room and out of sight. I wondered what Ron would do if I were to knock on the door. The last time he saw me, I was a gangly teenager, glasses where there were now contacts, mousy brown hair where there were now blond highlights.

Just then, Ron emerged from the house, hopping into his car and backing out of the driveway. I turned my face away, still pretending to be on the phone, hatred bubbling up inside of me. All these years, he'd been living in my house while I'd been sleeping in a car. While my mother lay dead in the ground.

I waited until he was gone and then shoved my car door open, making my way toward the tall hedge that bordered the southern edge of the property.

I glanced over my shoulder once, just to make sure no one was watching from the street before disappearing alongside the house. A tall iron gate separated the front yard from the back, and through it I could see Nana's rose garden, just beginning to bloom. I tried to open the gate, hoping I could take just five minutes to say goodbye to a place I'd loved.

But it was locked. I rattled it a few times, reaching over it to see if I could find a latch, but all I could feel was a padlock.

As I emerged back onto the sidewalk, I nearly collided with a woman in a track suit. She glanced between me and the side yard, as if trying to figure out where I'd come from.

"Did you lose a dog?" I asked, my tone urgent. "Small, black, with a white patch on his chest?"

"No," she said, her suspicion melting away.

"I almost hit him with my car. I pulled over and tried to catch him, but he ran into those bushes and now I don't know where he went." I gave her a worried look. "I hope he's okay." Then I checked my watch. "I've got to run, but maybe keep an eye out for him? See if he returns?"

"Sure," the woman said.

I felt her watching me as I made my way back to my car, grateful for Cory's generous clothing allowance—7 For All Mankind jeans, Franco Sarto boots, and a Rag & Bone sweater. I fit into this neighborhood better than I ever had before.

I gave the house one last look, knowing it was unlikely I'd ever return. But instead of feeling sad, I felt a lightness bloom inside of me. Life was long, and a lot of things could happen. Circumstances might bring me home again, back into Ron's circle. And if they did, Cory had taught me how to be ready for him.

# LOS ANGELES

Present Day

# KAT

I stay at the fundraiser, keeping a loose eye on Meg, but she and Ron don't talk again. She leaves around eleven, and I wait fifteen minutes before retrieving my own car. Then I text my mother, the only person still awake who might care.

I saw Meg Williams tonight. She's back.

Even though it's 1:30 in the morning in Chicago, I know she's up. When I was a kid and would wake in the middle of the night, she'd be in her study, reading newspapers, magazines, and political blogs. Anything she could get her hands on.

As I make my way down the winding street and back toward Sunset, I try to imagine Meg on her way home, only thinking about her introduction to Ron. Not knowing I was there too, watching her.

A couple months after Nate, I called Connor, one of the nicer reporters who had worked alongside me under Frank. "Did the police ever talk to Nate Burgess?" I'd asked. Even saying the name made me sweat, but I needed to know.

"Oh yeah," Connor said. "An anonymous tip was called in, shortly after you left, about an attempted rape. The police investigated, but didn't find anything. Since there was nothing to back up her story, they wrote it off as a crazy ex-girlfriend, looking for revenge."

Connor's words hit me like a punch. Meg never mentioned anything about an attempted rape. Not even a warning—*Don't go alone* or *Watch your drink around him*. Instead, she'd led me to believe that if I concealed who I was and what I wanted from him, Nate would share all of Cory's secrets. She didn't care that it might put the young female reporter on the other end of the phone at risk.

My mother's reply buzzes as I turn onto the freeway that will lead me home. I've kicked off my heels, and the gas pedal vibrates against my bare foot.

This is your second chance. Don't squander it.

A familiar pinch of disappointment. With just a few words, she's reminded me that most people don't need a second chance at all.

I never told my mother what happened with Nate. All she knows is that I was on the Cory Dempsey story, and then I wasn't. I was a young, promising reporter working at the *LA Times*, and then I wasn't. I'd gone to the high school the following morning, gotten the quote for Frank, and delivered it on the edge between *late* and *too late*. But as the story developed, with new and horrific details being released every day, I couldn't stomach it. I kept seeing Nate's face, blurry around the edges, the last thing I remembered before I passed out. There's a special kind of hell in not remembering trauma. It becomes a dark and faceless fear that lurks in unexpected places—the smell of whiskey, a certain type of bar stool, a song, a laugh—reaching out to grab you when you least expect it.

I slid off the story and another junior reporter from Frank's team stepped in, no one aside from my mother seeming to notice or care.

"What were you thinking?" she'd asked when I told her I'd quit the paper. "I pulled a lot of strings to get you that job."

"It's done," I'd said. I couldn't tell her that I was sick every morning, terrified that, despite the empty condom wrapper, I'd somehow gotten pregnant or caught an STD. I began to isolate myself, declining dinner invitations, nights out with friends, until the only person I saw regularly was my best friend, Jenna, from journalism school.

"Things didn't work out," I told Jenna. "You know what it's like. Endless fact-checking. Twenty-hour days chasing someone else's byline. I want the freedom to write my own stories."

Leaning on my time working at the *LA Times* allowed me to get a few decent freelance jobs at the beginning, but Nate had changed me. For years, I had to fight down panic attacks every time I had to meet a source in person, always choosing a crowded place. Never eating or drinking anything. I felt safer behind a computer screen, eventually settling there permanently.

As a result, research became my specialty. I know how to take a deep dive into someone's financials or to dig up old records from small claims court for a property dispute. Over the years, I've used these skills to learn as much as I can about Meg Williams.

I'm not the naive reporter I was back then. If I'm going to pull myself out of the professional hole I've been in for the last several years, exposing Meg and unraveling a decade of her cons and thievery will be how I'll do it.

She owes me that.

---

Being an investigative journalist is like traveling through a maze backward. I start at the end and try to find my way back to the beginning, discarding false leads and dead ends until all the signposts are clearly marked. And to understand anyone, you have to start with their family of origin, which informs every choice they make.

I started my search years ago, using public records. In 2001, Meg's mother, Rosie, inherited a house in Brentwood from her paternal grandparents. Brentwood is a pocket neighborhood, between Santa Monica and Westwood, filled with an eclectic mix of high-end condominiums and large estates. Home to twentysomething tech bros as well as megastars like Jennifer Garner and Gwyneth Paltrow, properties like the one Rosie inherited on Canyon Drive sell for millions of dollars.

In 2004, Rosie put a developer named Ron Ashton on the title to the house. Eight months later, she'd signed a quitclaim deed, giving him sole ownership. She'd died a year later.

But public records will only provide a framework. They can't tell you anything about the people behind them. For that, you have to talk to those who might have known them.

I needed a busybody. Someone who paid attention to the comings and goings of their neighbors. Who was moving in, who was moving out. Who had rip-roaring fights in the driveway at five in the morning. Who came home drunk in the middle of the night. Every neighborhood had one; you just had to knock on enough doors to find them. I spoke to a lot of housekeepers and ladies who lunch, all of them refusing to acknowledge whether they'd known the Williams family or not.

But finally, I found Mrs. Nelson, who lived in the house directly behind the Canyon Drive property. "I've lived here for nearly fifty years," she said, after I'd introduced myself as an old friend of Meg's, trying to track her down. "I remember the Williams family well."

We'd settled into white rattan furniture on Mrs. Nelson's sunporch, overlooking a flat expanse of grass leading toward a tall hedge at the back, behind which stood Meg's family home. "I remember Meg's mother, Rose. She was a spunky and sparkly young lady." Mrs. Nelson lowered her voice. "Rupert and Emily's son—Rose's father, Dean—had some trouble with drugs. In and out of rehab for years." She sighed. "They never said so, but I'm certain that's why Rupert never retired. He worked until he was almost eighty."

"What happened to Dean?" I asked.

"Oh, it was tragic. He died in a car accident right after Rose graduated high school, I think. All those years, all that money they spent trying to help him, and that's how it ended."

I took a sip of the lemonade she'd offered, imagining the kind of heartbreak that would cause. "Is that when Rose inherited the Canyon Drive house?"

Mrs. Nelson shook her head. "Not until her grandmother, Emily, finally passed away in 2001."

Meg would have been thirteen. "When I knew Meg, they didn't live in this neighborhood, that's for sure."

"After Emily died, Rose and Meg lived there off and on, in between renters. I got the impression they couldn't afford the mortgage, and I imagine there was a sizable estate tax as well," Mrs. Nelson said. "They left in 2004 or 2005, though I don't think it was on good terms."

"What makes you say that?" I asked.

"I was in my garden, and I heard Rose yelling through the back hedge. 'You lied to me!' She was screaming it, over and over again."

"Who was she screaming at?" I asked.

"The man who lives there now. Ron Something-or-other." She gave a dismissive wave of her hand. "He's a fancy fellow, with his sports car and slicked-back hair. He said, 'You have seven days to clear out or the sheriff will do it for you.' Well, it just about broke my heart. Rose loved that house." Mrs. Nelson gave an indignant sniff. "Every now and then I'll see him. He'll say hello, but I just ignore him. I *never* say it back."

"Do you know where they went?" I hadn't been able to dig anything up on them beyond 2004. No address, no utilities. I knew they hadn't left the area because Meg finished high school. But where had they lived?

Mrs. Nelson shook her head, her rheumy eyes sad. "No idea."

———————

I never could fill in those blank years. But for $12 a month and Meg's mother's maiden name, I was able to track her for a short while after she left Los Angeles. First to Seattle, where she lived for six months. From there, she went to Salem, Oregon, and after that, Phoenix. The people she'd conned described a woman who'd fallen on hard times, or a woman coming out of a bad relationship. And she always seemed to leave with something that didn't belong to her.

*She stole $50,000 and my mother's engagement ring.*

*She sold my Harley, right out from under me. She kept the cash too.*

Meg Williams seemed to be whoever she wanted you to think she was, twisting and turning in your mind like a hologram, never solid, never fully clear. In Seattle she'd been a college student. In Oregon a photographer. In Phoenix she'd been a dog walker. And after Phoenix, she simply vanished. No new locations, no new cell numbers, no death or marriage certificates, no court records. I've learned over the years that if a person doesn't show up in one of those paid databases, it's because they're working very hard not to.

In addition to setting that Google Alert for Meg, I also continued to keep tabs on Ron Ashton. Watching him grow his construction business into one of the largest in Los Angeles County, his successful bid for city council, and most recently, a run for state senate.

Con artists don't like to be conned. The loss of her childhood home is Meg's core wound. Every criminal has one, a beacon calling them home. Of course, it's possible Meg grew up, got therapy, and moved on. But I don't think so.

At home, I unlock the door as quietly as I can, my shoes dangling from my other hand. The apartment is dark, save for the table lamp Scott left on for me. I drop my keys on the table and veer into my office, not even bothering to take off my dress. I want to get my impressions down as soon as I can. What Meg was wearing. Who she talked to. How long she spoke with Ron. When it comes time to write the piece, I want my readers to be able to taste the canapés, to hear the music, to feel the soft breeze from the open french doors.

Another text from my mother. Happy to read anything you have so far!

"Jesus, go to bed, Mom," I say into the quiet room, regretting my earlier text.

I'm a visual thinker, which is why I work on paper and not a computer. My notes are like a complicated map with arrows connecting ideas to names and dates. I've got over a hundred pages—handwritten jots, outlines, interviews—but ten years out, it's all old news.

I ease open the bottom drawer and pull out what I do have—fifty-three pages, double spaced, Times New Roman—the start of a novel I haven't had time to work on in over a year.

What would my mother think to know this is all I've got? I'm a cliché, a frustrated journalist taking her useless research and turning it into fiction. A story about a female con artist traveling the country, the different ways I imagined she targeted people. The things she stole. If I can't expose her in the *New York Times*, maybe I can expose her on their bestseller list instead.

I shove it all back in the drawer. It's a ridiculous dream and one I can't afford to pursue.

I creep into the bedroom, where Scott is just a dark lump under the covers. I change quickly and slide in, fitting myself up against him. I'd met Scott five years ago, when an online data breach had compromised my bank account, the thieves stealing nearly $1,000. Scott had been the detective to work my case.

"These are becoming more and more common," he'd told me when he took my statement. "Everyone says their website is secure, but that's really an impossible thing to promise."

"I'll be paper-only from now on," I told him.

He'd laughed, and I loved the way his eyes crinkled around the corners, like happiness enveloped his entire face. "I'm not sure that's any more secure," he said. "I'll keep you posted on any developments, but don't hold your breath."

We never caught the thief, but Scott and I became friends, eventually even working on a few cases together. I'd worked hard over the years to deal with the trauma of what Nate had done, but trusting men was still difficult. When Scott invited me to go to the LA County Fair, my therapist encouraged me to give it a try. And when I told Scott I'd go if I could buy my own food, he only shrugged and said, "I don't care if you go behind the counter and make it yourself. I'm just happy you said yes."

I thought he'd last a few months and then grow weary of my insistence on sleeping at home—alone—every night. How sometimes dark places like movie theaters or dive bars made me nervous.

"Take your time," Scott had said, over and over again. "You're worth it."

And after a while, I began to trust him, telling him a little bit about what happened to me. Not specifics, just enough for him to know that I'd suffered an assault. "Did you report it?" he'd asked, as I knew he would.

"It's complicated," I said. "It was part of a larger story I'd been working on. I was somewhere I wasn't supposed to be, talking to someone I wasn't supposed to be talking to. I was young and scared, and I only wanted it to be over."

But the truth was, I had no proof. I'd gone to work the following day and pretended nothing had happened. There were no witnesses. No rape kit or police report. *If it really happened, why did she wait so long to tell someone?* It would have been my word against Nate's, and I never wanted to see Nate again.

Scott's voice softened. "Statistically, only 35 percent of women report an assault. Even fewer get a conviction." He looked grim. "I always think it's worth trying to prosecute, but I acknowledge that I'm not a woman or a victim, so I don't get to have an opinion."

I never told him that I felt Meg was partly to blame. Instead, I concealed my anger beneath a determination to find her. To tell her story and take back a little bit of the agency I'd lost.

I fell in love with Scott's calm demeanor, his steadiness, his sense of humor. And while my mother wasn't thrilled to see me tie myself down—*just remember how quickly a career can end before it even starts*—I didn't care. Scott allowed me to finally start healing.

Which is why, when he ran into his own trouble a couple years ago, I didn't think twice about supporting him. After everything he'd done for me—giving me the occasional lead on a story, helping me come out of my shell and trust again—I wasn't going to walk away when he needed me.

But lately, Scott's been pushing me to start planning our wedding. Wanting to talk about things like name changes and joint bank accounts. The more he pushes, the slower I want to go. I feel safe in this space we've created. Committed to each other, but still separate. And I can't tell if it's because I don't trust him, or I don't trust myself.

I snuggle in close to him and close my eyes, but my mind keeps working. He isn't going to be happy to hear I'm back on the Meg story, reluctant to lose me down this rabbit hole again—one he thinks is a dead end.

"She didn't break any laws," he's always happy to remind me.

"She took $30,000 and a car."

"He gave her access to the money. It would be impossible to prosecute, which is why he never did. She's not a con artist; she's just a pissed-off woman. And for good reason."

I can't explain to Scott that it's more than a story to me. I want to climb inside Meg's mind, inside her life, and piece it all together, dot by dot. Figure out how she manipulates people, infiltrates their lives, getting them to trust her. I want to know where she's been for the last ten years, and why she's returned. And then I want to tell everyone about it. Take something from her, the way she took everything from me.

# KAT

*June*

As I guessed, Scott isn't thrilled. "Do you think that's a good idea?" he asks over breakfast the following morning.

I pick apart the muffin in front of me and say, "What do you mean? This is a real story, not one of those content-mill pieces I've been churning out for the past two years."

But I feel a prickle of irritation, because what he's really asking is whether we can afford for me to step away from the piecework and copyediting jobs that have replaced the investigative stories that sometimes take months to write and sell.

Two years ago, shortly after we got engaged, Scott got into some trouble gambling. He'd managed to accrue over $15,000 in credit card bills, and together we've been slowly paying it off.

"Meg's story would put us within spitting distance of wiping the debt out completely." I've mastered the nuances of this topic, hiding my resentment that a percentage of my income goes toward it as well. Money I earn, not by researching and pitching real stories to real publications, but by writing crappy content that pops up at the bottom of websites. *How to Make a Backyard Butterfly Garden* or *Ten Genius Hacks for Your Next Trip Abroad.*

"That's not what I meant," he says. "I'm worried about what it will do to you. To go back to all of this again—the people, that time in your life. You've worked so hard to put it behind you."

"I can handle it," I tell him. Even as I say the words, I wonder if they're true. Already I can feel the heat of Meg's proximity pulling me backward.

"I still think you should finish your novel. What you've got so far is great."

I brush away his words. "We'll never pay off the debt that way."

When I'd agreed to marry him, I knew I'd have to sacrifice some of my own dreams and focus on being a good partner. Scott helped me deal with my shit; it wouldn't be fair for me to let him flounder alone with his. But there was a fair amount of trust that he destroyed when he finally confessed how much trouble he was in. How much he'd already pilfered to cover himself. Things he'd sold, desperate to hide the truth from me.

For a long time, I went to weekly Gam-Anon meetings. Aside from the strategies I've learned to support him, I also know how lucky I am, how much worse it could have been. The stories I've heard are enough to make me swallow my frustration—a double-mortgaged house, bankruptcy, college funds squandered; $15,000 is a small price to pay.

But it's been enough for me to put off the wedding, claiming that Scott needs more time in recovery. And with the return of Meg, I'm glad we're not in the middle of guest lists and centerpieces and menu tastings. There will be plenty of time to get married after my piece releases. After *Meg Williams* becomes a household name.

The Google Alert that had landed in my inbox three months ago sent me to a real estate website for Apex Realty, a Los Angeles-based company, featuring Meg's photograph in full color in the upper right corner.

Meg Williams—Bringing You Home. Beneath it was a brief bio that touched on the few facts I already knew. Born and raised in Los Angeles, California, daughter of a single mother who worked hard to support her child, Meg brought that work ethic with her to the Midwest, where she has been a top agent for the last ten years. She's won numerous awards, including the President's Award, given to agents who earn in the top 1 percent of commissions quarterly. Meg specializes in finding just the right property to match a client's needs, and her tough negotiating skills have saved her clients millions of dollars over the past decade. I snorted. Ten years ago, Meg was blowing up Cory Dempsey's life, not embarking on a successful real estate career. Newly relocated back to the Los Angeles area, Meg looks forward to partnering with you for all your real estate needs.

Beneath her statement was a gallery of properties in Michigan she'd supposedly sold, the cheapest one just under $4 million. Below that were nearly twenty client testimonials.

At the bottom was a Los Angeles area phone number and a link to the real estate firm she'd been affiliated with in Michigan. When I clicked on it, it took me to a boutique agency website, located in Ann Arbor, and a picture of a cute storefront. But there were no links to any other agents, just a phone number, photos of featured properties for sale, and their list prices.

When I called, it went straight to voice mail. A woman's voice said, "You've reached Ann Arbor Realty. We're out showing properties to clients, but please leave a message and we'll get back to you as soon as we can!" I hung up without leaving a message.

I'd been certain the license number listed on Meg's website had been fake. Getting a real estate license takes months of studying, several exams, and the submission of fingerprints. I'd been stunned when I found her on the California State Real Estate Board site, listed as an active agent working out of the Beverly Hills Apex office.

———————

I wait a couple days after the fundraiser to call Meg. She answers on the third ring.

"Hi Meg, my name is Kat Reynolds," I say, offering up the fictional last name I sometimes use. "I'm hoping you can help me... I'm looking to buy a home in the area, and you come highly recommended."

"That's fantastic," she says. "But I'm pretty slammed with clients right now. Can I refer you to one of my colleagues?"

According to the state of California, Meg's license was granted six months ago. No matter how good she might be at selling houses, there's no way she'd be turning away new business this early. "That's too bad," I say. "Ron Ashton gave me your name. I was hoping we could set up an appointment for later this week."

Her tone shifts immediately. "You're friends with Ron?" I hear her shuffling some papers, and then she says, "You know, I can probably fit you in. Let's talk through what you're looking for, how much you want to spend, and I'll try to set up some appointments for Thursday afternoon. Would that work?"

"That sounds great," I tell her.

———————

On Thursday, Meg and I meet at the Apex office. She guides me into a conference room where a single file folder sits on a large glass table. When I open it, there are five properties inside, all of them on the Westside. The cheapest one is a tiny white bungalow, listed at $1.2 million.

Meg is dressed in a pink silk top and black dress pants, spiky heels peeking out beneath the hems, her hair pulled into a loose chignon at the base of her neck. She looks nothing like the high school photo I saw of her so long ago, and I feel the thrill of being close to her. She slides into a chrome and leather chair across from me and says, "All of these properties have been on the market for at least six months, so don't let the prices scare you off. I think they're pretty soft."

I flip through each page, pretending to read the details of each home—the square footage, whether there's inside laundry or attached parking—but I'm not processing anything. I'm watching her watch me. Does she even remember making that call to the *LA Times* ten years ago? Would it bother her to know where it sent me? When I get to the last page in the file, I close it and say, "Shall we ride together?"

Meg beams. "I'll drive."

---

Her black Range Rover is a far cry from the used Honda that Cory Dempsey bought for her. "So, tell me about yourself," she says as we pull into traffic on Santa Monica Boulevard. "What do you do?"

I thought long and hard about a backstory I could give, something that would allow me to be flexible with my time, but nothing that she could Google to verify. "I'm actually not working right now," I say, casting a sideways glance at her to see how that lands. After all, she's about to show me several properties listed for over a million dollars. "I used to work for Bank of America as an account specialist, which really meant I tried to get people to upgrade their checking accounts. I hated it. But then my great aunt Calista died, and she left me a sizable amount of money. Enough for me to tell them to get lost."

Scott had argued against this. "You have no idea how these people operate," he'd said when I told him my plan. "They shake your hand with the right and reach into your pocket with the left."

"The only way I'm going to get this story is to get close to her. To see firsthand how she works. You know this."

"There are so many different cover stories you can use," he'd argued. "Pose as another real estate agent, or someone with a lot less money, looking for a rental instead of a million-dollar home. You don't have to set yourself up as her next mark."

"I have to be someone worth her while."

I could tell he still wanted to argue, but he sighed and said, "Fine, but don't let your guard down. If she thinks you have money, she'll have you turned inside out and backward by dinnertime."

"She can't con me if I'm expecting it," I told him. "I think I can befriend her. Get her to trust me. Maybe even tell me where she's been all these years."

"I think you're confusing real-life Meg with a character you've invented. In the real world, con artists don't have friends. Every word they say is a lie, and their only goal is to scam as many people as possible."

Meg's voice pulls me back. "If only everyone was lucky enough to have an Aunt Calista," she says.

I smile. Calista is actually my favorite aunt on my father's side. Not rich, but thankfully, also not dead. "She was pretty special," I tell Meg. "Calista never married. She worked as a paralegal, putting herself through law school, and was the first female partner at her law firm back in the seventies." I shift in my seat so I'm facing Meg. "Investing in property would have been something she'd want me to do."

The thrill of dropping below the surface of my life and pretending to be someone I'm not rushes through me, and for a moment, I can understand why Meg does it. The allure of a new life, a new backstory, is seductive. How easy it might be just to stay here.

She turns left off the main boulevard and into a pocket neighborhood of small houses and large trees, and pulls up in front of a white house with large windows and a dying lawn out front. "This one needs a little rehabbing, but it's got good bones."

She trails me as I walk through the house, pointing out original features. When we're back outside, she says, "What'd you think?"

I wrinkle my nose and say, "It's a little too much of a fixer for me."

The next property is in Venice. "My mother and I lived in and around this neighborhood when I was growing up," she says as we navigate through downtown Santa Monica, the buildings growing shabbier the further south we travel.

The admission catches my attention. "Really? Where?"

"Never anywhere long enough to memorize an address."

"Have you always lived in Los Angeles?" I ask.

She shakes her head. "I was in Michigan for the past ten years. I just moved back."

"Must be nice to be home."

She gives a rueful laugh. "Yes and no," she says. "You have this vision of how your life back home used to be, and you think that's what it'll be like when you return." We've hit a red light, and she looks at me, her expression sad. "But it's not. No one is in the same place. Nothing is as you left it. It's disconcerting. The people I knew before are gone. I've not only had to start my business from scratch, I've had to find a new community. A new group of friends." She's quiet for a moment. "I miss my mom," she admits. "Even though I lived here for a number of years after she died, the hole she left feels bigger somehow. More obvious."

I know how loneliness can seep into your life, the realization that there isn't anyone who understands you, or the things that keep you up at night. "How old were you when she died?" I ask, though I already know the answer, having tracked down her mother's death certificate several years ago.

The light turns green, and we accelerate. "It was December of my senior year in high school. Close enough to eighteen that I could fake it for a few months. My biggest regret is that she died thinking she'd failed me."

What a heartbreaking thing to have to live with, if it's true. "In what way?" I ask.

"We lost our house," she says. I notice how her hands grip the steering wheel, white knuckles visible beneath the skin. "We ended up with nothing." She gives me a quick glance. "We lived in our car for a while."

Scott had warned me Meg would do this—make herself vulnerable by telling me something that would elicit sympathy, and I work hard to step around it. Her admission explains why I couldn't find them, but her words don't match what happened. They didn't lose their house; her mother signed a quitclaim deed over to Ron Ashton.

"Enough about my sad story," Meg says, gesturing to the engagement ring on my finger. "Do you have a date set?"

I glance down at the one-carat solitaire on a platinum band that took us six months to pay off, and twist it on my finger. "Not yet."

"What's his name? How did you meet?"

"His name is Scott and he used to work with me at the bank," I tell her.

"How long have you been together?" she asks. "Does he get a say in what you buy?"

It's so easy to take the truth and turn it a few degrees, shifting things just enough to rewrite our struggling finances. Paying rent on our credit cards turns into an inheritance from an aunt. An engagement that's been dragging on for two years is suddenly new and exciting. "We've been together five years, and no, he insists this is my money, my decision."

"He sounds like a keeper."

It's been a rough road, with a couple setbacks and one relapse at the beginning, but Scott and I are on the other side of it now. "He's the best," I say, fighting harder than I want to fit inside the words.

"Let's get lunch when we're done," Meg suggests. "My treat."

———

We find a restaurant on Sawtelle, a Japanese fusion place with an out-door patio in the back, crisscrossed with vines and twinkle lights. It's nearing two o'clock, and we have our pick of tables. Meg leads me to one in the far corner, orders a half bottle of white wine, and we study our menus while we wait for it to be delivered.

"So how do you know Ron?" Meg asks.

I answer carefully, mindful that I can't give her something Ron might refute. "I met him at a fundraising dinner, not too long ago. In the Hollywood Hills. It was pretty spectacular."

She gives me a quick look. "You're kidding. I was there too."

I study her thoughtfully, as if trying to place her. "I thought you looked familiar. Don't be too impressed with me though. Scott's parents bought the tickets months ago, but his dad got sick so we went instead. I doubt Ron would even remember me; I only spoke to him for about five minutes. Long enough to tell him I was in the market for a property, and he gave me your name. Sorry if you thought I had a more official connection…" I trail off.

Meg reaches across the table and squeezes my arm. Her hand is warm and soft. "Not at all. I was only there to support my friend, Veronica, whose husband is his campaign manager."

Our server arrives with our wine and takes our order.

"What did you think of Ron?" I ask when she's gone again.

She shrugs. "I'm hoping to pick him up as a client. Like you, we only spoke for a few minutes." She looks away, her gaze landing on a muted television mounted on the wall, showing a women's march. Fists in the air, they silently shout, their #metoo posters bumping up and down as the crowd moves forward. "Men will always show you who they are." Her voice is quiet, and she gestures toward the television screen. "Doesn't it ever just exhaust you?"

A lot of things exhaust me. Paying down a gambling debt that shouldn't be my responsibility. A job that sucks my soul dry. The shadow of what happened to me, always nibbling at my periphery, because even ten years out—well past the daily panic attacks and night terrors—I still wake up sometimes, flooded with shame. Not that I let it happen, but that, in not reporting it, I've let it continue. I've let it happen to other people, the way Meg let it happen to me.

Meg's voice is quiet. "Don't you wish you could take some of that power back?"

I look at her, wondering what she's really trying to say. "What would you do with it?" I ask.

"Hold them accountable."

Back in the car, she turns to me and says, "I got the feeling you didn't love any of the properties we saw today."

"I didn't," I admit. "It's all so expensive." I'm wondering how long I can carry on the charade of me looking for a house to buy.

"That's Los Angeles for you," she says. "I'll see if I can find anything cheaper, though you might have to push out to Culver City or down into Westchester."

"I'm okay with that," I say. Anything to stay next to her, to keep her talking.

———

Over dinner that night, I bring up the topic of real estate fraud.

"Is this about Meg?" Scott asks.

I think about what I know. From Mrs. Nelson, overhearing Rosie's accusation—*You lied to me*. And Meg's own confession—*We had to live in our car*. "I don't have anything more than a gut feeling, but too many pieces are overlapping with Ron Ashton to ignore. Right now, I'm thinking it might be some kind of real estate scam."

He shoots me a warning look. "Careful what you tell me."

"No, this is just broad strokes stuff. She hasn't done anything, as far as I can tell. But let's keep this off the record, just in case."

"I'm not a reporter, Kat. There is no off the record with me. If a crime is going to be committed, I have to do something."

I hold up my hands. "Right now, I'm in information-gathering mode. Looking at all possibilities."

Scott nods and helps himself to a slice of pizza. "Real estate fraud could be a lot of things," he says, taking a bite. "A signature forgery on a quitclaim deed to pull money out of a property."

A quitclaim deed is how Ron got the property. It's unlikely he would fall for something like that.

Scott continues, warming up to the topic. "Or sometimes people find abandoned properties, change the locks and try to sell them to unsuspecting victims. Most of the good scams require several people to pull off—property appraisers willing to appraise a property at a much higher value, loan officers willing to file false or inflated loan documents."

I take a bite of pizza, thinking. I suppose it's possible Meg has assembled a team, but she doesn't strike me as a collaborator. She would need local people already in place, established in their chosen fields. And I don't think she has them.

"But banks put in a lot of safety measures when they're loaning money," Scott says. "They require appraisals. Inspections. Proof of insurance."

"How about in the context of all-cash deals?" I ask.

"Then the options open up significantly."

"Why is that?"

Scott wipes his mouth with a napkin. "With an all-cash offer and a corrupt agent's encouragement, the buyer can waive the contingency protections—like the inspection and appraisal—and get stuck with a property that could have major issues."

"Why would an agent do that?" I ask.

"The buyer's agent might be getting a kickback. Her commission, plus a percentage of the money the seller makes on the sale." He chews, thinking. "Or maybe she uses a legitimate transaction to get his personal information. Social security number. Banking information. Most everything is done online, but a smart agent could find a way to get access." Scott gestures at the last piece of pizza and I decline. He takes it and says, "If it were me, I'd try to find out where she's been, what she's been doing. Con artists pull the same scam over and over. It's likely whatever she has planned is something she's done before."

---

After dinner, Scott turns on the TV, and I sit at my desk, flipping through my folder, rearranging the pages to give myself a new perspective. I stop when I find notes from my source at the Contractors State License Board. I'd called him after my interview with Mrs. Nelson, the neighbor who'd lived behind the Canyon Drive house. He'd described Ron as *sketchy*. "Or maybe more like predatory," he'd said. "He used to find people in financial trouble, get them to refinance their homes under the guise of big renovations. When the money ran out, he'd disappear."

"Used to?"

"He cleaned up his act about a year ago. No complaints since then."

I doodle a starfish along the edge of the page, imagining Rosie, a young single mother with no family left, trusting a man like Ron and losing everything. What had that done to her? What had it done to her daughter?

For every story I write, I keep a legend—a quick glance at important facts, names, dates, and locations. Meg's is a scramble of information going back ten years. I trace my finger across the names I gathered so long ago. *Cory Dempsey. Cal Nevis. Clara Nelson.*

*Nate Burgess.*

I stare at the name now, remembering his face, and the way his apartment smelled, until the letters blur and I have to look away. Remind myself that it's been ten years, and I'm not that person anymore.

My therapist had been the one to suggest writing fiction as a tool in my recovery. "When you write a fictional account of something, you're in control. You get to decide how it ends. I want you to write what happened to you that day, but I want you to change it so you have all the power."

The first scene I wrote was short—me waiting in my car instead of the bar, watching Nate enter, and then driving away. The next one had me tossing my drink in Nate's face. The one after that had me kneeing him in the groin and using his tie to yank him to the ground.

It was empowering, but it didn't erase what had happened. It showed me that, like fiction, justice was an illusion for men like Nate.

But then I turned my attention to Meg and kept writing, giving her a backstory similar to the one I'd researched, wondering what her tipping point had been. The trigger that had sent her in the direction of Cory Dempsey, and then turning that into a career.

I gather my notes back into their folder and tuck it away. Long ago, when Scott moved in, we made the agreement that our workspace was sacrosanct. That neither of us would breach the other's work documents unless invited. Even though I haven't had a big story in over a year, I still put things away, on the off chance that Scott might see something unintentionally.

On the desk next to me, my phone buzzes with a text from Meg. It was nice getting to know you today. I do a yoga class every Wednesday morning in Santa Monica. Want to join? As I read the text, she sends a follow-up. This is me, trying to make a friend. She includes a laughing emoji to keep it light, but I feel a pulse of sympathy for her, which surprises me.

I'd love to, I type back. Then I add, This is me, trying to be a friend.

# MEG

What are the most important traits a con artist might need? Many people would say charisma. Others might say intelligence, or the ability to lie and manipulate. Some might also talk about being able to think on one's feet. To pivot quickly when something goes wrong.

Those aren't wrong answers, but they're not my answers.

The ingredients of any good con are patience and trust.

In every job, every identity I've inhabited, I always have to start with something true. Something real. Take Veronica and David's transaction, for example. Ask either of them and they will swear up and down that I am exactly who I say I am. It took me forty-five days to earn that trust. Most con artists aren't interested in—or able to—stick around for that long.

But this is how you embed yourself in someone's life. How you become one of their people, a member of their innermost circle, which will open up all kinds of opportunities.

---

Today is my first outing with Ron, and I'm taking him to look at a beachfront duplex in Malibu. It's been on the market for over two years due to significant structural issues. The listing agent is someone from over the hill in the valley, and he told me up front what to expect. "I'll be thrilled if I can finally sell it," he confided. "I've been sitting on this listing forever. But I've got to disclose that the pylons below the house have begun to erode. No matter what, those are going to have to be replaced. That's why it's priced so low at $5.5 million."

"That might not matter to my buyer," I told him. "He's a developer, so something like that won't scare him off."

I chose the property for many reasons, not the least of which was its remote location, requiring a long drive from Beverly Hills, through Santa Monica, and up the coast highway. That time in the car with Ron will allow me to build my backstory, shading some of the Michigan transactions with just a hint of corruption. Letting Ron know my professional ethics are as soft as his.

But I wouldn't be human if I didn't admit I'm nervous. I've spent years vilifying him in my mind. Making him out to be the monster who stole the last of my childhood. Now I'm going to need to cozy up alongside him and engage in flirty banter, openly admire him for his business acumen and intellect. Allow him to define who he thinks I am and then live inside that assumption. It will require a level of acting I haven't had to do since I discovered the truth about Cory.

I'm still gathering information, learning how Ron works, discovering his habits and blind spots. But there's one thing I do know—Ron has a lot of money and a lot of power, and my goal is to use Canyon Drive to take both away from him.

---

Just north of Pepperdine University, we turn off PCH and onto a small access road. Houses here push right up to the water, built on concrete pylons suspending them high above the sand and breakwater. Properties along this stretch sell for at least $10 million, depending on square footage and whether someone has come in and converted everything to glass, chrome, and white marble. Gone are the beach cottages of the sixties and seventies with their wooden stilts, warped hardwood floors, and sticky sliding doors.

"This place has been converted into a duplex, and some of the finishes aren't as high-end as the zip code requires, which is why it's priced so low at $7 million," I tell him, deliberately adding a couple million to the list price. Anything lower and he'd know something was wrong with it.

We enter a bright space with vinyl wood flooring and light fixtures from Home Depot. "The second unit upstairs is an exact footprint of this one. Access is an outside staircase along the south side of the property. Garage parking for two."

Ron walks toward sliding glass doors and opens them, stepping onto a redwood deck. For a split second, I fantasize about the pylons giving way right at that moment, tumbling him one hundred feet to the rocks and shoreline below us. He turns and smiles. "I could rent each unit for at least six thousand a month. Is there laundry?"

I lean against a tiny kitchen island and point down a hallway to my left. "Stackable washer and dryer in a closet there."

We make our way slowly through both units, Ron commenting on the light. The high ceilings. The kitchens in each, both of them clean white tile with clean white appliances. "There's almost nothing to be done," he marvels. "How long on the market?"

"One month," I lie. "I got the impression from the listing agent that the sellers are beginning to get antsy. They thought it would have sold by now."

"If it were a single-family home, I'm sure it would have," he says. "I think it's priced a little too high for what it is."

"The market sets the price, not the seller," I recite. Seven million, two million, ten million…it doesn't matter because I'm not going to let this transaction get that far.

Our eyes meet across the room, and I feel the same jolt I felt that first night at the fundraiser—I can't believe I'm finally here, after so many years.

"Let's put in an offer," Ron says. Beneath us, waves crash against pylons that are slowly disintegrating. "Let's do five million even."

I nod once and slide the door closed, the ocean sounds now muffled. "I'll go back to the office and draw up the paperwork."

———————

Two days later, I call Ron. "We have to pull out of the Malibu property."

"What? Why?" I can hear the sounds of a busy campaign office behind him, a low rumble of voices, the ringing of phones.

"My inspection guy knows the property. Apparently, there's major structural damage to the pylons below the house. Something to do with the concrete not being done right and saltwater erosion. You don't even want to know what it would cost to repair them."

He breathes out hard. "Jesus. Why didn't they disclose that?"

"I don't know, but I've already spoken to my office manager about it. He's reaching out to the listing agent's manager, and I can guarantee you there'll be hell to pay." I lower my voice just a touch, though I'm alone in my house, with only the sound of a neighbor's lawn mower in the distance. "Look, there are a lot of agents out there who would push this deal through, earn their commission, and leave you to handle the fallout. But that's not how I work."

"I really appreciate that. Trying to litigate this would be a nightmare right now. Do you need me to do anything? Sign any paperwork?"

"Don't worry about a thing," I tell him.

"You're the best, Meg. Thanks for looking out for me."

I disconnect the call and draft a quick email to the listing agent. *I did my best, but unfortunately, my client decided not to make an offer after all.* I hit Send and lean back in my chair, satisfied with how well this first part went. I've gotten everything I wanted from our initial excursion, the most important being that Ron now believes I will protect his interests over my own. This will make it easier for him to take my advice later.

*Patience and trust.*

# KAT

July

Yoga turns into a weekly thing, which then turns into brunch afterward with Meg's friend Veronica.

"You're in the best hands," Veronica always says, anytime the conversation turns toward my house hunt. "She'll find you something great."

One morning, we're lingering over the remains of lunch, empty plates scattered around us, when Veronica asks, "Why the long engagement, Kat?"

Her question feels like a test. Meg had just finished telling us a story about how someone once tried to break in to the car where she'd been sleeping, and Veronica had told us about the time her husband, David, got a DUI. Women forge friendships around shared confidences, and in order to stay on the inside, I need to give them one of my own. Scott's voice in my head warns me. *Nothing personal. Not your parents' names, or even the name of your childhood dog.*

Here's the thing about the truth—it makes everything surrounding it seem like the truth as well. One tiny fact—one true thing—can spread out and legitimize all the lies I've told. "Scott used to have a gambling problem," I say, hardly believing I've said the words out loud. But as I say them, I know it was the right decision, because I feel them drawing nearer, lowering their own walls. Being vulnerable is the fastest way to connect with another person. "Mostly online stuff. But we worked through it, and he's two years in recovery. So we're taking our time with the wedding. Letting things gel before shaking them up again."

Meg looks concerned. "Is your aunt's inheritance a problem for him?"

Veronica chimes in. "Aunt? Inheritance?"

I quickly fill Veronica in on Aunt Calista, legal superstar and benefactor to her struggling niece. Then I turn to Meg and say, "Large amounts of money aren't really a trigger for Scott," I riff. "It's more the adrenaline of winning that gets him. But he's been working the program, and we have some really strong guardrails in place. It would have been easy for me to quit, to walk out, but he got me through something really tough a long time ago and it would've been hypocritical of me not to stand by him. He's a good person, and a hard worker. I believe in him."

Meg's eyes are wistful. "I love a good redemption story."

The conversation moves on, but I'm stuck on what I've revealed, trading something true about myself in exchange for a sliver of Meg's trust. It was a calculated risk, but I had to take it.

---

Meg has continued to take me to see properties—usually about three or four a week. I always find some reason why I'm not ready to move forward on any of them. We're walking through another tiny house in need of major rehab in Westchester when Meg says, "Be honest with me… you're not really interested in buying a house, are you?"

I'm peering into a utility closet when she says the words, and I freeze, trying to compose my face to be more *true confession* than *oh shit*. I turn to face her and say, "You're probably right, although I *want* to buy a property," I admit. "It's just…I like seeing that huge number on my bank statement. For the first time in my life, I don't dread opening that envelope every month. I spent my whole life living check to check. It's nice to have that kind of breathing room."

Meg leans on the counter separating a tiny galley kitchen from the laundry room. "I get it," she says. "There's something really powerful in knowing you've got security."

"I like the company though." Which is truer than I care to admit. Meg always has stories to tell—about deals that almost fell through, a client with absurd requests—*a wine cellar and a sex toy room, if you can find it.* I don't believe a word of any of them, but a part of me is impressed with how well she's developed her backstory. How easy it might be for someone who didn't already know who and what she was to believe her. This is how people like Meg operate. They build an incredible fantasy world, and when you're living inside of it, you stop caring about what's real and what's not.

"I'm kind of relieved, to be honest," Meg says. "The houses at this price point are depressing. I wouldn't have wanted you to spend your money on any of them."

Back in the car, we pull away from the curb and head back toward the Beverly Hills Apex office where my car is parked. "Perspective is a funny thing," she says. "My mother would have killed to have lived in any one of those houses. I would have too."

About a year ago I wrote a piece for an online psychology blog titled "Ten Simple Ways to Build Trust," and I've been employing as many of them as I can. Things like being on time, mirroring her body language, and being generous with my own information, like my confession about Scott. All of it leading up to my next question. "What exactly happened?" I ask, hoping she's ready to answer. "You mentioned that you lost your home?"

"It's a cliché, really. My mother fell in love with the wrong guy," she says, keeping her eyes on the road as she talks. "Her biggest regret was getting involved with him, and for what he put me through."

"Did he...?" I trail off.

"No, nothing like that. He barely looked at me. I was awkward and bookish and mostly hid in my room when he was over. But because of him, we lost our home. Our family history, really. There's only so much you can take with you when you're living in your car."

"Did your mother have any legal recourse?"

Meg shakes her head and looks over her shoulder to change lanes. "My mother barely had a quarter for the pay phone. She was terminally ill. By the time any of that got sorted out, she would have already been dead."

"How did he do it?" We still haven't named him, and I'm careful not to reveal that I know it's Ron we're talking about.

She's quiet, and I worry I pushed too far. But then she says, "My mom needed to refinance the house—get cash out of it. But her credit was shit. She couldn't secure a loan on her own, so he offered to cosign in exchange for putting him on the title."

I sit up straighter, intuiting where this is going. Meg must see my expression because she says, "I know. She believed him when he said they could co-own it. He'd do all the repairs—and believe me, it needed a lot. There was mold in the downstairs library. Earthquake damage from the '94 quake that never got addressed. He said he'd fix it at no cost and then they could either rent it out or sell it, and split the profits. It would have been a life-changing amount of money for us."

"But that's not what happened?"

Meg shakes her head. "He spun some story about how the banks wouldn't allow him to refinance the loan so long as she was on the title.

'Forty-five days,' he told her. 'Just long enough to secure the loan. Then we'll put you right back on the title.'"

"That's not how it works," I say, remembering a case Scott worked on several years ago, a young man who convinced his elderly grandmother to do something similar and then sold the house out from under her to fund his drug habit. "Banks don't care who's on the title; they only care who's on the loan."

She looks grim. "I know that now. But back then? I was just a kid and my mother was in over her head." She's quiet for a moment and then says, "That was the hardest year of my life, living in our car with my mother. She tried to make it feel like this big adventure—'We can go anywhere we want, on a moment's notice'—but the reality was, we cycled through beach parking lots and the occasional shelter. In the fall of my senior year of high school, my mom got sick. Urgent care sent her to the ER and…" She trails off. "It was pretty fast after that. By Christmas, she was gone."

All the ways I've pictured what could have happened to push Meg and her mother out of their home, I never imagined this. A part of me wishes I'd never asked, because it's hard not to empathize with her. To imagine a younger Meg and her mother, sleeping in their car, knowing the man responsible for putting them there lived in their home. Still lives there to this day. I can't pretend this is another one of her stories, because enough of the pieces fit with what I already know. "I'm so sorry," I say.

Meg shrugs. "It was a long time ago. Time to move on, you know?"

This is a lie. This is why Meg has returned.

"How do you not want to kill him? Or make him pay somehow?" My words hang there, an invitation.

"Men and accountability," she says. "They rarely go together."

We travel in silence for a few blocks before she says, "What's next for you? If not a new house, then what?"

"I'll have to find something else to fill my days," I say, though I'm having trouble moving past what Meg has just told me. The rage that must have consumed her for so many years, bringing us to this moment.

Meg shoots me a quick look. "A life of leisure isn't suiting you?"

I stare out the window, trying to step back into the role I've cast for myself. "I guess I could pick up a few more yoga classes. Volunteer at the animal shelter." I'm struck with the irony of two women, each of them trying to spin a web of lies and manipulation around the other, never knowing whose strings are wrapped around whom.

Meg laughs. "Just remember, work is a drag." She hits the brakes, traffic piling up behind a broken light. I can make out the edges of the traffic cop at the center of the intersection, white gloves flashing.

I shift in my seat so I'm looking at her. "It must be fun though, having access to fancy houses and rich clients. What else are you working on? Anything interesting?"

"Ron's taking up most of my time. He says he wants an income property, but he's got me all over the map. Apartment buildings. Duplexes. Triplexes. But he hates them all. An investment property isn't what he really wants."

"And what would that be?"

"What all men like him want. Power. Status. The respect and envy of his peers. Which he won't get from a duplex in Culver City." Meg keeps her eyes on the car in front of us, masked behind her sunglasses, so it's hard to read her expression. "He's an all-cash buyer, so that keeps me hanging on. 'Why get the banks involved,' he says. But Ron's no different than any of the other rich and powerful men I've worked with a hundred times before." She gives a small laugh. "I know how to handle him."

"And how's that?" I ask. The traffic cop beckons us forward, and we ease into the intersection, the car picking up speed.

She smiles. "Tell them what they want to hear."

———

Meg calls me after dinner. "I've been thinking," she says when I answer. "I know you don't need to work, and I know you're weighing your options, but how would you like to be my assistant for a little while? It would probably be about twenty hours a week, searching for and previewing properties and some assorted paperwork. Everything's online now, so you wouldn't ever have to set foot in an Apex office. Plus, flexible hours, so we can still do yoga and brunch with Veronica on Wednesdays."

A friend of Scott's used to work undercover in the drug unit. *Definitely better than a desk job*, he used to say. He'd get up in the morning, put on a pair of jeans and a hooded sweatshirt, and head off to whatever neighborhood he was working that day. Sliding alongside junkies and drug dealers, hoping to gain their trust so that they could lead him to the person at the top.

In the past, I've always investigated from a distance, using my sources, the internet, and public records to piece a story together. But I'm realizing that won't work with Meg. I don't have any sources, and the internet is yielding only what she wants people to see. The only way to know what Meg's up to is to step out of my comfort zone and become a part of it. "I'd love to," I tell her.

# MEG

Let's talk about Kat for a moment. Young, flush with new money, adrift and unsure of the direction her life should be taking.

Also, a pretty accomplished liar.

From the moment she called me, claiming to be a referral from Ron, I suspected Kat wasn't who she said she was, and I confirmed it by following her home shortly after our first outing together. I sat in my car outside her duplex and watched her neighbor, a young woman in her late twenties who smiled at three different people between the front door of the building and her car.

My favorite kind of person.

"Hey," I said to her the next morning as we waited in line at Starbucks. "You're Kat and Scott's neighbor, right?"

She looked at me, her eyes bright and trusting. "Yes," she said.

"I knew I recognized you!" My delight at the connection became hers. "I've always loved your building," I confided. "How long have you lived there?"

The woman furrowed her brow, thinking. "Three years maybe? I moved in right before Scott."

The line inched forward. "Scott's such a doll. I wish they'd set a date already. Did Kat tell you how they met?"

The woman smiled. "Of course. Very sweet."

"What are the chances though?" Vague questions implying knowledge can yield a lot.

She shrugged. "I remember Kat saying something about meeting Scott on a case, but I don't remember the details. I'm sure on most of his fraud investigations, there would be journalists involved as well."

My stomach slid sideways. Even though I'd suspected Kat wasn't who she said she was, I didn't expect a reporter and a fraud detective. I kept my tone thoughtful, as if I were trying to remember something. "Didn't he work on her last story too?"

"I don't know," she admitted. "To be honest, I can't recall the last big piece she did. I think it was a while ago. But I'm sure if you Google Kat Roberts, it'll all come up."

*Kat Roberts.* Not *Reynolds.* I marveled for a moment at the similarities between us—each fully ourselves, with only a few select details swapped out. It's not easy to inhabit a facsimile of yourself, and despite my racing heart and sweaty palms, I could still appreciate how well she did it.

"What can I get for you?" the barista asked me.

"Black coffee, please." Whatever would get me out of there the fastest. To Kat's neighbor I said, "It was really great running into you!"

She smiled as she slid up to the counter to take her turn, and I grabbed my coffee and hurried out, as if I had somewhere important to be.

Instinct is a funny thing, a whisper of trouble that we can never quite name, never quite define, that allows us to locate danger. Women are taught from a young age to ignore theirs. We're forced to justify our instincts with evidence, or we're taught to ignore them—as a way to keep the peace, to prioritize other people's comfort over our own.

It's taken me a long time to override those impulses. To pay attention when something seems off. And my instincts weren't wrong about Kat. The inheritance story was a good one—impossible for an outsider to verify—but it lacked the background details that might have fooled me for longer. An inheritance large enough to purchase a home in Los Angeles would show up in your life in other, smaller ways. Maybe as a new car, or nicer clothes. Jewelry. Even expensive highlights from the salon. But Kat had none of those things. She drove a ten-year-old Honda. Her yoga wear was from Old Navy, not Lululemon. Her makeup was from Sephora, not Neiman Marcus.

My mind began circling through ways to cut her loose. Become too busy to show her any more properties. Avoid her calls and texts, build a wall that would keep Kat separated from what I was planning.

But then my instincts kicked in. Casting her aside wouldn't stop her. She'd continue to target me, follow me, possibly feeding information to Scott. But if I held her close, I could control the narrative. Make sure the only things she saw were curated by me. So I made her my assistant instead.

I'm not a fool. I know Kat plans to write about me, exposing who I am and what I do. I see beneath her soft sympathy and the delicate questions she's likely known the answers to for years. But I have a plan too, and Kat will be a useful part of it.

It'll be easy to pull her in and feed her the pieces I need her to have. And because she'll be so close, it'll be impossible for her to see the whole picture. Like standing under the Eiffel Tower—when you're inside of it, it's just a bunch of crisscrossed steel. It's only from a distance you can see it for what it really is.

# KAT

*July*

Scott's reaction is predictable. "You have no idea how hard undercover work can be. It's 24/7. We still have bills to pay."

What he's not saying: *How will we be able to live and pay down my debt if you're not cranking out six or seven shit articles a week?* I swallow down a sharp reply. "I'll work in the evenings. Carve out pockets of time when I'm not with Meg. It doesn't take a lot of brain power to write one thousand words about the power of positive thinking, or to come up with five new moves to super-sculpt your abs. Besides, Meg is going to pay me."

He rolls his eyes. "She's not going to pay you to hang out with her. It'll be twenty hours of actual work a week, if you're lucky."

"We can economize. Eat out less often. Stay home more. It's only for a couple months," I say.

"You don't know that."

But I do. Meg isn't back in Los Angeles to sell real estate to people like Veronica and her friends. I'm almost certain she's after the Canyon Drive house, and she's using the distraction of the election as cover. Taking advantage of a time when Ron can't possibly be as focused as he should be.

"It'll be over by Thanksgiving," I hedge. "Four months. And if it's not, I'll step away and get some paying work."

Scott nods and I pull him into a tight hug. By the new year, everything will be different. I can feel it.

---

The job turns out to be mostly property searches for clients Meg supposedly picks up from Veronica or her friends. I use the MLS—the Multiple Listing Service—which is a real estate database that has every house for sale, along with its purchase history. I can look up any property in Los Angeles and see all the buyers and sellers, going back decades.

The first thing I did was look up the Canyon Drive property. But it didn't show me anything I didn't already know. Bought in 1954 by Rupert and Emily Williams, refinanced in 1986 and again in 1993. Default on the loan in 2004, and a quitclaim deed to Ron Ashton that same year.

---

I'd worried that Meg might want to keep me separate from Ron, the better to shield whatever she has planned for him. But shortly after I start, she invites me along on a showing with him. He enters the Apex office in a wave of cologne and importance.

"It's nice to see you again, Mr. Ashton," I say, hoping to head off any indication this is the first time we've met. In my experience, politicians will never admit to not remembering someone, and Ron proves no different.

"You too," he says, his eyes lingering a little too long on my chest. I cross my arms and plaster a smile on my face.

"I'm taking you to see a multiunit property that's USC-adjacent," Meg says as we walk toward the Apex parking garage.

"That's real estate speak for low-income," Ron says, making a beeline for Meg's front seat.

I'd always intended to sit in the back—not just in my role as assistant, but to better view the two of them side by side. But the fact that he didn't even make a show of offering the front seat to me tells me that Ron is here as a consumer, and he plans to consume everything.

I buckle in and say, "What exactly are you in the market for, Mr. Ashton?"

Ron doesn't bother looking at me as he responds. "My dream scenario is to find something in need of repair—I'm a developer and contractor at heart—evict the welfare queens and drug addicts, do a quick and cheap rehab, double the rents, and lease to college students too dumb or drunk to know better." He laughs. "David, my campaign manager, would kill me if he knew I just said that out loud. 'Optics are everything.' I'm not even allowed to compliment Meg's outfit or tell her she has the best set of legs I've seen in twenty years. Because once the media gets ahold of something, it's impossible to walk it back."

I don't know if it's Ron's tone, or the casual way he objectifies Meg, but it yanks me back in time, images like a broken filmstrip flashing through my mind. The way Nate looked at me, his eyes raking up and down my body. The way his knee pressed against mine under the table. A hand on my lower back, guiding me toward a dark car, the smell of his expensive leather seats so similar to the smell of Meg's car I almost vomit.

I crack my window, quietly practicing the breathing technique that helps to regulate these attacks before they can take hold. I haven't had an episode in over a year, and as I breathe, I remind myself that I'm safe. That as awful as Ron might be, I'm not alone with him. He's not Nate.

"Running for public office means you have to follow the rules," Meg teases, unaware of my growing anxiety.

We ride in silence for a little while, but when we reach a freeway underpass with several homeless tents under it, Ron has to comment. "These encampments are everywhere," he says. "Druggies, rapists, crazies."

Meg glances at him. "What's your plan for that?" she asks.

He sighs. "Since we can't scoop them up and dump them somewhere else—like out in the desert—my plan is to let the mayor and city council deal with it."

"What, no social service platform?" she asks.

"We've got the bare bones of one," he admits. "But only because we have to. I'm big business; that's why people are going to vote for me. Oh sure, LA is a liberal enclave, but a majority of the residents in Malibu, Brentwood, and the Palisades are in the top 1 percent income bracket. While they like to put signs up in their yards about 'Black lives matter' and 'Love is love,' they don't actually want to fund those initiatives if it will cost them more in tax dollars. Los Angeles is the capital of lip service and illusion."

Meg is taking surface streets, the late afternoon traffic making the freeway almost impassable, and the start and stop of the car as we move through Culver City and beyond adds to my queasiness. That and Ron's cologne, which feels as if it's seeping into my skin.

"I'm assuming all of this is covered by agent-client privilege, correct?" he says to Meg.

Her eyes meet mine in the rearview mirror and hold. "Of course," she says, giving me the smallest of winks as she pulls up in front of an apartment building just off Normandie Avenue—a stretch of concrete, graffiti, and decay.

"Kat and I will wait out here and enjoy the sun," Meg says. "I called ahead and had the manager open up Unit 4 for you."

"Back in a flash." He bounds up the front steps, his expensive suit in stark contrast with the cracked stucco, rusted hand railing, and trash gathered at the base of the building. When he's gone, I say, "He's awful. How can you stand spending so much time with him?"

Meg sighs and leans against her car. "Believe it or not, I've worked with worse."

*Who? When? What did you do, and are you doing it again?* The questions dance inside of me, aching to be asked. "There's no such thing as *client privilege* with real estate agents, is there?" I ask instead.

"Of course not. The only thing I'm not allowed to do is disclose his financials—assets, bank account information, routing number—to anyone outside the context of a deal."

I search her face for a hint of what she might be thinking. Emptying his bank account? Making it vulnerable somehow? But her expression is unreadable as she tips her face toward the sun.

We stand in silence for a while, the sound of traffic and the distant crash of a trash truck somewhere behind us, before she says, "Were you okay back there, in the car? You looked like you were going to bolt at the next red light."

She looks at me, waiting, and I wonder what she'd say if I told her about Nate. How she'd played a role in it, and whether she might want to make amends. She'd had no trouble tearing Cory Dempsey's life apart, and it's obvious she's planning something similar with Ron. What might she do on my behalf? The question jolts through me, electric and raw. "Men like him make me feel boxed in," I finally say. "Like I can't think clearly enough to get away."

"Did someone hurt you?"

I savor the warmth of the sun on my shoulders, glad to be out here instead of trapped inside somewhere with Ron. "Yes, but it was a long time ago, and I don't like to talk about it." I have to remind myself that I'm not here to confide in Meg. She hasn't earned the privilege of my secrets, no matter how much I might want to tell her this particular one.

Meg's expression softens into concern. "I never would have brought you along if I'd known."

"Why did you?" I ask. "You certainly don't need the help." Meg isn't someone who would do anything on a whim; there must be a reason for my presence here today.

"Appearances matter to a man like Ron. Hired help, personal chefs, valet parking, and assistants scurrying after him. It's all part of the facade I have to build."

I give her a sharp look. "For what purpose?"

She grins and says, "A big commission, of course." When I don't return her smile, she says, "You look disappointed."

My cheeks flush. "No, I just hate people like him, sliding through life always getting what they want."

She glances toward the corner of the building, where Ron emerges from a side walkway. She bumps her shoulder against mine. "Me too," she says, pushing off the car and making her way around to the driver's side.

It's only later, when I'm home again, after the hot shower I took to wash off the clinging scent of Ron's cologne, that I realize the entire outing felt like performance art, Meg serving Ron up to me on a platter, garnished with his most horrible traits, aligning me alongside her, despite my best intentions.

She claimed it was Ron who needed to see me working for her on his behalf. But maybe her true purpose was for me to see firsthand what kind of a person Ron is, so that when she's done, I'll understand.

Regardless of who her audience was, there's no question that Meg's performance was flawless.

---

But in the meantime, a woman like Meg still has to earn a living. I don't see her selling any houses, just sending me on endless searches for buyers who always seem to vanish before they ever look at a single property, leaving me to wonder if they'd ever existed at all.

As promised, I spend a few hours every evening getting some writing work done. Tonight, while Scott's watching a baseball game, I'm finishing up a story on menopause and belly fat for an online women's health magazine that's 90 percent paid advertisement and 10 percent shitty content.

When I'm done, I turn to the pile of mail Scott tossed there earlier. Several bills and a note from Scott—*Your mother called my cell because you haven't returned any of her calls or texts. Please let her know you're still alive so she'll stop bothering me.*

I've been avoiding her for a couple weeks now. She'd come across a story I wrote—"No Time to Cook? No Problem!"—and her text had stung. Do you really think it's a good idea to affiliate yourself with content like this? As if I had a choice.

I throw away a few pieces of junk mail and turn toward the bills. When Scott moved in, we'd decided to split them, Scott paying the gas and our cable/internet bill every month while I'd pay the water and power. We take turns paying the rent, and I'm relieved that this month is his turn.

But the arrival of the gas bill makes me realize what's missing. I flip through the stack again, double-checking, then look in my drawer where I keep all my important paperwork filed, just to make sure I'm not mistaken.

Our bank statements haven't arrived. Which is odd because they always arrive a few days before the bills, and I always check mine before paying anything. Though we still keep separate accounts, Scott and I use the same bank. Our accounts always post on the same day, and I can't remember the statements not arriving near the beginning of the month.

My stomach coils, as it always does when something like this happens.

Even after two years of Scott being completely transparent, of working the program, it's still so easy for my mind to leap back again to a time when he'd stay out all night, gambling with friends. To the unpaid utilities and service disruptions. And the loss of my grandmother's engagement ring, sold to pay his bookie.

We'd worked through it in therapy, and Scott has granted me full access to everything. His bank statements, his cell phone and computer. I used to check every night, but I've grown tired of the constant monitoring.

Which is exactly when Scott might backslide.

Through the doorway I check to see that he hasn't moved from the couch, then open his laptop. A quick search of his history shows nothing unusual. His emails are likewise uninteresting. I wander into the kitchen, where his phone sits on the table, and scroll through his messages and history there.

Again, nothing. His last text with his sponsor, Karl, was this morning at nine.

I wander back into the living room and say, "Our bank statements haven't come yet."

He keeps his eyes on the game. "Maybe it's time to finally sign up for online banking."

"If you recall, the last time I did that, someone stole $1,000. Do I also need to remind you why online banking is a bad idea for your recovery?"

Scott doesn't respond, but I can see his jaw flex.

"Where do you think they are?" I ask.

His expression grows defensive. "What makes you think I know?"

I try to pick my way carefully through a mix of fear and worry. Had he taken them, perhaps to conceal something he didn't want me to see? Maybe his account is overdrawn to pay a new gambling debt, or maybe he's trying to figure out a way to borrow money from me without having to ask. Is this how it starts again? "I'm just wondering what you think, that's all." I hold my breath, studying his face looking for any trace of guilt.

But I don't see any. He pauses the game, his expression serious. "Have you considered the possibility that your con artist friend followed you home? Feeding her a bullshit story about an inheritance from Aunt Calista might have been a mistake."

"Why would she risk being caught?" I ask.

He sighs. "Mail fraud is some of the easiest to perpetrate. You can get all kinds of information with the right piece of mail. A bank statement would be like gold to someone like Meg." He glances toward the front of our building, with its drafty vestibule and broken outer door latch. "It's not like our lobby is exactly secure," he adds.

I sit down hard on the couch, thinking back to what I'd said the day I told her I wasn't going to buy a house after all. A throwaway comment now comes back to haunt me: *I like seeing that huge number on my bank statement every month.* An invitation to come and take a look.

My heart begins to race at the chaos a compromised bank account would create in my life. In Scott's. Neither of us have much—Meg would surely be disappointed by what she'd find there. And then a new worry comes crashing in.

"If she stole them, not only would she realize there's no inheritance, she'd see that the name on my account doesn't match the one I gave her. All she'd have to do is Google me to figure out who I am and what I do. All that work I put into building a relationship with her, gone. Along with the story."

"If she knows who you are, you've got bigger problems than losing the story," Scott says. "You're actively trying to expose her. A con artist isn't going to just let you walk away. She's going to want to make you pay."

For the first time, I consider the possibility I might be in over my head.

# KAT

July

I'm finishing up a paid copyediting job that's due this afternoon, my mind foggy with exhaustion. I'd woken up at two in the morning with a night terror—heart racing, drenched in sweat—and hadn't been able to fall back asleep again.

"You okay?" Scott mumbled.

"Bad dream."

"It's this story," he'd said. "It's putting you around all of the same people again, and your body is reacting. It remembers."

"Maybe," I'd whispered. In my dream, I'd been in a car with Ron and Meg, and they'd taken turns trying to get me to drink from a flask. "Go back to sleep."

But I'd remained awake, catching up on paid work I'd let slide, only taking a break to drink the cup of coffee Scott had poured for me before he left for work.

When Jenna, my best friend from journalism school, calls at ten, I'm grateful for the break.

"Hey," I say.

"Is now a good time? I've got a window before I have an editorial meeting."

It's been a year since Jenna moved to New York to take a staff position at the *New York Times*. After she left, I dropped away from our small circle of grad school friends who'd settled out here. It's hard to be happy about someone's piece in the *Atlantic*, or their byline in the *Times*, when I'm still struggling at the bottom. My mother is always on me about networking. Meeting people. *You can't hide inside the cocoon of your relationship with Scott or rely on Jenna's contacts forever.*

"That story you did on corruption inside the SDNY was great," I tell her now.

"Thanks. It almost didn't run. Long story. But tell me what's going on with you. What are you working on?"

"Meg's back," I say.

I hear her sharp intake of breath. "Really? Tell me everything."

I fill her in, telling her about the Google Alert and tracking Meg down at one of Ron Ashton's fundraisers, then posing as a potential buyer and befriending her. "She's hired me as an assistant," I say.

"How's that going?"

"Depends on who you ask," I tell her. Then I explain about the missing bank statements. "Scott thinks it's possible she knows who I am and that now she might be targeting me."

"Seems pretty risky for her if she is," Jenna says.

"That's what I think. Plus, in the two weeks since they've gone missing, nothing's different. We spend at least four hours together every day, and I don't see any change in her behavior or attitude toward me. I don't care how good she is at what she does, no one's that good."

"Where do you think the statements went?" Jenna asks.

"Maybe they just got lost in the mail," I offer. Though even as I say the words, they don't ring true. That it's possible the woman who didn't think twice about encouraging a young female reporter to meet with Nate might easily be the kind of opportunist Scott thinks she is.

"So, after all these years of wondering, what's she like?"

I think about how to answer. The careful dance we're both doing—each of us lying about who we are and what we want, always one careless comment away from the edge. Then I think of Meg's sharp humor. The vulnerability she's shown.

"If I didn't know who she was and what she did, I'd probably be her friend."

"I think Scott's right to be concerned," Jenna says. "Whether she knows who you are or not, you need to be careful."

"Don't worry."

But since Meg's return, a different version of her has emerged. She isn't the one-dimensional con artist who'd lived inside my imagination for so many years. She's a woman who hates men like Ron as much as I do. Who always insists on paying for lunch and ends up tipping 30 percent. Who rolls her window down at red lights to give $5 to the homeless person standing there.

"Where are you going to pitch the story? And when?"

"I don't know," I hedge. I'd been thinking about *Vanity Fair* or *Esquire*. This is exactly the kind of big, splashy story they would love—a beautiful, mysterious female con artist—but all I have are some ten-year-old claims and a lot of empty space. "I need to know where she's been and what she'd done to get an idea of what she's doing now."

"Where does she say she's been?"

"Michigan. Selling real estate," I say. "She's got a website, with photos of houses she's sold and client testimonials."

"Fake?"

"Almost certainly. But it's a dead end." In the weeks since Meg's return, I haven't been able to find any company in Michigan operating under the name Ann Arbor Realty. An image search of the listings from her website were all traced back to Zillow or Redfin with other agents' names attached. "I'm stuck," I admit. "None of the databases I have access to are going to turn up what Meg wants to keep hidden."

"Let me put one of my researchers on it, off the books. See what we can turn up."

I'd been hoping she'd offer. "Really?" I say. "That would be amazing. All I need is a lead—a name, a location. I can do the rest."

"Your mom must be loving this," she says.

I sigh into the phone and stare out the window. "She's constantly at me, texting suggestions, and offers to read pages. When I told her I was going undercover, she practically had kittens."

Jenna laughs. "She means well."

I know Jenna is right, but it runs deeper than that with my mother. The expectations I always seem to fall short of, the disappointment that my big break at the *LA Times* resulted in a career writing piecework while my grad school friends have gone on to write for major outlets. When Jenna got hired by the *New York Times*, instead of being happy for Jenna, the first thing my mother said was *Why didn't you go for that job yourself?*

"Other than worrying about you, how's Scott?" Jenna asks.

"He's doing well," I say.

"When are you guys going to set a date?" she asks. "I want to make sure I put in for time off."

"I don't know. We're both so busy. Maybe after I sell this Meg story, we can sit down and get something calendared."

"You make it sound like you're booking a gynecologist appointment. Try to be a little excited."

I laugh. "I'm excited. I just have a lot to do. I'm basically working two jobs."

Jenna's silent for a minute, as if she's weighing my words. "Just make sure that's all it is. I know I've said it before, but there's no shame in changing your mind."

"Scott's been doing great," I tell her. "Working the program. All is well, I promise."

Jenna waits a beat before saying, "I gotta run. Call me this weekend?"

"Will do."

After we hang up, I stare at the phone. I miss having a friend. Someone to meet for lunch or a quick coffee. Someone I don't have to always be on guard around, looking for lies and manipulation slipped into conversations. All the pretending, all the role-playing takes an emotional toll. I think back again to Scott's undercover friend, to what he'd always say. *After a while, if you're not careful, you can lose sight of the line. You no longer think in terms of* me *or* them *and only in terms of* us.

# MEG

Six weeks into the job and I will admit, I'm starting to worry. I've never had a deadline like the one I have with the election, and like any deadline that starts to loom…the closer you get to it, the more you begin to panic that the pieces might not come together in time.

And I can't help but wonder if I've got a blind spot. Never before has a job been so personal. So raw. Never before have I had so much invested in the outcome. This is my magnum opus, and I am flat-out stalled.

I've got Kat, bless her heart, keeping us busy with properties Ron might like. If she thought this job was going to be mostly yoga and lunches with a few contracts here and there, she's got another thing coming. I actually need her to work.

I'm out with Ron at least three times a week, carving out an hour here, an hour there from his busy campaign schedule, ostensibly looking for the perfect property to add to his portfolio. But my real job is to keep him talking. I can't execute the first part of my plan—the one that centers around Canyon Drive—until I know for sure what decisions Ron will make in the second half.

Despite all the apartments and duplexes we've seen, I have no intention of selling him anything. But this entire job hinges on Ron's belief that I will.

———

I've had Kat dig up properties in price points ranging from $3 million to $10 million. Ron has looked at all of them with an open mind. Every time I ask him how he feels about the price, he gives me a throwaway comment about his business manager, Steve, who keeps him in cash and out of jail.

Not helpful.

So in mid-July, just a week away from when I absolutely must launch the Canyon Drive piece, I decide to turn things around. Instead of me asking questions and hoping he'll tell me what I need to know, I've figured out a way for him to want to give it to me. Because if I don't get this information soon, it'll be too late to launch anything.

"I've always wanted to invest in real estate, not just sell it," I tell Ron. We're sitting in traffic on the 405, heading back into Santa Monica from the valley, where we'd looked at an apartment building for $3 million. The car is where we've had our most productive conversations. And by productive, I mean conversations where Ron spouts misogynistic, racist bullshit while I nod along, fantasizing about how it all will end.

"You should buy the building we just looked at," he says. "It's too far outside LA for my portfolio, but it would be a nice little investment for you."

I look over my shoulder, contemplating the diamond lane, which is as backed up as the one we're in. "A good idea in theory," I say. "But I don't have the cash to put up for something like that, and my credit's not that great."

I wonder what Ron would think if he knew how much money I really have. That my credit score is perfect, because when you're busy conning people, it's important to always pay your bills on time.

"I looked you up online," I admit. "Right after we met. I read that you took over your father's business when you were twenty-five and turned it into the biggest construction company in Los Angeles." I glance at him. "It's pretty impressive, what you've done. But not everyone has that kind of seed money. And if the banks won't give it to me…" I trail off, hoping he'll finish my sentence for me.

"If the banks won't give it to you, then you have to get creative. You should start your own real estate firm, not work for another company. Then you can structure the money how you want."

Heat fills my chest, remembering how Ron *creatively* stole my family home. How my mother and I had to live in our car, showering at shelters or the high school locker room. How we would get our food from the food bank, Big Macs from McDonald's a once-a-month splurge. I squeeze the steering wheel as tight as I can, then force myself to relax, knowing that, when I'm done, Ron will have lost Canyon Drive as well. "I don't understand what you mean by 'creative,'" I say. "You either have the money or you don't."

Ron shifts in his seat so he's facing me, in what I've come to think of as his *true confession* stance, where he spouts off about politics (*Democrats and their socialist liberal agenda*), the homeless problem in Los Angeles (*You have to round them all up, sort out the crazies from the druggies, and then arrest as many as you can*), and women (*I'm not sexist, but I'm sorry, now I can't even compliment a woman without getting slammed for sexual harassment?*). "It's a delicate dance," he says. "And a quiet one. One of the easiest ways I keep the cash circulating is to undervalue my properties with the IRS, and overvalue them with the banks. This keeps my tax liability low but my borrowing power high."

I give him a dubious look. "Isn't that tax fraud?"

He laughs and says, "Believe me, if the IRS cared, they'd be prosecuting it. But they don't have the time or the money to come after everyone. And we all do it, every single one of us."

Traffic begins to open up and I accelerate.

"If you own your own business, there are other ways you can get cash quickly," Ron continues. "Six or seven years ago, I had an investment opportunity, but I didn't have the liquid cash to invest. It was too good to pass up, so I pulled it from my company's retirement fund."

I glance at him, eyebrows raised, and he holds up his hands. "I paid it back. But the money was sitting there in an account I controlled, so I borrowed it, just for a little while. No harm, no foul. Those are the kinds of things you have to be willing to do to get ahead."

"I'm sure the campaign has opened up a lot of opportunities for you as well. Your fundraising is incredibly strong."

He shifts in his seat, facing forward again, and I worry he's done sharing for the day. That perhaps the campaign is off-limits. But then he chuckles. "That lunch we had? Paid for by a credit card set up to be paid through campaign donations."

I laugh. "Now, I *know* that's illegal."

He gives me a wink. "It's only illegal if you get caught."

If my life were a movie, this would be the moment the heist soundtrack kicks in—bass guitar first, then horns and drums joining in—an upbeat tempo propelling us all forward toward Ron's inevitable end. The camera would zoom in on me, a tiny smile on my face, showing the weight of my worry lifting away. And just like in a movie, there isn't a moment to spare.

"I think I've heard enough," I say. "Plausible deniability and all of that."

He grins back at me. "Oh no. You're in it now. If you're going to be my long-term agent, you also have to be the keeper of my secrets."

I give him a questioning look. "Are you going to make me sign a nondisclosure?"

"I don't need one. With the number of properties I buy and sell, you'll be making at least a million in commissions annually. In my experience, that's enough of a nondisclosure for anyone. This time next year, you'll be paying cash for something. You just wait and see."

*You just wait and see.* The words flutter around in my mind, like butterflies taking flight.

# KAT

July

Meg and I are at post-yoga sushi with Veronica when I see how good Meg is at what she does, and I get my first glimpse into what she might be up to.

"Where is Ron having next week's fundraising dinner?" Meg asks.

"A house in Beverly Hills. A huge estate in the flats."

"Has he ever hosted anything at his house?" Meg asks.

I look up at the mention of the Canyon Drive property, but Meg keeps her eyes on Veronica.

"It's too small," Veronica says. "The crowd we're after prefers modern chrome and clean lines. Ron's house is more English estate."

Meg looks concerned.

"What?" Veronica asks.

"I just think it's too bad Ron doesn't live somewhere with more status. There are so many properties on the market right now that have more of a pedigree, you know?"

"I suppose," Veronica says.

"I'd tell him myself, but I'm a salesperson. Everything we say is suspect."

I dip a piece of sushi in soy sauce and watch the exchange.

Meg continues. "His neighborhood is nice enough, but everyone knows that those with real money and power live north of Sunset Boulevard."

"I doubt Ron will want to move so close to the election."

"Sure. It's just..." Meg trails off, as if she's not sure how to say what she needs to say. "At that fundraiser you took me to, I overheard a conversation that got me thinking." She looks out the window, as if trying to remember the details. "They were an older couple...she had sort of shortish gray hair...you know who I'm talking about."

Veronica shakes her head, and I almost laugh. Meg is describing 90 percent of the people at that event.

Meg says, "God, I can't believe I don't remember their names. Not just rich, but really wealthy. And he's some kind of big deal..."

"The Morgensterns?" Veronica offers.

Meg snaps her fingers and says, "Yes! Thank you. Anyway. I overheard them say something about how Ron was low class masquerading as high class." Meg wrinkles her nose. "She said, 'He's supposed to be a successful developer and yet he lives in a neighborhood with houses so close together you can hear when people are in the pool or grilling at their barbecues.'" Meg takes a salmon roll and pops it into her mouth, chewing. When she swallows, she says, "One thing I've learned over the years is that rich people care about really weird shit."

Veronica looks worried, but Meg shrugs and says, "I'm sure it's fine. I mean, who cares where he lives, right?"

Then she changes the subject to our yoga teacher's upcoming vacation to Cabo. "I guess if you're looking for a spring break vibe, Cabo's great."

But Veronica isn't listening. Not really. Meg's careful comments have framed the outline of what she wants Veronica to do. Tell David that Ron's major donors don't see him as one of them. And she very quietly laid out what was holding him back: his house.

———————

After lunch, Veronica catches an Uber in front of the restaurant, and I wait with Meg while the valet brings her car, though I'd parked my own at a meter three blocks away. On the street next to us, traffic slows to a stop as the light turns red.

"Hey, blondie, does the carpet match the drapes?" The voice comes from a convertible next to us. Three men—boys really—look back at Meg, smiling.

Irritation passes through me, and I put on a stony expression most women would recognize, ready to pretend I don't hear the sexual harassment being hurled our way by boys who have already learned that their passage through life will be largely unobstructed.

But Meg turns toward the one who spoke, a smile plastered on her face. "In my living room, you mean?"

Confidence drains from his expression as Meg takes another step toward the car, and a bubble of a laugh wells up inside of me at how easily she's turned the tables on him.

"Do people even do that?" she asks, looking back at me. "Matching carpets and drapes would be a lot of the same color."

"Most people don't even have drapes anymore," I say. "They have some kind of blinds."

Meg nods and leans down toward the passenger, whose cheeks are growing flushed. "Some people have plantation shutters," she says.

"Put the top up," the kid mutters to the driver.

His friend laughs and says, "The light's about to turn green."

"Plantation shutters are really nice," I say.

Meg edges even closer to the car. "So, you want to know if the flooring in my house matches my window treatments. Are you looking to buy a place? I sell real estate and I can add you to my weekly newsletter if you want."

Just then, the light turns green, and the boy's face melts with relief. As they accelerate, we can hear the sound of his friends' laughter. "She worked you," one of them says.

Meg steps back from the curb, grinning. "Someone has to teach them," she says.

Regardless of whether or not she knows who I am, regardless of whether or not I've placed a target on my back, being around Meg is always entertaining.

I turn to face her. "So Ron's house," I prompt. "It would be great to get that listing."

Meg gives me a smile and says, "It's a great house."

*It's* your *house*, I want to say.

She crosses her arms and continues, "I might have the perfect buyers for it. I'll have Veronica plant the seed first and then bring it up with Ron."

I give her a sharp look. "Can you represent both ends of the deal?"

"Technically? Yes, though some consider it a little shady. Fiduciary duty, and all that. But my thinking is that we can probably keep it off the market and get a quick sale if my buyers can make a competitive offer. I doubt Ron will be excited about open houses twice a week."

The valet pulls her car forward, and she hands him a tip.

"I didn't realize you had new buying clients," I say, wondering where she's picked them up. She doesn't do any of the things other new agents have to do, like door knocking or open houses. "Who are they?"

She gives me a tight smile and says, "Can't disclose, sorry. They're industry people and want to remain anonymous." Before I can ask where she found them, she checks her phone for the time. "And I'm late. Chat later?"

She slides behind the wheel and is gone within seconds, leaving me standing there, thinking through all the ways this could be the beginning of her plan.

---

I arrive home just after one o'clock, eager to research the ways a listing agent could manipulate a sale. Especially one that never hits the market.

I settle at my desk and open my computer, typing the parameters into the search bar. My computer is slow to load, so I get up and grab a Diet Coke from the kitchen. When I return, the page is still blank.

Cannot load page. Check your internet connection and try again.

I look to our router, which is blinking green, and try again. Still nothing.

I move into the living room to see if our cable is working. Maybe there's an outage. I turn on the TV and am greeted by a black screen.

"Shit." Back in our office, I pull out the box where Scott and I put things we want to shred and dig out an old bill. I dial our cable company and punch my way through several automated choices, until I finally get a live person on the line. "Yes, I'd like to report an outage," I say.

"Zip code?" a woman's voice asks.

I offer it and hear her typing in the background. Finally, she says, "I'm not seeing any outages in your area."

"Well, there has to be, since neither my internet or my cable are working." I look out the window, as if I might see a pole fallen down into the middle of the street. But everything looks normal.

"What's your account number?" she asks.

I read off the number from the statement and wait. Finally, she says,

"I'm going to connect you with an account manager who will be able to help you."

I'm on hold again, and I return to the box to find the cable statements, going back five months—all with the bottom portion torn off, presumably paid. But a small voice in my head reminds me that gamblers are very good at deception.

The account manager comes on the line, and I run through the situation again, feeling a headache build behind my eyes. Finally, she says, "Your account is sixty days past due, so service has been turned off. You can pay right now with a credit card, or come into our office with a money order. The total due to resume service is $473.94."

I collapse on the couch and close my eyes.

"Ms. Roberts?" the woman prompts. "What would you like to do?"

"I'll pay with a credit card," I say.

———————

As soon as I'm done, I call Scott's cell.

"I just paid over $400 to reconnect our cable and internet," I say when he answers.

"What?" Scott says.

"Why didn't you pay the bill?"

"I *did* pay the bill."

"Don't bullshit me, Scott. It was sixty days late."

Scott blows out hard and says, "Look. I admit, I lost track of one month. Thought I'd paid it, but I didn't. But when the next bill came and I realized I hadn't, I paid it then. In full."

"Well, that's funny, because when I spoke to them on the phone just now, they never got the payment."

"You know, if you'd let me pay the bills online like every other fucking person in the world, this wouldn't have happened."

"Don't turn this around on me," I say. "We agreed, along with Dr. Carter, that online payments of any kind could be a trigger for you. Keeping your financial stuff offline is the best way to protect your recovery." Before he can argue with me, I push on. "What concerns me more is that you put the stubs in the box anyway, making it appear as if you'd paid them. It's not that you forgot; we all get busy. But it's the way you worked to conceal it that's the problem."

"Because I knew you'd turn it into something it wasn't."

I stare out the window, feeling unsettled. Scott's story makes sense. There's been no evidence of gambling. His phone and computer are consistently clean. He's always where he says he'll be, and I'm more likely to be in front of my computer in the middle of the night than he is. When he'd shown me the new bank statement he'd requested the other week, there'd been no unusual activity. The balance had been lower than I'd hoped, but there weren't any large cash withdrawals or any of the other red flags that would indicate he wasn't doing exactly what he said he was—working the program.

And yet, this is how it starts—with unpaid bills and creditors calling.

He continues. "You're ignoring the bigger problem, which is that you refuse to consider Meg is the one behind all of this. And now it appears she's targeting me too."

"What would Meg want with our internet and cable bill?"

"You'd be surprised," he says. "Washing checks, using the account and router number to buy something else."

I try to see things from Scott's perspective, but my instincts are telling me this isn't how she works. Meg doesn't need our money. "I know you're worried, but I don't think that's what's happening here."

"Fine," he says, his tone sharp. "I guess you know more about this than I do."

"I spend hours with her, every day," I say. "Do you think you're the only one who has the ability to read a person?"

"I know you think you know her," he says. "But you don't. Not really."

# KAT

Scott began pushing me to get my banking back online, and after a week, I agreed. "Just because I can't be online doesn't mean you shouldn't be," he'd said. "And it's better than it used to be. You'll have complete control, no middleman, no opportunity for someone like Meg to interfere."

He'd also warned me to continue being careful around Meg. "If you're out to lunch with her, don't leave your purse unattended. Don't let her borrow your phone, or even let her sit in your car unless you're there too. She might get ahold of your registration and cause all kinds of problems."

"I don't need you to hold my hand," I said, but the truth was, when I was with her, I found myself forgetting for longer and longer stretches of time that Meg wasn't who she said she was. That huge parts of her past were completely fabricated.

But every outing with Meg shows me something new. Tonight, I'm on my way to meet her for an outdoor concert at the park, and the prospect of sitting in lawn chairs with a bottle of wine is an appealing opportunity to see if I can find out more about her mystery buyers.

I meet up with her on a grassy expanse that slopes downward, where a stage and lights have been erected. People are filtering in, carrying blankets, chairs, and coolers. Tall sycamore trees arch overhead, and as the sun begins to set, the air takes on a chill.

"Cold?" Meg asks as I suppress a shiver. Below us, the band takes the stage. People around us quiet, conversations falling off one by one.

"A little," I whisper. "It's been so hot these past few weeks, I didn't think I'd need a coat."

I'd left my coat at home on purpose, remembering the one Meg always kept in the back of her car. *Michigan winters leave an impression*, she'd once told me.

"I have one in my car, if you want," she says, digging her keys out of her pocket. "It's in the back."

I feel a flash of triumph and take her keys, jogging back to the parking lot, eager to have ten minutes to look around. When I was Meg's client, she had a folder with my name on it with listings she wanted me to see. She also has one for Ron. I'm hoping there will be something—if not a folder, then a business card or a phone message, jotted on a scrap of paper—that might tell me who these buyers are, and from there, maybe I can figure out how they might be collaborating with Meg.

I unlock the doors and start in the backseat, which appears empty. When I check the seat pockets, all I find is a pack of travel tissues and a ballpoint pen.

Next, I reach under the seats, hoping she's tucked her purse under there, like I had with mine. I imagine what I might find in her wallet: Business cards with names I can look up tomorrow. A receipt shoved in the side pocket of her purse with a restaurant name I can visit. Something that would point me in the right direction. All I need is one lead I can chase.

But there's only dirt, a few old leaves, and an old coupon for a dry cleaner.

Behind me, the band leads off with a Fleetwood Mac song.

I move on to the glove compartment, which contains a car manual, a map of California, and underneath it, a piece of paper. It's an old listing from one of the homes Meg showed me that first day. And at the top, in her now familiar script, is a note. *Aunt Calista—$$—unclear how much.* I stare at the words, trying to imagine what she was thinking when she wrote them. What she would do with the information if she got it.

The rest of the car turns up nothing. I put everything back the way I found it and make my way to the trunk, where I find the coat tossed into a corner. It's a little heavier than people wear in California, but the minute I put it on, my shoulders release, my body warming up quickly. I scan the trunk for anything interesting, but it's empty as well. Locking the doors, I check the time on my phone before dropping it into an interior pocket, and make my way back to the concert.

As I weave through the parking lot, the click of a lighter just to my left startles me, and I jump back, swallowing down a scream.

A man stands, hidden between two SUVs, smoking a cigarette.

He must see the terror on my face, because he holds up his hands, the ember of his cigarette glowing in the dark. "Sorry to startle you," he says. "Just sneaking a cigarette."

I offer a weak smile, but grip Meg's keys in my fist as I scurry through the remaining rows of cars and back to the park. I take several deep breaths and try to center myself. *Just a guy having a smoke. Nothing more.*

By the time I get back to Meg, I've mostly recovered. "Thanks," I say as I slip into my chair, tossing her car keys back.

She hands me a plastic cup of wine and says, "I need to run to the bathroom."

She grabs her phone and hooks her purse over her shoulder, and I watch it bounce against her hip as she walks away.

———————

The band is phenomenal, energizing the crowd with hits by Blondie, the GoGo's, Fleetwood Mac, and Joan Jett. Soon, we're on our feet dancing, singing at the top of our lungs along with everyone around us.

For a few hours I let myself drop my questions. I forget about Scott's concerns and missteps, and set aside my growing unease that I've acclimated so much to who Meg is as a person that I'm no longer able to see her clearly. At one point, I catch Meg watching me with a smile, and I wonder who she sees when she looks at me. A wealthy woman at loose ends, trying to figure out her next step, or a journalist who let herself get too close?

I close my eyes and decide I don't care.

———————

When the concert ends, my voice is hoarse and my body aches. "That was great," I tell her.

She hooks her arm through mine and says, "Thanks for coming with me." She squeezes my arm and says, "Want to get some pie?"

"Yes, please." We've reached the parking lot, where overhead lights give off a dim glow, headlights of exiting cars sweeping across the ground.

"Follow me," she says. "There's a great place in Santa Monica that's open all night."

When I climb into my car, I pull my phone from my pocket, setting it on the center console, and notice a text from my bank.

A new device is trying to access your account. If this is not you, contact an account manager.

I look toward Meg's car and see her pulling her seat belt across her body and then down at my phone again. The time stamp shows the attempt was made just after I'd searched her car and tucked my phone away. Right about when Meg made her quick trip to the bathroom.

A car horn toots, pulling my attention back. Meg, gesturing me to follow her.

I drop my phone back into the center console and fall in behind her.

---

I follow her to Main Street in Santa Monica, anger bubbling inside of me—not just at Meg, but at myself, for letting my guard down. All the stories Meg told me about her past, tiny threads of empathy weaving between us, pulling me close. Keeping me distracted. Investing me in her heart instead of her mind.

Scott tried to warn me. *You're actively trying to expose her. A con artist isn't going to just let you walk away. She's going to want to make you pay.*

I pull into a parking spot and remind myself that the attempt had failed. And now I've been warned.

There's a twenty-minute wait despite the fact that it's nearing midnight. We stand outside with everyone else and make small talk, but my mind is far away, imagining Meg huddled in one of the bathroom stalls at the park, the cold concrete forever wet and murky. The sounds of the concert floating through the windows and echoing through the barren space, staring at her phone, using my stolen bank statement to try to log in to my account. Knowing it would be at least two hours before I'd get the notification. Believing her proximity to me would rule her out as a potential suspect.

"What will you do next with your life?" she asks. "I mean, besides your exciting career as a real estate assistant." Her cheeks are still flushed from the concert, and she buzzes with energy.

Fed up with the endless lies, I decide to tell her something true. "I've actually been working on a novel."

She looks surprised and is about to ask a question when her name is called. We're led through the center of the restaurant, the room stuffy after we'd been standing outside. We slide across from each other as the server hands us menus.

"I'm thinking apple," Meg says, flipping the menu over. "With a decaf latte."

"I'll have the same, except cherry pie instead."

We hand our menus back and look at each other across the table. "So, a novel! What's it about?" she asks.

A recklessness possesses me, and I'm suddenly curious to see just how clever she is, how quickly she can pivot and conceal who she really is and what she's doing. "It's a thriller about a female con artist."

Meg's eyes widen, and her laugh lifts above the noise of the restaurant. "That sounds amazing. What's the big twist? Or do you not want to say?"

My smile matches hers. "I haven't figured it out yet, but I'll let you know when I do."

If what I've just said worries her, she doesn't show it. Her arms rest on the table, completely relaxed, as late-night diners at the tables surrounding us eat, their conversations coming to us in pieces and snatches of words.

*And then she said to me...*

*I'm telling you, you need to quit that job.*

I miss Jenna with a near physical ache, and I imagine what it would be like if she were here instead of Meg. To be able to let my guard down and enjoy a concert and a piece of pie without needing to secure all my edges. Without needing to think through how much or how little to say.

Instead, Meg sits across from me. A woman who looks like a friend. Acts like a friend, but is not a friend.

"Are you okay?" she asks. "You seem quieter than usual."

I look at the giant chalkboard hanging above the counter with menu items and prices written in giant, colorful letters, then back at her and say, "Someone is trying to hack into my bank account."

I study her expression, keeping my eyes locked on her face, but only see surprise and concern register there. "You'd better change your password immediately." She gestures toward my phone on the table. "Do you want to do it now?"

I shake my head. "They can't get in. I have two-step verification. But I'll call tomorrow, just to make sure."

She lifts her glass of water and takes a sip before saying, "Why do you still look so worried?"

"We've had some mail go missing. Bank statements. Paid bills that never got to where they needed to go. Scott thinks someone is targeting us."

Her eyes widen. "Have you called the police?"

"Not yet," I say. "But Scott's going to want to, after tonight." I let the threat hang in the air, searching her face for a reaction. A flash of worry. A flinch. Something that might betray her. Again I see that jotted note. *Aunt Calista—$$—unclear how much.*

Our pie arrives and we begin to eat in silence. Finally, Meg says, "I don't want to overstep, but do you think Scott might be gambling again?"

I look up from my plate, a dark realization washing over me. The secret I shared, the truth I revealed so long ago, has now come back to haunt me. This is what con artists do—squirrel away information and use it when you're at your most vulnerable. As if to say, *It's not me you should be worrying about.*

I could have made up any reason why Scott and I might be prolonging our engagement. But I'd settled on offering up the truth, never knowing how expertly she might use it against me.

Meg gestures toward my ring. "How often do you take that off?" she asks. I must look confused because she clarifies. "I'm just wondering if it's possible he could have swapped out the stone without you noticing." She holds her hands up and says, "I'm sorry, but if he's gambling again, that's exactly the kind of thing he'd try to do."

My mind flashes back to my grandmother's engagement ring. How long it took me to notice it had gone missing, and how hard Scott argued that the house cleaner must have taken it before finally admitting he'd sold it to cover a debt.

"I'm overstepping. I'm sorry," she says. "But if you want, I know a guy in the diamond district downtown. He can take a look at it just to make sure."

I take a bite of pie, but I can barely taste it, imagining the kind of guy Meg might have, and how quickly he would swap the stone out himself. "I don't ever take it off," I tell her. Though that's not exactly true. I take it off to go to the gym. I take it off when I get a manicure. There have been plenty of times I've taken the ring off, where Scott could have done something with it.

"I don't want to make things worse," Meg continues. "But I also want you to be careful. If your instincts are telling you something's off, you should listen to them."

"You're right," I tell her. "But I don't think it's Scott."

Meg nods, accepting my words, and slips a piece of pie into her mouth and chews. Finally, she says, "Well, I guess that's good then."

---

When I get home, I creep into the house, careful not to wake Scott, and go straight to his computer, unable to fully discard Meg's suspicions until I can see for myself. A long list of websites come up, but they're all legitimate, and none of them are the bank. Then I check his phone, where again I find nothing that indicates he'd been the one accessing my account. I feel a thread of relief, followed by a wave of exhaustion, wondering if there will ever be a time when I won't have to check up on him. If there will ever be a time Scott isn't the person my mind always leaps to first.

I hear him shift in bed and realize how careless I've been. I ignored his warnings, believing I could handle Meg. If her strategy is to foster doubt in my relationship with Scott, to grow the divide between us so wide I start to question him, it's working.

But I'm still in control. I know who Meg is and what she's doing. My account is locked down. Her attempt failed.

I shrug out of Meg's coat and log back in to my email, wanting to double-check the time stamp on the attempt. An email from Jenna sits at the top, subject line reading *Reading, PA*.

Curious, I click on it.

My researcher found a DBA under the business name Life Design by Melody, and the name Melody Wilde attached to it. Backtracking with the state of Pennsylvania showed that the DBA was filed by Meg Williams. But here's the thing…there's a house involved. That's how my researcher found her. It was sold to Meg's company for $20,000. I don't know much about Pennsylvania real estate, but that's not a lot of money.

I sit back in my chair, thinking. A DBA—also known as a *fictitious business name*—and a property transfer for well under market value. And then my mind flies to Meg's mystery buyers. Maybe they're not industry people, committed to protecting their privacy, or collaborators working alongside Meg. Maybe they're Meg herself.

# TWO YEARS AGO

Reading, Pennsylvania

# MEG

Renata's house was two stories with leaded windows that, upon closer inspection, needed the trim refreshed. As I walked up a path lined with hurricane lamps, music and laughter floated out, the September evening air chilly.

I stood on the porch and straightened my skirt. No one inside knew that the clothes I wore had been purchased a few weeks ago at a consignment store in Philadelphia, or that the name on the solitary business card tucked into my otherwise empty purse wasn't my real one. I'd laid the groundwork, going back weeks, layer after layer, carefully constructing my backstory so that this moment—this party—would go exactly as planned.

The people inside were expecting a woman named Melody Wilde—recently divorced, home decorator and life coach to New York City celebrities. The person responsible for Renata's miraculous family-room makeover, which was nothing more than a couple sample books purchased online, a high-end upholsterer subsidized with my own money to give the illusion of a steep discount, and a throwaway comment about Sarah Jessica Parker.

My stomach was a jumble of nerves, as it always was when I was about to meet a mark for the first time. So many details had to be in place; so many things could go wrong. *Miracle worker* is what Renata had been saying to anyone who would listen. With every retelling, she tied me to the lies I'd told. Polishing them until they held the bright shine of truth.

———————

Six months ago, I'd been ready to quit. The constant relocating. The isolation the job required. How long until I made a mistake that would blow it all up?

But then I found Celia.

---

**Celia M > Divorced Mamas**

**July 8**

Here's the thing I'm learning about abuse—it never ends. Even though I've left Phillip, he still finds ways to torment me. No, he's not kicking me out of the car and forcing me to walk home at one in the morning, but every day is a new legal challenge from his lawyers. Some ridiculous way to delay, to prolong. It's not the physical abuse I endured, but it's no less damaging because I'm still constantly terrified. He still has power and control over me, and will continue to have it as

long as this divorce drags on. I'm running out of
money, and in a few months I won't be able to pay
my attorney. My credit is shot. I don't know how
much longer I can live this way.

34 comments

I'd felt a familiar stirring of interest, a feather tickling the back of my mind. *This one.*

That was how it always started. Someone pouring their heart out online, and me, taking notes. The divorce support group was one I'd stumbled into a couple years ago (a fertility group that led to a parenting group that led to this divorce group; the progression depressingly predictable). I'd joined as Margaret W, with a profile picture of a sleeping cat. A thirty-year-old woman whose deadbeat husband left her with two young kids and the ability to give great advice.

Celia's page had led me to Phillip's page, which had finally led me to his sister, Renata—midforties, no kids, and an unhealthy obsession with interior design.

———

Renata would tell you we met at a political rally. She'd been there registering voters, and I'd been there, new in town, looking to make new friends. But I'd been tracking Renata online well before arriving in Reading—cataloging her interests, scouring secondhand and consignment stores for clothes similar to hers, building a fictional business that would dovetail so seamlessly with Renata's interests that meeting me would feel like reconnecting with an old friend.

These are the small details that make or break a job. There can never be any question you aren't who you say you are. And it doesn't matter what backstory you build for yourself. If the visual details don't match, it's like an out-of-tune piano. Hit a wrong note enough times and people are eventually going to notice.

I'd literally bumped into her, pretending to be searching for something in my purse, the contents of it spilling on the grass around us. As she helped me gather my things, I gave her all the basic pieces I needed her to have—that I'd been at a crossroads after my divorce, that my mother had grown up nearby, and that my move had been more sentimental than practical.

"Meeting people will be easier when I have my business up and running and I've got an excuse to get up and out the door every day," I told her.

"What is it you do?"

"I'm an interior decorator and a life coach," I said, then laughed. "I know, it sounds pretentious, even to me."

"I don't know much about life coaching, but I love decorating," she said. "In fact, I'm kind of obsessed with it."

I smiled. "There's something special about taking a room and giving it an entirely new look. I do more than just decorate though. I redesign a client's physical and emotional space." Then I leaned forward, confiding. "I've worked with many celebrities, but my favorite jobs have been the small decorating ones. The ones where you know the cost is dear to them. It matters more."

As I spoke, I could see Renata's interest growing. I already knew about her inability to afford the look she wanted in her home and her husband's reluctance to pay for what he called *frivolity*. "Do you have a card?" she asked. "I'd love to talk more with you about this."

Renata's party was well underway by the time I arrived. As I stepped through the front door, I couldn't help but appreciate that she really did have a good eye for design. The room was lit with candles clustered on surfaces, giving the space a flickering magic. The yellow fabric I'd chosen to re-cover her chairs and couch glowed golden in the light, and people stood in small groups, holding wine glasses and nibbling on passed hors d'oeuvres.

Renata hurried to greet me. "I'm so glad you could come," she said. "Everyone loves the pieces and I'll bet you get at least three new clients just from tonight alone." She lowered her voice. "I hope it's okay I let slip that the fabric was originally bought by Sarah Jessica Parker—it was out of my mouth before I could stop it."

I smiled. "Totally fine. It's not a secret that I've done some decorating work for her. I think we had a spread in *Vanity Fair* a couple years back. She'll be happy to hear it's been put to good use." My eyes scanned the space until I found Phillip, standing near the edge of the room, talking with another man. He was taller than I expected, wearing a button-down shirt and navy slacks that strained around the waist, making it clear life without Celia was one of indulgence.

Renata followed my gaze and said, "That's my brother, Phillip. He's the CEO and founder of Prince Foods—you know, the grocery store chain?"

"I love that market," I told her. I'd walked the aisles earlier that day, noting the high prices and organic, non-GMO labels. "They have the best produce."

Renata's voice softened. "He's a really great guy, but he's going through a tough divorce." She looked back at me, a gleam in her eye. "Maybe you should meet him."

I shook my head. "I'm not ready for anything like that," I told her. "It's too soon."

Renata waved away my words. "Who says anything has to happen right now? Just meet him."

"Let me at least get a drink first."

Renata directed me toward the bar, where a uniformed bartender was serving various types of wine and beer. "I'm going to play around with the seating arrangements," she told me.

With a glass of white wine in hand, I hugged the perimeter of the room, taking small sips. Approaches needed to be flawless, striking just the right note. I went through the steps in my mind again and tried to imagine Celia among these people. Laughing at inside jokes, making plans to meet for lunch or for a tennis game at the club. I wondered what she was doing tonight while all her old friends gathered to celebrate an overpriced pair of chairs and a couch. How many of them had checked in on her, or thought about what Phillip was doing to her? Did any of them think it was unfair? Did they worry about her, or had she fallen off their radar, only set to power and influence?

"Dinner is served," Renata called from the other side of the room. "Please find your seats." She looked at me from across the room and gave me a tiny wink.

---

The table felt both formal and intimate, with centerpieces of flowers that looked as if they'd been cut from her garden and arranged in low crystal vases. Next to me, Phillip took his seat and shook out his napkin, placing it in his lap. "Renata tells me you're a decorator and a life coach?" he said, holding out his hand. "That's a combination I haven't heard before. Phillip Montgomery."

"Melody Wilde," I said, shaking it.

We each picked up our forks and began to eat our salads as

conversations around us ebbed and flowed, bouncing from one topic to the next. Finally, he asked, "So, Melody, what brings you to town?"

I set down my fork and took a sip of wine, as if considering how much I wanted to tell him. "That could either be a long answer or a short one."

He tilted his head and said, "Why don't you start with the short one?"

I fed him the line about my mother, about how she'd always wanted to come home. "I'd just ended my marriage. It was becoming clear for various reasons that it wouldn't be a good idea to stay in the same town as my ex-husband, and Reading seemed as good a place as any to start over."

"Now the long version."

A server took my nearly empty salad plate away and replaced it with a bowl of tomato bisque soup. I picked up my spoon, thinking. Finally, I said, "The long version is that my ex-husband wasn't very happy with the financial terms of our divorce. He felt I owed him more than what he got. And so, instead of living out this next phase of my life with him constantly accusing me of taking what was rightfully his, I decided to start over somewhere else." I smiled and tasted my soup. "I guess the long version is also pretty short."

Phillip had been eating while I talked, but now he turned to me and said, "Sometimes, when a relationship ends, it's best for all involved if one party moves somewhere else."

"Tell me about yourself," I said. "Have you lived here long?"

"My whole life. I went to college at Penn, then moved back home. Got married, started my business, had kids." He looked down at his nearly empty bowl of soup and said, "I, too, am going through a fairly contentious divorce."

I placed my hand on his arm, just a light touch, for just a moment, and said, "I'm so sorry."

From across the table, Renata caught the gesture and raised her eyebrows.

"It was long overdue," he said. "But she's having a hard time with it and making things difficult."

I pumped the brakes. "Let's change the subject to something a little happier," I suggested. "What do you do for fun around here?"

Phillip pushed his bowl aside and said, "The usual. Dinners with friends, poker games with the guys, fishing trips, golf at the club."

"I dated a golfer in college," I told him. "I used to be pretty good."

Actually, it was a golf pro in Boise, and at the end of that relationship I had $43,000 and the large diamond earrings I now wore in my ears, but that was just a detail.

Phillip turned to me, intrigued. "We should play a round."

"I'd love that," I said.

The soup course was finished, and we started in on our salmon and asparagus, lightly seasoned with garlic butter and lemon.

"Renata won't shut up about that deal you got her on those armchairs," Phillip said.

"I fear that she's creating a bit of an unrealistic myth. I have some high-end clients who occasionally change their minds. Now I'm getting calls from everyone she knows."

He took a bite of asparagus and said, "That's a good thing, right?"

I sighed and pushed some of the food around on my plate. "I'm grateful, but I was hoping to take a little time off."

"Tell me more about this business of yours."

"I started the decorating side of it when I was twenty-five, right out of design school, with just a few clients, and built it up over time. There are some pockets of real estate in New Jersey that would rival Philadelphia and the surrounding areas, and people who are willing to pay a premium for a foyer rug or high-end table lamps." I took a sip of wine. "The life coaching evolved out of that. I had a few B-list celebrity clients in the city and realized they needed more than just a redecorated townhouse. They needed a total life overhaul. Get out of the bars, stop sleeping around, go to yoga a couple times a week, and do a cleanse, you know?" He nodded. "The thing about famous people is that they pay so much attention to the exterior of their lives, the interior can fall apart due to lack of attention. So I got certified as a life coach and marketed myself as a life designer." I shrugged. "It grew from there, rather quickly. At its height, I was pulling in over a million dollars in profit per year."

Phillip looked impressed. "Amazing, for someone who couldn't be much older than thirty."

"Thirty-two," I lied, taking the three extra years. "But thank you. Age doesn't matter if you have the right idea and are willing to work hard."

"I doubt you'll find very many celebrities in Reading."

"My list is deep enough that I don't really need new life coaching clients. I'm happy to go to New York when needed and do the occasional decorating job here. Projects I'm passionate about." I let a slow smile spread across my face. "At this point in my life, I can afford to be selective."

As I said the words, I felt a spark of pride. The statement itself was true, and it was quite a claim for a woman who'd never gone to college. Who'd spent several years living in her mother's old minivan.

"Do you have a card?" he asked. Then he held up his hands, laughing. "To set up a golf game. Not for design work or, god forbid, 'life coaching.'" He put the words in air quotes.

"Don't knock it until you try it. I actually specialize in life transitions, and divorce is one of the biggest you can have."

"For now, let's just start with a golf game. In my opinion, there's no better way to clear your head than playing eighteen holes."

I set my fork down and smiled. "That sounds fantastic." I pulled the solitary business card from my purse and handed it to him. "I look forward to hearing from you."

---

It took a couple weeks, but Phillip and I finally got that golf game sched-uled. By then, the air had the bite of late fall, and as we stood in the pro shop waiting for my borrowed clubs, Phillip said, "There's probably only another month or so before the course closes for the season."

"What do you do for fun during the winter?"

"Watch golf on television," he said.

A man wearing a green sweater vest with the logo of the country club stitched over his heart set a golf bag next to me. "I have Stephen all ready to caddy, Mr. Montgomery."

"I think we'd like to caddy ourselves today," Phillip told him. To me he said, "I hope that's okay?"

I shrugged. "It's pretty much the only way I've ever done it."

It had been a few years, and I hoped the feel of the game would return quickly. I never really enjoyed it but had tolerated hours on the course every weekend in the service of connecting with a man who'd had an extra $90,000 of his elderly aunt's money burning a hole in his pocket.

I set up at the first hole, my club hitting the ball with a satisfying smack, arcing into the air over the fairway. I turned to Phillip and said, "I was worried I'd shank it."

"You look like a pro," he said. "You say you played in college?"

"My boyfriend was on the men's golf team. He got me hooked on the game, and I played for a few years after we broke up, but then life got in the way. I started dating someone who wasn't a golfer, and we spent our weekends doing other things."

I caught a tiny smirk on Phillip's face as he set up his next shot. We played the rest of the hole in silence, Phillip coming in one under par and me one over.

We hefted our bags over our shoulders and walked to the next hole. The wind gusted and the trees around us swayed at the tops, white puffy clouds scudding across the sky.

Phillip looked at me and said, "The other night, at Renata's, you shared that your divorce was contentious," he said.

I balanced my ball on the tee. We had arrived at the reason we were here today. "There were a lot of assets to divide, and it got heated," I said. "There were winners and losers and feelings got hurt. It worked out fine in the end, as I'm sure yours will too. You're in the worst part of it right now. The negotiating. The fighting over every little thing."

I set up over my ball, swinging hard, and watched it hook left, into the rough.

"You'll want your pitching wedge for that," Phillip advised, before returning to the topic at hand. "I'd be interested to hear more about your settlement. You mentioned at Renata's it was favorable to you."

"It was," I said, sliding the driver back into my bag. "My ex-husband wasn't really the kind of guy who liked hard work. And yet he was asking for 50 percent of everything." I turned to face Phillip so he could see the righteous anger on my face. "I worked my ass off to build that business. Why should his share be equal to mine? Where was he when I was working seven days a week? Or when I was litigating against one of my clients who refused to pay me? He was sleeping late, going out to lunches, and taking trips to Vegas. Buying cars and clothes and I don't even know what." I took a breath. "So yes, I made sure my settlement was favorable to me."

As I spoke, I saw vindication in Phillip's expression. I was hitting all the right notes. Saying aloud all the dark thoughts that must have swirled inside his head at night after meetings with his own attorney. I knew what to say because Celia had already told me.

Phillip took his shot and then said, "I'm sorry if I'm being intrusive, but how did you do it? My lawyers are telling me there's no way around the shared property laws, and I'm already going to have to pay her a substantial amount in alimony."

"It's not something I like to talk about, to be honest," I said. "Let's just say I had to get creative."

He looked intrigued. "Anything you can tell me, I'd appreciate it. It'll stay between us, I promise."

I let his request hang in the air between us, as if I were considering it, but then I shook my head. "I really want to help you. But what I did was just a shade beyond the legal line, and it would put me and a very good friend of mine in jeopardy. I hope you understand."

I wanted his imagination to run with that, puzzling out different scenarios, each one more outrageous than the last, so when I finally told him, the simplicity of it would be irresistible.

As we played through several more holes, Phillip talked about his job, about the way the food industry worked, and about his now adult children.

"They have their own lives. I'm grateful that Celia and I don't have to be fighting over custody."

"It could be worse," I agreed.

As is typical of a certain type of man, Phillip did not respect my *no*. He kept pushing. Nudging. Keeping what he wanted at the center of our conversation.

*If it would make you feel better, I have a lot of experience keeping privileged information confidential.*

*If I can't figure this out with Celia, I might have to sell the house that's been in my family for three generations.*

I made him wait until the seventh hole before giving in.

I sighed, as if I were making a decision I might regret later. "What I did was simple in execution, but you should understand, there would be serious consequences if you're caught." I wanted to make sure I outlined the risks early on, so there wouldn't be any second thoughts later. "There are better, legal ways to keep the bulk of your money from her, like gifting it to your children."

He shook his head. "Kids should build their own wealth, not inherit it."

A foursome approached from behind. "Phillip!" one of them called. "Mind if we play through?"

"Go ahead," Phillip said. "Sorry we're so slow today."

The men—all of them wearing some combination of khaki and pastel—eyed me but offered nothing more than a muted greeting. Phillip and I stood to the side until they'd disappeared down the fairway before resuming our conversation and game.

"I'd like to know how you did it," he said, wiping one of his clubs with a soft green towel.

"I had a close business associate in New Jersey," I told him. "She was a furniture designer, and I bought a lot of pieces from her over the years. What I did was simple, commissioning several things from her over the course of eight months. Paid her up front, held on to the invoices. The money sat in her account, and I was able to give my ex-husband accurate financial statements, and our financial negotiations were based on those amounts."

"How much did she hold for you?"

I adjusted the glove on my hand and said, "I'd rather not disclose that, if it's okay with you."

Phillip looked intrigued, and I imagined him filling in the blank with an obscenely large number.

"Surely your husband's attorneys would have demanded half of whatever you'd 'purchased'"—air quotes—"from your colleague."

I pulled my driver from my golf bag and said, "We didn't use attorneys."

Phillip looked impressed. "How did you pull that off?"

"I pretended to be collaborative. 'Let's make this easy and figure it out without paying lawyers the bulk of our estate.'" I shrugged. "Why do you think I needed to leave town and move my entire business? The only people who benefit from a prolonged divorce battle are the attorneys. Once they get involved, it's a year—minimum—until you're settled."

Phillip was silent so I could set up my next shot, and I took my time, letting him think that over. I swung, feeling the muscles in my back starting to tighten up. "When's your valuation date?" I asked. The valuation date is the day—usually set by the court—where parties have to turn over a statement of their assets to be split.

"In about eight months," he said. "Right before our hearing. Because of my stock options, the court set it then, as a way to address any fluctuating value."

"So you have some wiggle room."

"I'm supposed to be gathering a list as we speak."

We walked to the green, our balls six feet apart and fifty feet from the hole. I pulled out my putter and made my shot just as a gust of wind blew from behind us, nudging my ball beyond it.

Phillip was quiet as he tapped his ball to within range.

When he was done, I said, "Your attorneys will want to look everything over, so you can't put your money into fictional goods that never show up. You'll have to give her half of any asset—whether it's cash or a Chihuly chandelier. What you need to do is use your money to pay for a service. Something she can't demand you sell or give her half of." I gave him a bright smile. "Like life coaching."

Phillip groaned.

I laughed. "Let me explain why this might be ideal for you."

I pulled my phone from the side pocket of my golf bag, entering the web address to *Life Design by Melody*, and handed it to him.

Phillip pulled a pair of readers from his bag and started scrolling. Then he held up the phone and said, "It's asking for a password."

"Sorry," I said.

I'd spent a week building this website, stealing photographs from interior decorators all over the country. Under the testimonials tab, I'd settled on several celebrity clients whose media presence was consistently saturated. Jennifer Lopez, Sarah Jessica Parker, Neil Patrick Harris, and Lin-Manuel Miranda. It took a few days to create the images I'd need to support my story—one of me laughing with Neil Patrick Harris in a sunny café, another one of me arm in arm with J. Lo on a Brooklyn street, and a third one of me inside Sarah Jessica Parker's gorgeous brownstone on the Upper East Side.

I took the phone and entered the password. "My clients are pretty well-known and value their privacy. I trust I can count on your discretion?"

"Absolutely," he said, clicking on Jennifer Lopez's glowing testimonial. Melody changed my life, inside and out. Life isn't just about the stuff you accumulate and how you arrange it. It's about the internal landscape as well. Your mental approach to your relationship with things. With people. She's a life designer.

He flipped through a couple more before handing my phone back. "Impressive," he said. "Explain how this will work."

"It's very simple. You'll hire me as your life coach. We'll do some decorating too, since that's how I generally work. The goal is to lower your liquid assets. The less you have in the bank, the less you have to split." I thought of Celia, counting on Phillip's fat bank account to cover her bills. Pay off her attorney. I'd like to think I was doing her a favor. The tighter I could wedge Phillip in now, the more leverage she would have when the truth came out later. "I charge $30,000 a month for full access—24/7, plus the decorating and space renovation, though we can adjust that depending on how much you want to shelter. The bulk of your fee will go toward coaching, under the guise that this is a big life transition—it's the end of a thirty-year marriage. I'll provide documentation of our sessions together, and of course, any time you want to check the account, you can. When your settlement is finalized, I'll transfer the money back to you, into an offshore account that you'll set up later."

Phillip blew out hard, gesturing toward the phone. "People really pay $30,000 for that?"

"Mental health is a big market. I'd like to say I really help them. They certainly think so."

"I wouldn't have to do any of that, would I?"

"Not unless you want me to keep your money—which I'd be happy to do," I said, winking.

Phillip did some mental math. "Over the next eight months, that would only be $240,000. Could you inflate your fee to $50,000? That would get me a lot closer to what I want to set aside."

*Set aside. Shelter.* Euphemisms of a corrupt man with an urgent deadline. My favorite kind.

"Of course." I paused. "In order for this to look legitimate, you're going to have to tell people that you've hired me. It's important you demonstrate—especially to your attorneys, who will be watching every move you make—that all of this is in good faith." I grabbed my golf bag and slung it over my shoulder. "Let's finish this round."

After returning my clubs at the pro shop, Phillip offered to buy me dinner. The sun was sinking in the west, and the air had a real bite to it. I crossed my arms over my chest and said, "I had fun today. And dinner sounds lovely." I looked down at the white golf shoes I paid over a hundred dollars for, then back up. "Full disclosure, I'm attracted to you. But it's too soon for me to jump into something. I just wrapped up my own divorce, and I don't want to step into the middle of yours." I looked into his eyes and saw a flash of anger. Just a flash, there, and then gone again. Phillip wasn't used to hearing *no.* "I'd like to keep spending time with you," I continued. "But for now, can it be just as friends? I'm trying to start my business, and I'd like to do it on my own terms, not as the girlfriend of the most powerful man in town." I reached out and brushed my fingers down the length of his arm. "I'm not saying *no,* I'm saying *not yet.* I hope that's okay."

He nodded and said, "Of course. I'd like that." He cleared his throat, looking uncomfortable. "I really appreciate your honesty earlier. I know it wasn't easy, and I'm grateful for your help."

I took his hand and squeezed it. "I'm honored to be trusted. This is a really stressful time, so try to go easy on yourself."

He looked across the emptying parking lot. "Now all I have to do is sort out the lake house," he said.

My head snapped up. "What lake house?"

---

The lake house was an hour out of town, the only major asset Celia wanted. I did a deep dive in the divorce group to see if she'd talked about it, and pulled up a post from several months ago.

**Celia M > Divorced Mamas**

I did it. I asked for the lake house as part of the settlement. The thing is, Phillip doesn't even want it. He hates the place with its outdated appliances, mismatched furniture, and, according to him, "Nothing to do there but stare out the window." But I love it. I used to take the kids for the entire summer, and it would be eleven weeks of heaven. No Phillip. No outbursts about how much I tipped the gardener, or whether I should get the house-keeper in an extra day each week. Just the three of us playing games, doing puzzles, going for long walks around the lake. Once, when Phillip had to travel over the holidays, we even spent Christmas

> there. It felt like a fairytale. Like a dream. That lake
> house is my home, in a way our Reading house
> never was.

When we spoke again over the phone, two days after our golf game, Phillip told me the deed was in his name only, but had been acquired during the course of the marriage. No loans or liens on the property. Worth about $250,000, it was his to give away if he was so inclined.

Which he wasn't.

"Maybe you could gift it to the kids," I suggested.

"Absolutely not. They'd just let her live there for free."

Ron's parting words to my mother floated into my mind: *There are winners and losers, Rosie.*

I'd done a little research since our golf game. I kept my tone casual, a favor being offered. "Here's an idea," I said. "I could buy it at a steep discount. Say, $20,000? Once the divorce is final, I can deed it back to you, and you'll be free to sell it. But we'll need to do it sooner rather than later, in order for the title to record before your valuation date."

Phillip was silent on the other end of the call, and I waited. We'd already walked so far beyond the concepts of fair and honorable, adding the lake house wouldn't be much more of a leap. Just one more thing I was helping him steal from his wife.

I rushed to fill in the silence, to show him I was willing to offer an out, if he wanted one. "If that feels too risky, *no* is a perfectly acceptable answer. I'm sure your lawyers could lock it down for you—force her to buy you out. Or maybe give her some stock options in the business in exchange for the property. But it'll be at full market value if you decide to go that way."

"Can we do that?" he asked. "Sell it so low?"

"Believe it or not, it happens all the time," I told him. "You can sell a property for as little as you want. There will be some tax liability on the other end, but there are ways to get around it if the property is worth it to you."

"I don't want it for myself; I just don't want her to have it."

Determination hardened into a tight stone inside my chest. "Then let's make sure she doesn't get it."

———————————

A week after our golf game, I showed up at Phillip's house with a moving van and movers. "What's this?" he said when he answered the door.

I gestured for the movers to wait with the truck for a moment, and Phillip and I stepped into the front hall. "I need you to pick two rooms you don't spend much time in so we can empty the furniture and get started."

"Wait, what?"

I glanced over my shoulder, the three guys I'd hired lounging in the frigid morning sunshine. "You can't just wire me money, Phillip. We have to actually appear to be doing the work, and part of that work is reconfiguring your physical space. Pick two rooms, we'll move out the furniture, rugs and window coverings, put drop cloths down, paint samples on the walls, and then if anyone asks, you can show them where we've decided to start."

Phillip looked around, as if the answer was going to appear in the marble foyer, before saying, "Okay. The living room and the den."

"Great," I said, gesturing toward the movers. "Lead the way."

Phillip hovered next to me, watching the men dismantle each room. Leather couches, antique armoires, end tables, Tiffany table lamps, artwork, expensive rugs. All of it got wrapped and carefully loaded onto the truck.

"Where are you taking it?" he asked me.

"I've rented a warehouse. We'll store it there, and after everything's finalized, we can move it back."

"Do you need money to cover your expenses?" he asked. "Movers, warehouses..."

"Nope. It's all covered by your retainer."

I waved as I drove down the long driveway, the moving van close behind me with a large number of Phillip's most valuable antiques.

Of course, I sold them.

---

I once conned a geologist (*$25,000 plus a Fender Stratocaster*) who told me the tectonic plates beneath us are always shifting. Always moving, even if we never felt them.

I'd thought a lot about that over the years. The idea that we were out there, living our lives, thinking only about the next thing we needed to do, never noticing the incremental shift that was happening below. That one day, we'd look up and realize everything had changed.

Taking Celia's lake house shifted things for me. I began waking up in the middle of the night, not thinking about Phillip or the job I was in the middle of working, but of Ron. Memories of my house on Canyon Drive. My mother's laughter. I began dreaming of possibilities I thought were long gone, back now with a fresh coat of potential. What I was doing here, I could do again for myself. For my mother.

I'd need a different approach for Ron, though. There was no way I could float into Los Angeles as a life coach and convince him to sell me Canyon Drive for $20,000. He had decades of experience buying and selling real estate, with hundreds of transactions behind him. I was going to have to level up.

My research started out as a jumble of ideas scribbled into my notebook. I began by exploring the circumstances under which a property might *not* be sold at market value. If the seller wasn't going to deliberately underprice it as Phillip was, you'd have to make them believe the property was worth less, through inspection reports outlining significant damage and appraisers willing to corroborate.

*The universe will always give you what you need.* Phillip became my case study. How to lay the groundwork. Figure out what worked, and if there were mistakes to be made, I would make them here. The other part of it—the *life coaching*—was just making sure I got paid for my time.

———————

Phillip and I stood side by side in front of a vision board I'd created, a mishmash of various words, inspirational quotes, and images. I'd gotten the idea off Pinterest, and Phillip seemed to think it was sufficiently new age to be legitimate.

"You're going to need to get an inspection and appraisal for the lake house," I said.

Phillip turned to face me. "Won't that defeat the purpose of selling under market value?"

I shook my head. "Look, a judge is going to want to see them. Your attorneys will too. I can make it so that the reports say what we need them to say. In the meantime"—I handed Phillip the contract with the $20,000 purchase price—"sign and initial where I've indicated. Leave the date blank for now."

Phillip scanned the document I'd downloaded from a do-it-yourself real estate website. "It's boilerplate," I said. "As an extra layer, I listed my company as the buyer, and I'll be waiving most of the contingencies. When I'm done with the inspection report, it'll lower the value where we need it."

Phillip signed and initialed where I'd marked, then handed the contract back to me.

"You're making great progress so far, Mr. Montgomery," I said, tucking it back into my purse. "Let's keep up the good work. Your next retainer is due at the end of next week. I'll email you the invoice."

We were three months and $150,000 into the job by then, not counting the $200,000 I got when I sold his furniture, and the stress of executing the plan was beginning to weigh on Phillip. He looked haggard, as if he wasn't sleeping well. "I'm worried this isn't going to work," he said. "What if they figure out what I'm doing? Not only would it ruin me financially, but my reputation in town would be trashed."

I placed a hand on his arm and squeezed gently. "Look at me." When he did, I said, "This is the hardest part. But remember, you're not doing anything wrong. You're spending money on your mental health. To find a better physical and emotional state. You're selling a house that will have a ton of structural damage—a property you can no longer afford to carry—and you'll split what you get for it fifty-fifty—ten thousand for you, ten thousand for her. There are a lot of ways to frame this so that you end up looking okay. But the one thing you cannot do is doubt. You have to believe that what we're doing is legitimate, because how you frame things in your mind is how you present them to the world."

He nodded, and I could see he was coming back around. The fear was subsiding. I needed him with me just a little bit longer.

---

The internet made it easy to keep track of Ron Ashton over the years. Public records showed he still lived in my house on Canyon Drive. Online news sites told about his upcoming run for state senate. But it was an article on a local Los Angeles real estate blog about a predatory agent who'd sexually harassed a client that gave me my approach. Mick Martin has been the longtime agent for Los Angeles developer Ron Ashton, who is rumored to be considering a run for state senate. Mr. Ashton declined to comment.

This job required me to see connections others couldn't. I had to think ten steps ahead and imagine several scenarios simultaneously. Over the years, my instincts had become razor sharp, and I was rarely wrong.

I looked up Mick Martin and found that there had been two reports of sexual harassment to the California State Real Estate Board. According to their bylaws, three would be enough to permanently suspend his license. My fingers flew across the keys of my laptop, opening new tabs, conducting several new Google searches. *How to report sexual harassment to the California Real Estate Board.* Another one, *How to get a California real estate license*, and finally, *Online real estate license classes, California.*

I looked around my tiny apartment, the shades drawn against the dark night, and I began another list in my journal of things I'd need to do to get ready. A website for a boutique real estate agency. Another one for me, outlining several years of high-end sales. An agency phone number with a friendly, outgoing message. I bought several books about real estate, knowing I'd need to arrive already an expert.

It meant leaving Pennsylvania as soon as the title for the lake house recorded, several months before I'd intended. Sometimes, you have to leave a job early—you either run through other people's goodwill or you realize the risk of finishing it isn't worth what you'd gain by staying. This time, it was because I had to be back and in position well before the November election.

A spark of excitement danced around inside of me as I realized I would end my career where it started.

They say you can never go home again.

This is a lie.

# LOS ANGELES

Present Day

# KAT

## August

The first thing I do the following morning is call the bank. They assure me my account is safe and that no money had been taken, but I ask them to give me a new account number anyway. Wherever that bank statement is, I want it to be completely useless.

Then I open Jenna's email again. A DBA—*doing business as*—is typically used when a person wants to set up a business under a name that doesn't include their legal name, like *Ace Dogwalkers*. But a DBA can also be a con artist's greatest advantage, allowing anyone who can pay the filing fee to hide their true identity behind a fake company and a different IRS number. If you know the company name, you can plug that into the state website and find out who set it up. But they don't work in the reverse. If you only know a name—in this case, Meg Williams—you're locked out.

I'm almost certain Meg's mystery buyers—the *industry insiders* guarding their privacy so carefully—are Meg, hiding inside of a DBA. Somehow, she's figured out a way to either steal her own property back or buy it at a steep discount.

I get to work trying to figure out exactly what she did in Pennsylvania. Jenna had given me the details of the sale—a property located on a lake and the seller's name. *Phillip Montgomery.* When I Google him, the usual hits come back: Facebook and Twitter handles for various people—a doctor, a carpenter, and the CEO of a grocery chain. Among the hits is an article from a local Reading paper. It's a filler piece, used to take up page space, and it's short. "Local Business Leaders Come Together at Thanksgiving to Feed the Hungry." It talks about the great turnout, how many people were served, and then it goes on to list the volunteers. Two names stand out: *Phillip Montgomery* and *Melody Wilde.* The article comes with a tiny photo that I have to zoom in to see. A group of about ten people, wearing aprons and hair nets, gathered behind a long counter. And there, in the back, is Meg. Though she's partially obscured by the large man beside her, it's unmistakably her.

I stare at Meg, trying to pick out details until she's nothing more than black and white pixels on the screen. What would she say if I showed her this article? Undoubtedly, she'd spin a story about visiting a friend in Pennsylvania for the holidays. Maybe she'd claim she was playing a joke on the reporter, giving a fake name and profession. Meg is a formidable storyteller, entertaining me not only with stories of former clients and deals gone bad, but other adventures as well. The time she went skydiving on a dare. The vacation she took to the Everglades where her boat was almost overturned by alligators. Even though I know better, I still find myself sucked in, having to constantly remind myself that every word she says is a lie.

I start making calls, beginning with Phillip, quickly ruling out the doctor and the carpenter and focusing on the CEO of Prince Foods. "My name is Kat Roberts and I'm a journalist in Los Angeles. I'd like to talk with Mr. Montgomery about a woman named Melody Wilde."

"Mr. Montgomery isn't available, but if you leave your number, I can make sure he gets back to you." His receptionist's voice gives nothing away. It's possible she'll pass on my message, but equally likely she'll drop it in the trash instead.

Next, I start making my way through the other volunteers listed in the article. I have no luck reaching anyone until Frederica Palmieri, the owner of a dance studio. "My name is Kat Roberts and I'm doing a story about a woman named Melody Wilde. I was hoping you'd be able to talk to me about her?"

Frederica's voice is wary. "What's your story about?"

I choose my words carefully. "Melody may have been involved with a fraud case here in Los Angeles."

In the background, I can hear piano music and a voice giving directions. "I've never heard of her. How did you get my name?"

"I found a photograph of you in the Reading paper, and Melody's in it as well. It was a group shot at the local soup kitchen for Thanksgiving two years ago. You'd volunteered to serve meals."

Frederica's voice clears. "Oh yeah. Well, if I spoke to her at all, it was probably just to say hello and goodbye."

"Do you happen to remember if she was friendly with any other volunteers that day? I'm hoping to connect with someone who knew her."

"As you said, it was two years ago," she says. "I can barely remember what I did last month."

"I understand. One last question," I say. "Do you remember who organized the event?"

"Renata Davies," she says. "She's the president of the local food bank. She's involved in a lot of community events."

I jot down Renata's name and thank Frederica before hanging up.

Renata is harder to reach. I call the food bank first, and while they're friendly, they're not inclined to give out Renata's contact information to a stranger claiming to be a reporter. I leave a message with my number, hoping they'll pass it on.

I find her on Facebook, and a quick search of her friends list reveals something interesting—Phillip Montgomery is Renata's older brother. My private message to her is a variation of what I told the others. My name is Kat Roberts, and I'm hoping to talk to people who may have known a woman by the name of Melody Wilde. Any information you might have would be very helpful. You can reply to this message or call me at the following number.

Most likely, Renata won't be inclined to trust someone on the other end of a telephone or in the vast ocean of the internet. People are far more willing to open up to someone known by a friend. Meg gains the trust of others first. Like Veronica.

I pick up my phone to text Meg. Did Veronica have any luck convincing Ron to list his house? Are your buyers still interested?

I see the three dots that show she's replying, and I wait, wondering what lie she'll feed me next. Veronica came through! We just opened escrow at $4.5 million. Buyers are over the moon happy and escrow closes in 30 days.

I don't need to log in to the listing service to know that $4.5 million is at least $500,000 below market value for that area. And though the numbers are exponentially higher than in Reading, it might fit with what she did there.

But the idea sits, uneasy in my mind. Even with the discount, $4.5 million is a lot of money for anyone. Paying that much for a house doesn't feel like much of a con.

And I still can't figure out what she might want from my bank account. I think back to the fundraiser, two months ago. By that time, Meg had already been in town six months, building a backstory and fostering a critical friendship with Veronica that would open the door to Ron. Why would she suddenly pivot and start targeting me? Regardless of what happened last night, I'm still having a hard time making that leap. Meg's been doing this a long time. Surely she would know she'd need more than ten minutes in a park bathroom to hack into my account.

Unless she didn't want to succeed.

If Meg really wanted to con me, I think she would have. But she's done just enough to get my attention. To keep both me and Scott busy, on the phone with the bank and the cable company, locking everything down. What I'm not doing is asking questions about her mystery buyers.

# KAT

Meg is late again.

I stand outside Le Jardin, midday traffic rushing by, waiting for her to show up for lunch. The exhaust fumes from a passing bus make me hold my breath, and I'm just about to step inside to wait when my cell phone buzzes with an unfamiliar number.

"May I please speak to Kat Roberts?" A woman's voice with a hint of a Midwestern accent, and my heart races. *Renata.*

I glance around, making sure Meg is nowhere in sight. "Speaking."

"Good afternoon, Ms. Roberts, this is Natalie with Citibank Card Services. I'm calling to inquire about your payment, which is past due."

I plug my finger into my other ear and turn away from the busy street. "I'm sorry, what?"

"This is Natalie, from Citibank," she repeats. "We haven't received a payment for two months. If you don't make one soon, we're going to have to send this debt to collections."

"I don't have a Citibank card," I tell her. "You've got the wrong person."

"Would you please confirm the last four digits of your social?"

I nearly laugh. "I'm not giving that to you because I didn't open an account."

But Natalie will not be deterred from her script. "The balance currently sits at $31,125, with a minimum payment of $500. You can make one right now if you like."

Panic begins to rise inside of me as my mind leapfrogs back to Scott's warning from a couple weeks ago. *Be careful with Meg. Don't leave your purse unattended. Don't let her use your phone.*

Is this Meg, still trying to keep me busy, a phishing expedition to get me to reveal information she can use against me, or is this something more? I look up and down the street, imagining Meg parked in a garage somewhere, pretending to be Natalie from Citibank.

"What's your name again?" I ask, straining to hear her voice, to see if it sounds familiar.

"Natalie," the woman says. It's impossible to tell against the street noise.

"Give me the account number," I say, scrambling in my purse for a pen and a scrap of paper. I use the brick wall behind me, my letters bumpy and misshapen. "I didn't open this account," I tell her again. "I'm not paying you $30,000."

Natalie remains calm. "I understand, Ms. Roberts. I can make a note in the file," she tells me. "But to clear it, you'll need to file a police report and submit it to us. Until then, you're responsible for the debt."

*Ms. Roberts.* The use of my real last name finally slams into me, and I realize Scott's been right all this time. This is Meg's way of telling me she knows everything.

Just then, I feel a presence behind me. I turn to find Meg standing there, a concerned look on her face, and my stomach plummets. "Thanks for your call," I say and hang up.

Pedestrians step around us as Meg says, "Are you okay?"

When I don't answer, she takes my elbow and guides me away from the fancy restaurant where we'd planned to eat and instead leads me over to a taco truck parked at the curb. She orders two tacos, and we walk to a nearby park and sit on a bench.

"Tell me what's going on," she says. "Is it Scott?"

I press my lips together, a mixture of rage and shame flooding me. At my belief that I could befriend Meg and live alongside her as an ally. How close I let myself get to her. When I finally speak, my words are stiff and cold. "That was someone claiming to work at Citibank, telling me there's a $30,000 debt in my name." Even though she wasn't the one on the phone, I'm certain Meg was behind the call somehow.

She sits back, shocked. "Oh my god."

Ever the actress. Ever the concerned friend.

"You need to file a police report," she says. I stare at her, trying to see her endgame. "Look," she continues. "I don't mean to stir up problems, but this, plus the bank breach and the unpaid bill…" She trails off.

I shake my head, disgusted with myself for telling her about Scott's gambling, for handing her such an important piece of me. "It's not Scott."

I let the weight of my certainty wrap around me. I'm not naive. I know the statistics of a backslide. But since the night of the concert, when Meg tried to hack my bank account, I've been back to nightly checks on all his devices, and there hasn't been anything. His work computer is out of my reach, but he'd be insane to try anything there, where every keystroke is recorded and monitored.

"I know that's what you want to believe," Meg says. "And I want that to be true too. But you have to protect yourself, even if that means facing some painful truths."

*Truth?* Every word she says is a lie. "I don't think that was a legitimate call," I tell her. "I think it was a phishing scam. Someone trying to get me to hand over my social security number. It happens all the time." Will she flinch? Look away?

But she pulls her phone out and opens her web browser, and I watch her Google Citibank, pulling up their website. She holds her phone up so I can see it. "Here's the number; let's call and check."

Is this some kind of test? Does she think I won't make the call in front of her? I dial and navigate through several automated options, until I'm placed on hold. While I wait, shrieks of laughter from the playground filter through my growing panic.

This time, I speak to someone named Paul. I read off the account number Natalie gave me and step away from Meg to give him the last four digits of my social security number. "The balance is $31,125," he confirms.

I close my eyes, the sounds from the playground growing fuzzy. Not a phishing scam, but real debt—one so large, I have no hope of paying it off.

"Ask about recent transactions," Meg says.

My eyes fly open, and I study the way she watches me, her eyes wide with compassion and worry. Why would she want me to ask this? What does she want me to hear?

In response to that question, Paul rattles off several large cash advances, all local to us, and a few charges at the supermarket. "Can you tell me what the billing address is?" I ask.

He gives me a PO box in Brentwood. I glance at Meg again, knowing how easy it is to set one up online.

Paul's voice cuts in. "The statements are sent to an email." He reads it slowly. "Calistasniece at Yahoo."

My gaze cuts to Meg, the breeze blowing strands of her hair across her face, which is open and concerned. I remind myself she's had years to perfect the expression. "Thank you," I say to Paul, then disconnect the call. Meg places a hand on my arm and I jerk it away, desperate to go somewhere I can think. Figure out how she could have done this.

"You need to file a police report," she says again. "I can go with you if you want."

I look at her, incredulous, imagining the two of us at a police station, Meg by my side helping to craft the narrative. At what point would she slip and share details of Scott's gambling? A subtle mention that would skew an investigation away from her.

I'm going to have to tell Scott. I can't conceal a $30,000 debt from him. A small voice floats up from deep inside of me. *What if Meg is right? What if it's Scott after all?*

Not for the first time, I wonder what my life would be like if Scott weren't an addict. Or if I'd left him instead of staying and working through the steps with him. Things would be so much clearer now, not having to navigate around the constant doubt, the voices that invade my sleep, always questioning what he says. Always wondering if it'll happen again. Pushing me to look for the cracks, trying to figure out what's real inside my own relationship.

Just then, Meg's phone rings. She glances at the screen and says, "It's the buyers for Ron's house. I have to take this."

She steps away, her back to me.

God, she just never stops. Even in the midst of stealing $30,000 I don't have, she's still trying to spin these mythical buyers. I wonder who's really on the other end of that call. Veronica? Someone else? I strain to hear her side of it, but the sounds from the playground and the breeze carry her words away from me.

She hangs up and returns to the park bench. "Sorry about that."

I stand and toss my mostly uneaten taco in the trash. "I need to go," I tell her.

She gives me a hug, her expensive perfume enveloping me, but my body remains stiff, my arms at my side. "Call if you need anything."

———————

I wait until Scott gets home, needing to see his face when I tell him what's happened. To reassure myself that my loyalty isn't misplaced.

I'd driven home on autopilot, and by the time I arrived, the tiny seed of doubt had grown into a small stone sitting inside of me. The possibility that he might have done this. Because it *is* possible. Just because I can't find the evidence doesn't mean it isn't happening.

When he arrives, he takes one look at me and says, "What's wrong?"

He keeps his eyes on mine as I give him the details, reading from a page where I'd assembled all the information. The date in June when the credit card was opened, shortly after my first outing with Meg. The debt in my name. The most recent charges and cash advances and, finally, the email address associated with it.

"That fucking bitch," he says when I'm finished.

I stare at him, searching for a hint of a lie. A flash of guilt before being shuttered behind the outrage building there.

My silence catches his attention, and he pulls back. "Wait a minute. You think it was me?"

"I don't know what to think."

He stands and begins to pace, his voice rising. "What more do you want from me, Kat? I've laid my life open for you to pick through whenever you want—my phone. My computer—which, two years out, you still search on a daily basis." He turns to face me. "You've become best friends with a fucking con artist, and yet *I'm* the one you suspect? This woman has infiltrated your life. She's got you wrapped around her finger, going to concerts and lunches and yoga. You're her goddamn assistant," he spits. "She's tried several times to access our information—the stolen bank statements, the missing cable bill—and yet each time something's happened, I'm the one you've looked at first."

He sits next to me and takes my hands in his, his voice nearly breaking. "I don't know what else I can do to prove that it's not me." Tears well in his eyes. "I'm beginning to believe this will never be okay. You will never trust me."

"Scott," I say.

But he holds up his hand, silencing me. "I won't let her do this to us." He grabs my page of notes and says, "I'm taking over. Tomorrow, I'm opening an investigation into Meg. Whatever she's up to, it stops now."

The pain I see on his face nearly breaks me. How hard he's worked, and how much it must hurt that no matter what he does, I still doubt him.

No more.

"Okay," I whisper.

# KAT

**August**

I stop taking Meg's calls, so she begins texting me.

Are you all right?

What's going on?

Please just let me know you're okay.

Finally, I text her back. I'm fine, just dealing with this credit card. I filed a police report. They're taking over.

And Scott? she texts back.

I don't respond.

---

Scott had printed the credit card statements and taken everything associated with it into the station, and I'm grateful not to have to look at it. But I'm unable to do anything else. My file on Meg remains in my desk, unopened, and I've missed several deadlines for content I couldn't bring myself to write, even though I need the money more than ever.

Another week goes by. Veronica calls and leaves a message. Meg says you've been sick. We miss you. Hope you're feeling better soon.

*Sick.* I shake my head, imagining Meg spinning a story to Veronica as they sit on their yoga mats waiting for class to start, about a trip to urgent care and antibiotics. Stories are what she does best.

Flashes of the Citibank call keep returning to me. The dirty street, the smell of the bus as it passed, the scratch of the wooden park bench. And the call Meg took, right before I left. Meg's *mystery buyers.*

I grab my phone and open the text thread with Meg, scrolling back three weeks until I find what I'm looking for. Veronica came through! We just opened escrow at $4.5 million. Buyers are over the moon happy and we close in 30 days.

While I've been busy putting locks on my social security number, talking to the credit reporting agencies, I haven't had the time to give much thought to the fact that Meg is about to take her house back. She probably doesn't even want my $30,000; she just needs me out of her way while the deal closes. I've accommodated her by doing just that.

I imagine Ron packing up his belongings, directing furniture into storage, never suspecting that Meg has orchestrated the quick sale of his house, the removal of him from her childhood home. And what will she do next? Will she quietly sell it, this time at market value, and pocket the difference before slipping out of town? Perhaps Veronica will show up to yoga and wonder why the space next to hers is empty. Wonder why Meg's number has been disconnected.

Ten years ago, Meg made a phone call that derailed my life. I lost my career and my place in the world. She stole my sense of safety and self-worth, and every day since then, I've had to live with the consequences of that call. I've had to accept fear as a daily part of my life.

And now she's returned and taken even more. Because Meg is a con artist, and con artists steal—however and whenever they can.

I'm done feeling sorry for myself. Done with the second-guessing and hand-wringing. I may have missed what she did while it was happening, but that doesn't mean I can't figure it out now.

Scott had filed the police report yesterday, bringing the paperwork home for me to sign—*Kat Roberts vs. Meg Williams*. Now that the police are involved, there will be a formal investigation, and Scott has promised I'll have access to everything they dig up on her.

Meg will not destroy my life twice.

# KAT

"Were you able to connect with Phillip Montgomery, or his sister Renata?" I ask Scott as he arrives home after work.

"You need to take a break," he says, kissing the top of my head.

I tuck a strand of hair behind my ear. "I'm fine."

He rolls his eyes. "You're going to burn out." He stands behind me and rubs my shoulders. "I think you need to give it some space. Let us run the investigation, and I promise, if anything turns up, you'll be the first to know."

His fingers knead the tight muscles in my neck, but I pull away. "And do what?" I ask. "Wait for her to open up another credit card in my name? Run up more debt?"

Scott pulls his office chair over and sits, turning me away from my notes. "You're not eating, not sleeping. All I'm suggesting is that you take a break—a day, a week—to clear your head. Work on something else, then come back with fresh eyes. You know better than anyone that sometimes patience and time are the only things that will crack a story."

"I have a $30,000 debt. I don't have the luxury of being patient."

What I can't bring myself to admit is that if I'm not working on Meg's story, all that's left is crap content about home decorating, gardening, and relationships. *Is Your New Friend a Con Artist? Five Signs to Look For.* The thought makes me want to weep.

"Well, you're taking a break tonight. Go get showered and put on something nice. I made a reservation at Magnolia for 6:30. Traffic is crazy, so we need to leave in forty-five minutes."

I glance at my cell phone, silent on the desk, and wonder where Meg is, imagining her out there thinking she got away with it. Not knowing that we've named her in a police report, and that Scott and his colleagues are hard at work building a case against her. Not knowing that I'm slowly building the story that will finally expose her.

---

After my shower, I get dressed while Scott jumps in. On my nightstand I grab the tube of my favorite lotion, trying to squeeze the last remaining drops from the empty container.

"Shit," I mutter, knowing it'll be months before I can afford another one. But then I remember the small travel-size tube Scott got me for my birthday last year. I'd left it in his glove compartment after a road trip we took to Tahoe.

"I'm getting something from your car," I call through the closed bathroom door.

"What?" he yells over the sound of running water.

I ignore him and grab his keys from the hall table where they sit next to his cell phone. The cool air outside envelops my wet hair, but instead of feeling the chill, I feel invigorated. A night out might be exactly what I need. I spot his car parked a few doors down and unlock it, sliding onto the passenger seat and opening the glove compartment.

I find my lotion behind the car manual and several old takeout napkins. I grab it and am about to close the glove compartment when I spot a cell phone wedged into a corner.

The lotion slips onto my lap as I take the phone and turn it over in my hands. It's small and black, one of those throwaway burner phones that look like a smartphone but only perform the most basic of functions—calls, emails, and internet. I click the screen awake, hoping to see a photograph of strangers, their lost cell phone safely tucked in Scott's glove compartment until he can return it. But it's just a plain blue background, showing the time, date, and an unlock button.

I tap it and the phone awakes, no password protecting it, as if whoever owns it isn't worried about stolen data.

There are no photos, no contacts, outgoing or incoming calls. I toggle over to the web browser to look at the browsing history.

My breath hitches in my chest as my eyes scan the list, the familiar names of gambling sites that have haunted my dreams and my darker moments lining up to reveal how well Scott lied.

I scroll down further to the date of the concert in the park. The time of the attempted breach at the bank. It was Scott who'd tried to access my account.

Quickly, I toggle over to the settings to see what email is linked to the phone. And even though I'm expecting it, even though I'm bracing for what I know I'll find, it still feels like a punch in the chest.

Calistasniece at Yahoo.

# MEG

All roads lead back to Canyon Drive. Once again, I find myself sitting in my car, staring at my childhood home. How many times have I parked in this exact spot? How many hours have I lost, remembering the way we were tossed out, clothes hastily shoved into garbage bags, no time to even put on my shoes as the sheriff stood in the foyer and neighbors wandered onto their driveways and wide lawns to watch.

But today is different. Today I'm doing the final walk-through with my buying clients, Gretchen and Rick. Clients I poached from a colleague after I overheard him talking about what kind of a house they needed. A few phone calls, a coincidental encounter at an open house, an off-the-record opportunity, not even listed yet. Who wouldn't jump at the chance to snag a property in today's competitive market?

Canyon Drive will be closing tomorrow, and Ron has moved into a hotel until we can find him something more fitting for a state senator, a necessary pivot away from income properties that were never part of my plan. And now I will be going back inside my home—not for the first time, but for the last.

The first time had been just over a month ago in early August, to show the house to Gretchen and Rick. Ron had been there as well, so I'd had to keep my expression curious and open.

I'd been surprised by how much had changed. The floors were now stained dark instead of the blond wood I remembered. The brick fireplace had been refaced in marble, and the kitchen was completely new. But as I'd stood at the sink staring out the window and into the backyard, the view had been exactly as I'd remembered it. The same lawn sloping down toward the tall hedges in back. The sycamore tree, the shape of its branches exactly the same, all the way down to the pocket where two of the larger limbs met, the width of my hips, the perfect spot to read or hide from my mother and Ron.

I'd led Gretchen and Rick through the rooms on the main floor, Ron opting to wait outside while we looked around. Upstairs, I somehow managed to show them the features — the primary bedroom and bath, a balcony off the seating area, gesturing to the doorway of my old bedroom. "Guest plus bath," I'd said, letting Gretchen and Rick enter alone, not wanting the memories of those last few months to clutter my mind.

Today, though, I'm early. I glance at my phone again, hoping I'll see something from Kat. She's been quiet for weeks, ignoring my texts and calls. Veronica hasn't heard from her either. A flicker of worry passes through me as I imagine her trying to figure out how to pay off that credit card on her own. There's no way she can manage it on what she's been writing lately—articles about cuticle care and the power of essential oils.

I'm almost certain Kat believes I was the one who opened the credit card and ran up all that debt. I don't know exactly how much she knows about where I've been for the past ten years, but every job I've done would indicate I'm exactly who she thinks I am—a con artist, an opportunist, twisting reality to suit my purposes. Setting up a politician with one hand while simultaneously stealing money from a down-on-her-luck journalist with the other. Which means she'll be even more determined to expose me. To write something that will not only pay well, but finally open the door to bigger publications. I knew this was who she was from the beginning; I can't be angry with her about it now.

I flip through my keys until I find the right one. "The front door is made of oak, milled from a forest in Virginia. A tree that probably greeted the colonists of Jamestown before arriving here to keep us safe." My words a quiet whisper under the covered porch that still smells exactly as I remember—grass and mildew from stucco that never completely dries.

I step into the cool foyer, taking in the space. The house is now empty of Ron's horrible chrome and leather furniture, and I can let the ghosts return. Take the time to finally say goodbye. I move through the downstairs, past the main staircase with a window seat on the landing, passing into a family room once lined with bookshelves.

The house may be different, but its landmarks are the same. The railing on the wall as I ascend the back staircase is the same texture, with the same divots and dips in the wood. I run my hand along it, reacquainting myself. The fourth stair still creaks in exactly the same way I remember, and I spend a minute there, passing up and down, just so I can hear it. I close my eyes, pretending my mother is still alive, still in the house with me, just out of sight around the corner; any moment she'll speak. *Hurry up, slowpoke.*

A dog barking from a distant yard snaps me back to the present. I continue up the stairs, making my way to my old bedroom, the one with the dormer window overlooking the backyard and the walk-in closet where the slant of the roof meets the floor at a 45-degree angle.

I stand in the middle of the space, trying to find my younger self, but it's hard. Nothing is the same. The paint, flooring, and moldings—it's all been replaced, though the upgrades are cheap. Plastic blinds on the windows instead of wood, fiberglass in the bathrooms instead of the original porcelain.

I turn toward the closet, hoping Ron has somehow left it alone, and reach for the knob, holding tight to the memory of the interior wall marked with scuffs from my shoes. The sagging rod where I'd once hung my clothes. And in the back, on the far wall, the scratches and hash marks of a height chart. I can still see them in my mind, horizontal lines, and next to them, Nana's faded handwriting.

> Rosie 8-27-78
> Rosie 12-17-82

And in darker marker, my mother's writing, as familiar as a song I know by heart.

> Meggie 2-4-93
> Meggie 10-26-98

But when I turn the knob and open the closet, a light illuminates automatically, revealing the laminate shelving of a California Closets installation. The air is sterile, the floor beneath my feet shiny, the wall I remembered and everything written on it relegated to a garbage dump years ago.

I exit the room quickly and make my way down the front stairs, through the dining room, and into the backyard, the only place left that carries a hint of the people I loved. I brush my hand along the trunk of the sycamore tree as I make my way toward the back corner, where Nana's roses still sway and dance in the slight breeze—eighteen bushes planted nearly sixty years ago, when she was a young mother herself. Before her only son's downward spiral into drugs and alcohol.

This is the only place left where I can still feel her—and the memories rush at me. Long afternoons spent turning the soil, searching the leaves for aphids with my spray bottle of soapy water. She taught me the names of each variety—Burst of Joy, Moonlight in Paris, Double Delight—and I whisper the names under my breath like a mantra.

It's a small miracle they're still here, that Ron hadn't pulled them out and installed a fire pit or a hot tub. I reach down and pick up a few fallen petals and smell them—the sweet fragrance carrying me back in time.

"Meg, are you here?"

Rick's voice from inside pulls me back to the present, and all the pain and resentment I've harbored over the last decade snaps back into place, fitting into the grooves and edges I've carved for them. I let the petals fall to the ground.

"Out here," I call, making my way into the house, where they're waiting in the foyer. Rick, a partner at a downtown law firm, and Gretchen, his homemaker wife. Not the anonymous industry power couple I'd led Kat to believe. Perception is everything. Nameless, faceless clients who value their privacy force a person to fit those details into a story. Because when you leave a trail of breadcrumbs, people expect them to lead somewhere.

"Shall we start in the kitchen?" I ask, my smile genuine.

---

"You can pick up the keys at the Apex office tomorrow. I'll call you the minute it's officially yours," I say when we're done.

I watch them drive away, and it isn't until I'm unlocking my car that

I see him. Scott, Kat's fiancé, behind the wheel of an older model Toyota sedan, watching me.

I recognize him from Kat's Facebook profile. Once I knew her real name, it was easy to find her online, and then him. *Scott Griffin, fraud detective.* I read about cases he worked. I scoured Facebook for photos—Scott at the beach, on a ski vacation, laughing in front of a giant cactus in the desert. There's no question it's him.

I let my gaze slide over him, keeping my motions measured and smooth. As I pull away from the curb, I let myself glance once in my rearview mirror, the pinch of betrayal sharp. They're working together.

# KAT

## September

I try not to notice the empty spaces Scott left, the absence of him obvious in every room of the apartment. I stand at the counter, my bathrobe pulled tight around my waist, and think through next steps. I fight the urge to call Meg. To tell her she was right and to ask her what I should do next. I understand better the powerless rage she's felt for years, so much sharper than the blame I assigned to her so long ago. That rage vibrates through me now, a low-frequency anger that pulses with every heartbeat. What lengths would I go to make Scott pay?

I lose hours wondering what Meg would do if she were me.

———————

When Scott had gotten out of the shower, he found me sitting on the couch, my hair drying into awkward clumps, my face still bare of makeup. "You're not ready," he said.

Then he saw the cell phone sitting on the coffee table in front of me.

Several emotions flashed across his face—first fear, then anger, and finally a stoic resolution, as if a curtain were closing behind his eyes. "What's that?" he asked.

"Don't." I was numb, miles away from the initial stab of shock and pain. Instead, I felt an icy calm envelop me, and I welcomed it. I wanted to live inside that pain-free bubble for as long as possible, because I knew the alternative was to relive every betrayal, over and over again, long after this moment had passed.

He collapsed in the chair across from me and cradled his head in his hands. "I'm so sorry," he said.

A familiar refrain, danced to again and again. I knew all the steps—the apologies, the self-flagellation, the regret. Then the promises. And we would drag ourselves out of the hole once again.

Instead, I bypassed all of it. The questions about what triggered it. How it started, and why. The recriminations, telling him that if he'd only told me he was struggling, we could have worked together to get him through the rough patch. The words floated out of my mind, there and then gone. I had nothing left to give.

I slipped off my engagement ring and placed it on top of the dark cell phone, and I wondered how much I could get for it. Was it even real? I should have taken Meg up on that appraisal when she offered it.

Scott lifted his head and said, "Kat, no."

"Thirty thousand dollars," I whispered, and he flinched.

"I was going to pay it back, I swear."

The script was exactly as I remembered it. "You worked so hard to make me believe I was the one who fucked up, that I led Meg here because I was careless. Too trusting. But you were the one who took the statements. Who didn't pay the bill, and then blamed Meg for that as well."

"I'll go back into treatment," he said. "Five days a week. We'll get through this together. I need you."

I gave a sharp laugh. "You need my credit score. You need the very little money I've got left in my savings account. But you don't need me."

"That's not true."

"I don't think you know what true is," I told him. All his lies, his fake outrage over Meg came rushing back, juxtaposed against Meg's quiet concern. How she'd tried to help me see what was right in front of me.

It says something when the con artist is more trustworthy than your fiancé.

"I need you to get out," I said. "Tonight. You have two hours to get packed. Anything left will be sold and put toward the debt you've accrued."

Scott's remorse flashed to anger. "What happened to *I love you*? What happened to *I'll support you in your recovery*?"

I looked at him in disbelief. "I'd hardly call running up a five-figure debt 'recovery,' would you?"

"Where the hell am I supposed to go?"

I shrugged. "Call your sponsor. Find a friend. Sleep on someone's couch. I don't care."

"And if I don't?" he asked.

"I'll call the police. One of your colleagues will show up, and I'll explain what you've done. Then I'll hand over the cell phone which has evidence of you trying to breach my bank account and the email linked to the credit card. I'm sure they can sort it out with you at the station."

"You wouldn't."

I felt pieces of my old self falling away. Chipped edges, brittle fears and suspicions. Worries that kept me up at night, imagining years of constant monitoring. Years of doubting and following up, the endless cycle of wondering, questioning, confirming—they all slipped off me, leaving behind nothing but a polished resolution.

"Clock starts now," I said.

While he packed, I stepped out, taking his burner phone with me. I waited in my car, making sure all the doors were locked, and hunched down in my seat, checking my mirrors to make sure no one could see the woman sitting alone in her car on a dark street.

I imagined him emptying his dresser, the closet, clearing out his desk in the office. Shoving his clothes into a duffel bag, taking everything he'd brought into the relationship. The framed artwork in the living room. The lamp on his desk that once belonged to his father. The fancy toaster oven he just had to have.

Finally, he left, his car piled high with his belongings, and I waited until he turned the corner and vanished before going back into the apartment. I walked through the living room and into our bedroom—my bedroom now—climbed into bed fully dressed, and fell asleep.

---

My phone rings, yanking me back to the present. It's a number I don't recognize, and my stomach twists. Another collection agency? Another credit card opened up in my name? "This is Kat," I say.

"Kat Roberts?"

I close my eyes, bracing myself. "Speaking."

"This is Renata Davies, returning your call."

My eyes fly open, all thoughts of Scott vanishing as I scramble to find a pen and a fresh piece of paper. "Yes," I say. "Thanks so much for getting back to me. I was hoping you could tell me about a woman named Melody Wilde."

There's a long pause. Finally, Renata speaks, her voice low and angry.

"I can tell you that she's a fraud and a fake. I can tell you that she came into town spinning lies about who she was as a way to ingratiate herself into my circle of friends. And I can tell you she stole $350,000 from my brother and convinced him to sign over a house to her. Is that the kind of information you're looking for?"

Maybe I'll get my story after all.

---

I spend an hour on the phone with Renata, who told me about a woman posing as an interior decorator and life coach to New York City celebrities and how she convinced Renata's brother, Phillip, to let Meg—or *Melody*—"coach" him through his divorce, collecting huge sums of money she promised to hold on to until after the settlement.

"Tell me about the house," I said, the one piece that could tie together what Meg was doing now.

"The lake house," Renata said. "I told him to let Celia have it, but my brother is stubborn and the house was in his name. It was his asset."

"How did Melody end up with it?"

"He sold it to her for $20,000, which is a fraction of what it's worth. Melody said he could buy it back after the settlement was finalized, then sell it again, this time at market value."

"Surely he would have known he'd be slammed with taxes," I said, my mind half on what Renata was saying, half on how she might have convinced Ron to go along with something similar.

"Melody said she knew a way to get around them. Another lie. But by that point, the only thing Phillip cared about was hanging on to what he believed was his," she explained. "He didn't think beyond the settlement. Melody convinced him it would work simply because she'd told him it had worked for her."

"Con artists often target people who are emotionally vulnerable," I said. "People who need to believe the reality they're selling, desperate for a solution to whatever problems they're facing."

"She ruined his life. His reputation," Renata said. I knew what Meg would say. *He ruined his own life. I just found all the cracks.*

"Has he contacted the police?" I asked her.

"He did, obviously, but they said she'd be 'hard to prosecute.' Their words. Because he'd been engaging in fraudulent behavior as well, it would be hard to prove she conned him. His divorce attorneys resigned and he was forced to represent himself. It was a mess."

It was hard for me to muster any sympathy for Phillip Montgomery. Renata gave me his ex-wife's name and number, and I called her next. Celia revealed a man who terrorized her and her children. "I stayed longer than I should have," she told me. "I left with just a suitcase of essentials. Phillip was livid. Changed the locks. Wouldn't allow me to enter the house to retrieve the rest of my things. By the time we got a court order, most of it was gone. Thrown out, donated, sold, I don't know. I didn't care about my clothes, but some of the more sentimental pieces—my mother's jewelry, notes and cards the kids gave me over the years—that gutted me."

So much of her story was familiar, Meg and her mother having lived their own version of it. "How do you think Meg found you?"

"No idea. But here's the crazy thing—a few weeks ago, I was contacted by a real estate attorney who was working on behalf of a counterpart in California. He told me the lake house had been deeded to me. And since I acquired it after our divorce was finalized, Phillip can't touch it. It's mine."

I sat up straight, my pen still. "Meg *gave* you the house?"

"And everything in it," Celia said. "Even the taxes were covered."

I was unable to speak for a moment, Meg's generosity unexpected, and yet, not surprising. Sure, she'd kept Phillip's cash. But she balanced the scales. Gave back to Celia a little bit of the power Phillip had stolen, and exposed him in the process. The same thing she'd done for Kristen. What she was trying to do now for her mother and for herself.

"The incredible thing," Celia continued, "is that right before all of this happened, I'd resigned myself to getting nothing. I was ready to quit. To let Phillip keep it all."

"Why?" I asked.

"Divorce is like a virus. It invades every corner of your life, every thought and every moment. Everything is viewed through the lens of *how will this benefit or harm my settlement*. It's toxic."

"But you'd have given up a lot of money," I pressed.

"How much is your freedom worth to you?"

---

I'm still trying to answer that question. It's a complicated shame to have someone you trust deceive you, the pain of that betrayal compounded by the unraveling of the life you thought you'd have. The removal of their belongings, the empty spaces left behind to remind you of all you never saw. Telling friends and family, the phone calls and texts where you have to carry everyone else's regrets alongside your own. Which is why the only person I've told so far is Jenna.

She'd said all the right things, been outraged on my behalf. "I hope you've gone to the police."

First, I had to drop the charges Scott filed against Meg.

---

I sit on hold for fifteen minutes before I get someone on the line.

"Hi, I filed a police report a few weeks ago, but there was a misunderstanding, and I want to drop it."

"Case number?"

I read it off and am ready to wait while she looks it up, but she says, "That's not a case number. It's generally a ten-digit number, found in the upper right corner of your copy of the police report."

I look at the report Scott had brought home for me to sign. Eight digits and a letter.

"Let me call you back," I tell her.

Of course, there was never a real police report. If he'd actually filed one, the investigation would have eventually cleared Meg and implicated him. But a bigger realization keeps me from being angry about another lie. No police report means I'm still the only person who knows who Meg is and what she's doing.

I grab my phone and text Meg, hoping it's not too late. That she isn't already gone. Thanks for giving me the space I needed to sort things out on my end. I'm ready to get back to work.

But my phone stays silent. I get up and go into the kitchen to grab a soda, and when I return, I decide to read through my notes from Celia and Renata, trying to see a thread between what Meg did to Phillip Montgomery and what she might have done to Ron. A forged inspection report? A falsified appraisal? Pretending to be private buyers guarding their identity, and then possibly stealing the Canyon Drive property back. I can't even be sure that the sale price was $4.5 million. Meg could have told me anything, knowing that information wouldn't be public for weeks.

It might help if I can see everything in order, starting with Cory Dempsey, moving through Phillip, and then adding what I've got so far with Ron. I also want to take another look at the few victims I'd been able to find shortly after Meg left Los Angeles the first time. Dig a little deeper to see whether they, too, deserved Meg's attention the way Cory did. The way Phillip did. The way Ron does now.

I pull the file from my desk drawer and open it. A blank piece of paper sits on top of the stack. I set it aside and am faced with another blank sheet. My hands begin to shake as I start flipping through the pages, blank page after blank page, my mind finally catching up to what's happened.

Scott.

While I sat in my car waiting for him to clear out, he was stealing my notes and replacing them with a fat stack of printer paper.

Everything I've gathered about Meg—names, dates, former addresses, and family information—is gone. Ten years' worth of work has vanished, and any chance I might have had to sell the story and pay the debt. Rage pounds through me, and I grab my soda can and throw it against the wall, where it explodes in a cascade of brown bubbles, puddling on the hardwood floor.

# MEG

I'm walking through a tiny house in Sunset Park, my fourth one of the morning, making sure I've been seen by enough agents from the Apex office before calling it quits for the day, when someone behind me says, "Hey, Meg."

I turn from the closet I'd been peering into and see Guy Cicinelli, an older agent from the Apex office who's poked his head into the tiny bedroom.

"Seems you're following me," I say, having seen him at the last three open houses I'd been to.

He grins. "Maybe we'll be up against each other." He peeks over my shoulder and into the closet. "My clients are going to love this house."

"Mine too," I say, referring to clients I've been pretending to have— the young couple looking for their starter home. The retired teacher looking to downsize into something that will better fit his crap pension. I'm weeks away from leaving town, but I have to appear to be hustling, looking for my next deal. *Always be closing.*

Guy sighs and says, "It never gets old—helping people find the place they'll call home, and then making it happen for them."

"I know what you mean," I say, and for once it's not bullshit. When I got confirmation that Celia's lake house was officially hers, I felt the kind of joy you get when you've done something completely selfless and completely right. It was a moment of peace, as if all the problems and heartache in the world have suddenly paused their spinning chaos and it's silent, for one blessed moment. *I did that. I gave that to her.*

We make our way back into the living room, and he gestures toward the street. "Is that your buyer sitting in his car? You know he can come inside. Even though it's a broker's open, buyers show up all the time."

"What do you mean?" I ask, looking through the front window. "My buyer isn't here."

"Well, there's a guy parked in front," Guy says. "I assumed he was yours, since he's been at the last three houses you've looked at."

Fucking Scott. I roll my eyes and say, "Not a client. He's my assistant's fiancé." I move back to the central hall and say, "Have you seen the kitchen yet? Amazing."

Guy wanders into it, and I use the opportunity to peel away from him and head to the backyard, a concrete slab with a large crack that Guy's buyers will need to repair. A path leads toward the back gate, and I follow it, pretending to be looking at the garage.

My phone buzzes with a text from Kat, and I pull up short. Thanks for giving me the space I needed to sort things out on my end. I'm ready to get back to work.

After weeks of silence, ignoring my calls and texts, now she wants to come back? I think of Scott parked in front, Kat asking to be let back in, and I want to laugh. If this is a coordinated effort, it's pretty clumsy.

I slip through to the alley and head south, planning to circle back to the street and approach Scott's car from behind. I imagine myself pounding on his window, startling him. *You're Kat's boyfriend*, I'd say. *The gambler.* Relishing the moment when he realizes he's been caught. But before I round the corner and make my approach, I stop, common sense taking over.

It'll be easier to keep track of him if he thinks what he's doing is working.

I turn and walk back up the alley and through the back gate, making my way through the house, waving at Guy as I go. Out the front door, nice and relaxed.

---

The following day, I sit at my desk, the afternoon sun arcing across the surface, the house silent save for the quiet fizz of carbonation from the soda I just poured. I have one of my notebooks from Pennsylvania open to the notes I made about the DBA I set up there.

On my computer screen, I have several tabs open. One shows Southern California escrow companies and the counties they serve. Another explains the limitations placed on filing a DBA under a business name already in existence in California. A third shows a receipt for the plane ticket I just purchased, a quick trip to Las Vegas, leaving tomorrow morning and returning that same day.

In every job, there comes a tipping point. A moment when there is no exit other than allowing events to unfold, hoping the work you put into the setup was enough. With Cory, that moment came late. It wasn't until I started withdrawing cash from his account that I had to keep my eyes forward. With Phillip, that moment was when I sold his furniture. If he'd changed his mind and asked to move it back, the whole scam would have been over.

This is the tipping point for Ron. I have a website to finish and a visit to a Las Vegas notary. Then a second stop at the county clerk's office before my flight home, where I'll be filing for another DBA, one of the last benchmarks I need to hit in order to meet my deadline, two weeks before the election. I had only thirty-five days left.

And then I'll take him to see the Mandeville property. Five acres in the heart of Brentwood, on the market for over two years with only one set of buyers who'd backed out unexpectedly a year ago. Dead weight hanging around the listing agent's neck, and on lockbox with a combination anyone can access.

Kat's text remains unanswered on my phone. I'm not sure what to think about it—what she believes, or what she wants. I think back to the flame of worry I felt when she told me about the bank account breach and then later the credit card. How certain I'd been that it was Scott and how frustrated I was when she refused to see what was obvious to me.

But who am I to judge? Every relationship I've ever had has been a lie.

I stare at the website I've just created, nearly identical to the legitimate one, with the exception of an extra underscore at the end.

I close my computer, wondering if I should have kept my name off a flight manifest. If I should have taken the time to drive the nine hours to Nevada and back again. But I shake off my unease. I need this DBA—and the bank account affiliated with it—sooner rather than later. By tomorrow night, it'll be done.

———————

The next morning, I'm on Sunset heading for the freeway that will take me to the airport, when I see Scott again. This time, two cars behind me. "Shit," I mutter, fighting the urge to take off. To try and lose him on one of the many winding streets that branch off Sunset. Even though I've given myself plenty of time before my flight, I don't want to waste any of it on a cat-and-mouse game through morning traffic.

My heart rate ratchets up as my mind spins out options that go nowhere. In any other situation, I'd be happy to let Scott follow me—to the market, to the nail salon, to the gynecologist. But he cannot follow me to the airport. To use his badge to get through security and see which gate I'm departing from. To make a call and have someone on the ground waiting for me in Las Vegas.

I think back to that confrontation with Nate so long ago, when he showed up at Cory's house, threatening to expose me. I didn't sneak away in the night or try to deny his accusations. Instead, I leaned in, escalating and making things too big for him to handle.

I check the time again. In my rearview mirror, the single car separating us changes lanes, putting Scott's directly behind mine. As if the decision has been made for me.

I slam on my brakes, my car screeching to a halt in the left lane. Cars on the right veer wide, and I brace myself for impact. Scott doesn't have time to react. He slams into the back of my Range Rover, and my car pitches forward, the impact vibrating through me.

I use the adrenaline of the moment, shoving my door open and stepping out, oncoming cars slowing down to see it all unfold. "What the fuck?" I yell, approaching Scott's car. As I pass my bumper, I note my fender bent inward, but overall intact. Scott's car, however, is a mess. The hood has crumpled inward, and his airbag has deployed, though thankfully he appears uninjured. The last thing I need is a lawsuit.

He steps out of his car, clearly rattled, and I suppress the urge to smile. Instead, I pull out my cell phone and start taking pictures. Of my bumper, of Scott's car, his license plate, and even Scott himself. "I want to make sure all of this is documented," I say. "My lawyers are going to tear you apart."

"What are you talking about?" he says. "You had no reason to stop."

"There was a dog. Didn't you see him?"

Scott looks confused.

Someone has pulled over to the side of the road and calls, "Are you guys okay? Do you need me to call 911?"

"No," Scott says.

But I say, "Yes. I want a police report that says this man was following too closely. He's at fault."

The good Samaritan hops on the phone, and within ten minutes, the police have arrived.

Scott looks jittery, as if he's unsure what role to play. Does he reveal that he's a detective following a suspect? Or does he play the private citizen card? I'm pretty sure the LAPD doesn't issue shitty Toyota compacts to their detectives, so I'm guessing he wasn't following me in an official capacity.

The officer approaches. "You folks okay? Think we can move the cars to the side and open up traffic again?"

When we're parked on the shoulder, I go in hard. "This man plowed into me. He wasn't looking where he was going. Every other car on the road saw that dog dart across four lanes of traffic. But this guy was probably on his phone."

Scott shakes his head. "Not true," he argues. "She slammed on her brakes for no reason."

I wheel around, my voice rising. "Why would I do that?"

I wait, wondering how Scott will answer the question. Instead, he looks at the officer and says, "Can I speak to you privately?"

"Hell no," I say, my voice close to hysterical. "You're not going to have some *bro convo* behind my back." I point at Scott, stepping closer to him. "I fucking see you. I know what guys like you try to do. You're going to put your heads together and make this my fault. 'Female drivers,'" I say, putting the words in air quotes. "I don't think so. Not today."

The officer holds up his hands. "Ma'am, please calm down. Let's lower the temperature a little bit."

I turn to face him. "Don't tell me to calm down. Write up the report. Please make sure your badge number is on it as well." I start taking pictures again. Of my bumper, of the officer, and more of Scott.

As I circle his car, I see a duffel bag in the backseat. A pillow. Crumpled food wrappers on the floor. A stainless-steel toaster oven tucked behind the driver's seat, and a toothbrush sticking out of the seat's side pocket.

I know what it looks like when someone's living in their car.

I want to punch the air, do a happy dance on the shoulder of Sunset Boulevard. I glance at the officer, busy copying down our plate numbers, and walk past Scott, letting my shoulder brush against his. "It looks like Kat finally kicked you out," I say, my words floating just under the sound of traffic behind us. "What's that saying? 'The bell tolls for you, mother-fucker.'" I give him a sweet smile. "Or something like that."

Scott's eyes widen in surprise, but he doesn't say anything more.

---

Less than an hour later, we're done. Scott is stuck waiting for a tow truck, and I linger long enough to make sure the police officer leaves. After today, Scott can follow me all he wants.

I ease back into traffic, making sure to keep my speed slightly below the limit, and soon I'm circling onto the 405 freeway, heading south toward the airport. It'll be tight—I'll have to pay for VIP parking—but I'll still make my flight. As I settle into the left lane, I let the adrenaline fall away. Once the DBA is set up, the second half of my plan can begin.

# KAT

October

Give me back my notes. My first text to Scott since I kicked him out, and he's quick to reply.

Meet with me.

If it's the phone you want, I don't have it anymore, I text back. I already gave it to the police when I filed a police report against you.

I'd gone to the police station and stood at the Formica counter, giving the detective details that seemed to bore her, until I got to Scott's name.

She looked up sharply. "*Detective* Scott Griffin?"

"That's the one," I said. "I've got credit card statements and the phone he used to open it."

When she opened the evidence bag and asked me to drop the phone in, I hesitated. "I think I'd prefer to hang on to that, if it's okay with you. I can let the detectives see it whenever they need to."

She'd looked at me over her black-framed readers and said, "That's not how it works."

Scott texts back. It doesn't have to be this way.

Please get the help you need, I respond.

---

As far as I know, Scott's still working. My report is most likely either last in a very long line of fraud cases or slowed down by Scott. I've got an appeal with Citibank, though they've told me that without the police confirming it was fraudulent, I'll have a hard time getting the debt forgiven because some of the charges—for food, and once, for our rent back in June—implicate me. No one seems to care whether I opened the account or not.

*Accept the things you cannot change.* A line from Scott's twelve-step recovery pops into my mind. "What a crock," I say aloud into the empty room.

I stare at my silent phone, then open up my text thread with Meg. My last message to her sits there, unanswered, and I worry that she's already gone. That she's disconnected her phone and quietly left town, feeding a story to Veronica to keep her from wondering about her abrupt departure. If the Canyon Drive escrow is closed, there'd be no reason for her to stick around.

My finger hovers over the call button. I have to know.

The phone rings, and I brace myself for an automated message informing me the number is no longer in service. Or a full voicemail box.

Instead, she answers.

"It was Scott," I tell her.

She's quiet for a moment, and I think about a conversation I had with her, back when she was showing me houses. *Men will always show you who they are.* Scott worked hard to distract me with things that weren't true, forcing me to question my own instincts, telling me I couldn't trust what I was seeing with my own eyes. He chipped away at my confidence, convincing me up was down, good was bad. Meg had been the one who'd tried to keep me facing forward, to help me see who Scott was, and in doing so, who she was as well.

"I'm sorry," she finally says.

"I should have listened."

"If you'd done something the moment you saw the missing bank statement, would it have made a difference with the credit card?"

I think back to what Citibank told me, about when the card had been opened. "No," I tell her. "Maybe a few thousand dollars less, but not enough to change anything." I exhale slowly. "I can't stop thinking about the betrayal. The sense of powerlessness…it keeps me up at night, running through all the things I chose to ignore."

Her voice is quiet. "It's not your fault Scott's a shitty person."

"He's going to get away with it."

"Probably," she says. "In my experience, men like Scott usually do."

I think about how long she's had to wait to hold Ron accountable. "Did you close on Ron's house?"

"We did," she says.

I feel the air rush out of me. All my work, the time I invested, hoping to see things from the inside. But I'd never been on the inside. Meg made sure of that.

And yet, if it were truly over, she wouldn't still be here, answering her phone, going to yoga. I step sideways in my mind, trying to look beyond the Canyon Drive house, and ask myself, *What would success look like for Meg?* Perhaps the answer isn't a house.

"Is Ron looking to buy something, or will he wait, now that the election is so close?"

"We're working on a few different options," she says.

"I'd be happy to help," I say. "Whatever you need. I'm dying to take my mind off things, and paperwork sounds like the perfect distraction."

Meg is quiet for a moment, as if she's thinking. "Tell you what," she says. "Let's go for a hike. I need to get out of the house, and it sounds like you do too. Temescal Canyon in an hour?"

I feel a zap of energy, as if someone's plugged me in again. "Meet you in the parking lot?"

"See you soon," she says, and hangs up.

I stare at the notes from my calls with Renata and Celia, focusing on the purchase of Celia's lake house. It's clear that whatever happened with the sale of Canyon Drive, Ron was fine with it. Which means that Canyon Drive wasn't her end point, but rather the starting point to something bigger.

# MEG

Temescal Canyon is close to where I live and a popular hiking spot for locals. The day is overcast, and because it's a weekday, the parking lot is mostly empty. I lock my door and scan the surrounding cars, pulling the collar of my windbreaker against my neck. It'll be good to feel the burn of a steep hill, to sweat out my nerves, which have been pulled so tight I feel as if they're sitting on top of my skin. Everything depends on tomorrow, on my ability to sell Ron a vision of himself that exists only in his mind. If I can't, there won't be time for a plan B.

Kat's car pulls in next to mine, and I wait while she pays her parking fee and slides the ticket onto her dash. Then we head through the lot and into the park.

"What happened to your car?" she asks.

I glance back at my bumper, still bent inward. "Some guy on Sunset. He was on his phone and plowed into me."

Kat's expression crinkles with concern. "Are you okay?"

"Sure. That thing's a tank. His car was pretty messed up though."

Our feet crunch on the dirt path as a few hikers pass us in the opposite direction. My breathing opens up, my shoulders release, and I allow myself time to enjoy the fresh air. I wait until the trail narrows and starts to incline upward to bring up Scott. "How are you doing with everything?"

"Okay, I guess. It's quiet at home with Scott gone, so I'm glad for an opportunity to get out."

"Did you file a police report?"

"Last week," she says.

"What did they say? Can they do anything?" We slide into single file as the path narrows, with Kat directly behind me. The trail drops off to the left into a deep canyon and I can't see her face, but I imagine her carefully arranging her expression, flipping through the things she can and cannot say in order to maintain the facade that Scott is a midlevel bank employee and not a well-respected member of LAPD's Commercial Crimes Division.

"They're *looking into it*. But since the credit card was used for some household expenses, it doesn't look good."

Between her words are all the things she cannot say. What it must have been like for her to report him to his colleagues and the very real chance that they might cover for him. We're quiet, our breath growing labored as the incline steepens. A group of laughing women approach us on their way down, and we step aside to let them pass. When we resume, I say, "You're tougher than you think. You'll get through this and be better for it." And she will. I know for a fact that when your heart gets ripped out, it'll reassemble into something stronger. More durable.

She doesn't respond, but I know she heard me.

We make it up to the waterfall and turn around. The trip down is quiet and fast, and soon we find ourselves walking through a large clearing dotted with sycamore trees and a picnic table in the center. I gesture toward it and say, "Rest a bit before we go back to the real world?"

She shrugs. "Sure."

When we're settled, I say, "So what are your next steps?"

"I've sent the police report to Citibank and frozen the account, so at least he can't do any more damage."

"Did you report him to his supervisor?"

She looks away and says, "He's got a copy of the police report, yes."

I like the careful way she speaks. She's better at this than she thinks.

"And the phone?" I ask.

"Also with the police." She shakes her head. "What I really need is to get back to work."

I look at Kat, thinking about how I want to respond. As much as I've enjoyed having her around, when Kat went dark, things got simpler. The next few weeks will require precise timing and a flawless performance. "Things are slow right now. I don't have anything for you to do."

"What about Ron?" she asks. "Won't he buy something else?"

"Right now, he's ahead in the polls, so he wants to wait. See if he might rather buy something in Sacramento." I turn and straddle the bench so I'm facing her. "Listen, forget about Ron. Forget about the shit-paying job I gave you," I say. "You have a chance to reinvent yourself. To step out of the person you've been told you are and become who you want to be. Write that novel. Go on safari. Buy a boat and sail to Hawaii. Do something big. Something daring. Surprise everyone, even yourself."

"Is that what you've done?" she asks. "Is that what you're doing?"

The weight of her question bears down on me. "I just sell real estate," I finally say.

Kat looks down. "What if I'm just not a big, daring person with big daring ideas?" she asks.

"You figure out how you got that way. Go back in time, to the person who showed you that you couldn't be one, and give yourself a do-over. You only get one life," I tell her. "How do you want to live it?"

"Why did Ron's house sell so far below market value?" she asks, ignoring me. "I did the research. It should have sold for at least five million based on comps in the area."

My eyes widen, letting my surprise show before looking down at my hands, clasped in my lap. I'm not surprised she kept working the story, even as she was sorting through her own problems. I wouldn't have expected any less from her. Then I look up, my expression steely. "Both parties were happy with the transaction," I say. "There's nothing to see there, Kat."

"Can you tell me now who bought it?"

House sales become public record as soon as the title is recorded, which can take anywhere from six to eight weeks. Rick and Gretchen Turner will be revealed to be the owners of the house, and I wonder how much time Kat will lose digging into their background. Like a magician, I've let her see just enough to believe she's watching the trick, when all the while the deception is happening out of sight. "I'm bound to my clients' request not to reveal that," I finally say.

I'm exhausted by how careful we each have to be, picking and choosing our words to reflect a reality that doesn't exist. But I've made a decision. When this is over, Kat will know everything. Not just about this job, but about all of them, the people I chose to target, and why. I want her to know that I've done my best to adhere to Kristen's *girl code*—that you help other women, whenever you can. That I never picked a mark simply because I could.

I check my phone. "I'd better go. There are several properties I need to see."

I'll be happy when the whole charade is over.

# MEG

October
Four Weeks before the Election

The Mandeville property is listed at just over $7 million and located up a small road off Mandeville Canyon. "It's a flat parcel of land totaling just over two acres, almost unheard of anymore," I tell Ron as we drive west from Beverly Hills. I'd waved my hand at Ron's concern over my dented bumper. *A fender bender on Sunset*, I'd said.

"Centrally located," I say now. "You'll be close to the amenities of Brentwood but have the privacy you'll need as a state senator."

"I'm definitely tired of hotel living," he says.

"It's not quite move-in ready," I caution. "But I don't think it'll take much work to get there. I know the price point is a bit high, but with the sale of Canyon Drive, you have more than enough for a healthy down payment if you decide to finance it." I give him a sideways glance and say, "If you ever run for governor, this would be the perfect place for campaign events. Fundraising dinners. The listing agent is a friend of mine, and she says the property was owned by Ronald Reagan for a time, back when he was working in Hollywood. The pedigree is top notch."

As expected, that grabs his interest.

I pull through an open gate flanked by ancient oak trees. A stone wall borders the property, extending in both directions as far as the eye can see. I've been here several times—on different days, at different times. And each time, it's been as deserted as it is today.

So many of these former trophy estates linger on the market for years, no buyer willing to take the time and expense of rehabbing them. Many of them, like this one, are on lockbox, and it's simple to get the combination and show it without an anxious listing agent ever knowing you were there.

I force my grip on the wheel to loosen, my muscles to stay relaxed. "A security gate can be installed pretty easily," I say. "The house is newly vacant; the seller is motivated, but it hasn't hit the market yet."

There's a long, winding drive bordered by more oak trees, and I ease the car forward, my wheels crunching on the gravel. We pull up in front of a single-story ranch house with a mix of brick and white clapboard siding.

As we approach the front door, I layer my comments carefully, like a house of cards, one alluring fact on top of another. "There's room for about thirty cars to valet park," I say. Then I point toward the back. "Behind the house, we've got a pool, pool house with an apartment above it, and a small stable if you want horses. They say Reagan rode every day."

Then I usher him inside. "It needs some updating—fresh paint and new appliances, but those things can be done in a week." I point out the hardwood floors, a river rock fireplace, and an open-concept living room that leads to the kitchen. "Five bedrooms, all on this level. Plus a maid's quarters."

I trail him, letting his imagination take over. "Huge kitchen, which can easily accommodate a full catering staff," I say as we pass through. "Hookups for a double washer and dryer through there."

Out back, we stand on an enormous flagstone patio with incredible views of the canyon dropping below in the distance. "Few city lights out here, so the stars at night are magnificent."

We spend an hour walking the property, and I feel his interest building, my own excitement growing. This is the centerpiece of my plan. Without it, I'll have nothing to show for my time here other than a commission on the sale of a house that should have always been mine.

"I know you'll be spending most of your time in Sacramento," I say when we're done and back in the car. "But you'll need a place to get away. To recharge. All the most influential politicians have something like this, and as the saying goes, dress for the job you want, not the job you have." At the light at the base of the canyon, I add my last layer of persuasion. "I think it's doable. With what you got from the Canyon Drive sale, you won't have to make up too much of the difference—three million maybe. My advice would be to think about it carefully. Run the numbers with your business manager, but don't take too long. There are three different showings on the property this afternoon, and it's going to sell fast. But my friend owes me a favor. She can make sure ours is the first offer on the table, and if we can make it all cash, that'll be competitive enough to take it off the market."

I let that sit while we drive back to the Beverly Hills office, where we've left Ron's car. His left elbow rests on the center console, and I think about how easy it would be to reach across and invite something a little more intimate. An extra layer of scandal that could come out at the worst possible time. Sexual harassment of his real estate agent, right before the election.

I'll be honest, I really considered it. Back in Pennsylvania, when I was researching the best entry point, I was tempted by how much damage I could do as his girlfriend. But no matter how many ways I tried to reconcile it in my mind, it felt like a bridge too far. The ghost of my mother would be too close, her voice whispering things I didn't want to hear.

By the time we get back to the office, Ron is ready. "Draw up the paperwork," he says. "I'll call Steve and put him to work gathering the cash."

I turn to him. "You sure?" I ask. "It's a lot of money." I hold up my hand and laugh. "I know I spent all morning talking you into it, and now here I am trying to talk you out of it," I say. "But I don't want you to do something you're not comfortable with. If it's too big of a risk, we can go back to looking for another apartment building. Add to your portfolio and proceed with the status quo."

It's the perfect thing to say. "Risk is what makes life worth living," he says. "Let's put in an offer for full asking price, all cash."

I give him a cautious look. "Will you be able to assemble it that fast?"

Ron looks out the window. "David and I set something up with the campaign that allows us to have an emergency reserve of cash."

"You sure you want to risk that so close to the election?" I ask. "If it gets out…" I trail off, letting him imagine the fallout.

"Let me worry about the money and you just focus on getting the deal done. I want a short escrow. It would be a great place to hold a victory party. If the house isn't ready, we can set up tents, get a caterer to bring in the food."

I smile. "You got it."

---

I wait twenty-four hours, then call with the good news. "They accepted our offer, and the seller agreed to all of our terms. We're set to close in fourteen days—two weeks before the election."

"How soon can we get the inspection done?" he asks.

"Already scheduled for Thursday and we should get the report early next week. The sellers have also signed, so the contract is fully executed. If all goes well, we close and have you in the house on election night."

"That would be amazing."

I read through the escrow documents on the screen in front of me, looking to make sure everything is exactly as it should be. Seven million dollars, all cash, a fourteen-day escrow contingent on the inspection not turning up anything too alarming.

Which it won't.

My next call is to Ron's business manager, Steve Martucci.

When he answers, I infuse my voice with warmth, tinged with an edge of flirtation. "Hey Steve, it's Meg Williams, how are you?"

"Meg!" Steve's been handling Ron's business affairs for over thirty years. "Congratulations on the new deal. You and Ron are turning into quite a team."

"I'm thrilled to finally find him something," I say. "He's a lot of work."

Steve laughs and says, "Don't I know it. What can I do for you?"

"I just want to touch base and let you know what we're going to need from you to get the Mandeville Canyon property into escrow." I soften my voice. "Although I know you're a pro and have done this a thousand times before."

Steve chuckles and says, "Two thousand times. But you're not so bad yourself," he says. "The Canyon Drive transaction was one of the smoothest I've ever seen. You're a huge improvement over Ron's last agent, Mick. I never liked him."

I think back to the afternoon shortly after I'd arrived in Los Angeles and the three properties Mick had shown me. The way he stood too close, waiting for a signal that I might be open to more. When I gave it, he didn't hesitate. "I'm so glad someone finally reported him. Thankfully, not all men are like that."

My allusion is clear—Steve is one of the good guys. And like most people, he will do everything he can to live up to that impression. "What escrow company are you guys using this time?" he asks.

I've done my research on all the different escrow companies Ron has used over the years and have selected one that will be familiar but not recent. "Orange Coast," I tell him.

After an offer has been accepted, the buyer will get an email from the escrow officer saying *Congratulations on your new home!* In that email will be a secure link to escrow and wiring instructions.

"You should get an email from the escrow officer within the hour, with the link to transfer funds," I say. "I've made sure they're ready to send the escrow docs and preliminary title report as well, since our timeline is so tight. We'll need the usual 3 percent of the purchase price as a deposit, and as soon as we get through the inspection, I'll get you a firm closing date." I've only closed two deals in the entirety of my career, but even to my ears, I sound like a pro.

I hang up the phone, a bubble of joy dancing inside of me. This is what years of hard work can get you, if you stay focused and dedicated to your craft. I wander into the kitchen to fix myself a sandwich and eat standing at the kitchen counter, staring into the backyard—a flat patch of grass, tended by a gardener who comes once a week, paid for by a landlord I've never met. A fire pit sits in the back corner, the cover dusted with pollen and dry bird droppings, four unused chairs gathered around.

Shrieks of laughter and then the splash of someone jumping into a pool float over the fence from next door, pulling me back to the task at hand. I dump the remains of my sandwich in the trash and return to my computer, my mind mapping out the next two weeks. If all goes well, by the time early voting starts, there will be no way for Ron to extract himself.

But first, I need to put together an inspection report that will back up what I've already told Ron, and I'll need to start packing. Once again, I'll be leaving almost everything behind. I scan the room, trying to imagine what it'll feel like after I'm gone. With everything left just as it is, for Kat to uncover.

# KAT

October

"Come visit. You have the time," Jenna says.

"I can't afford it." I push my earbuds firmly into my ears and walk along the bike path that cuts through the beach. I'd parked in a lot in Santa Monica and headed north, needing to feel the wind and sun wash away my frustration.

"All you have to do is buy a plane ticket. Once you're here, you won't have to pay for anything."

The bike path is empty at nine in the morning on a Tuesday, only the occasional cyclist passing by in a flash—on me and then gone again. The pounding surf beats a rhythm to my left, the early October sun gentle on my back. "The election is in four weeks. I need to stick around and see this through."

If Jenna thinks I'm wasting my time on a story that's slipped beyond my grasp, she doesn't say so, and I'm grateful. I reach the part of the bike path that lifts up off the sand and hugs the edge of PCH, glancing at the dark tunnel used by beachgoers to pass safely under the busy street, and give it a wide berth. Another road cuts a sharp right off the highway into the Palisades, and my gaze follows it upward where I imagine Meg, tucked away in a house I've never visited, planning the final stages of a scam I won't see coming.

"What do you think she's going to do?" Jenna asks.

"I have no idea. She's locked me out, saying things are slow right now and she doesn't need me."

"You don't believe her?"

I laugh and lean against a metal railing, looking toward the ocean and Point Dume in the hazy distance. "She may have been right about Scott, but she lies about everything else."

"Maybe she figured out who you were."

That's what Scott had wanted me to believe—that Meg had followed me home, stolen our mail, and launched a campaign to steal from us. None of it had been true.

Two seagulls fight over a half-eaten hot dog bun on the sand below me, swooping and pecking each other, tearing the bread to tiny pieces in the process. "I don't think so," I say. "If she did, she wouldn't keep me around at all. But we're back to yoga and lunches, texts and calls. Nothing is different."

But the truth is, there's no way to know for sure.

Jenna's voice comes through the line, gentle and cautious. "If you still want this story, Kat, I know you can get it."

"It's not as simple as that," I say. Everything I thought I wanted had been based on the assumptions of a traumatized young woman who needed to assign responsibility for what happened to her. To look at the chain of events leading up to her rape, find the link connecting *before* to *after*, and then cut it.

I'm ten years older now, and I understand that life isn't linear; cause and effect are often unclear. I still want the story, but at some point over the last several weeks, my motivation has shifted. What I want now is to see Meg succeed.

Jenna's voice pulls me back. "When it's over, call me. Maybe take the trip then. My door is always open."

"Thanks."

I hang up and turn around, the morning sun now directly in my eyes, and I close them, letting the brightness burn everything away.

———————

When I get back to the parking lot, I find Scott leaning against a car I don't recognize, waiting for me. My step falters, but only for a moment.

"Are you following me?" I ask.

He gives a tiny shrug of confirmation. "I need to talk to you."

"Whose car is that?" I ask.

"Rental. Your friend Meg slammed on her brakes, causing me to plow into the back of her car."

My mind flashes back to Meg's bumper, bent inward. "Maybe you shouldn't have been following her, since she hasn't done anything wrong." I unlock my car door and look at him across the roof.

"You don't know that," he says.

"If you had proof, you wouldn't be here. What do you want, Scott?"

"She took that guy to look at a property in Mandeville Canyon yesterday."

A flash of frustration passes through me. Like the horizon line, every time I think I know where Meg is going, she moves farther away from me, an ever-shifting illusion. "So? He's buying a house. She sells them."

"You know that's not true," he says. "I can help you."

"By stealing my notes? Stealing money you know I don't have?"

"Getting your notes back is the only reason you're still standing here

261

talking to me," he says. "Like I said, I've been following her. There's stuff I know that you can use."

"I could use $30,000."

Scott ignores my dig. "Remember how we used to bounce ideas off each other? Brainstorm new leads to follow?" His expression is pleading, and I have to look away. "Tell me you don't miss it."

"I don't miss it."

"If you drop the charges against me, we can work together. I'll do the detective work, and you can write the story you've been chasing for ten years. I can feed you exclusive information from inside the investigation. It could be life-changing for both of us."

I stare at him, the planes of his face so familiar, and wonder if he remembers making that same promise a few weeks ago. "And conveniently make a problem of yours go away," I finally say.

"Maybe," he admits. "But if you don't drop the charges, I'll lose my job and then I'll never be able to pay you back."

I know he believes what he's saying, but I also know he'll never follow through. The money he owes me will be an obligation that will bother him for a little while, until he becomes so accustomed to the weight of it, he won't think about it anymore.

A battered Volvo pulls up next to me, a surfboard strapped to its roof, and I watch an older man get out, a wetsuit unzipped and dangling around his waist. He releases his board from its bindings and locks his car, half jogging toward the water. My mind travels back to Cory Dempsey, the man who started it all, and I wonder what he would say if he could see his former girlfriend now, on the verge of taking down a future state senator.

Scott continues. "You'd have the advantage of department resources—surveillance, computer forensics. If Meg is doing anything online, we'll be able to see it. She's targeting a political figure. We can stop her before she does any more harm."

I want to laugh. The harm has already been done, by Ron. By Scott. "How is it they haven't placed you on leave yet?" I ask. "I filed a report against you over a week ago."

"Right now, I have friends looking out for me," he says. "Paperwork moves slow. But if you don't drop the charges, neither of us will get what we want."

Scott doesn't know what I want anymore.

"Here's my offer," I finally say. "I'll drop the charges, but you need to leave the department. Quit and get some real help."

"You can't be serious."

"Your call." I slide into the driver's seat and back out. Scott stays where he is, watching as I turn right onto PCH. As I blend into the traffic heading south, I hope I've made the right decision.

# MEG

Ron's deposit hits the escrow account without any problems, and in another five days, the rest of the money will transfer—$4 million from the Canyon Drive sale and $3 million from Ron's campaign—and I'll be on my way out of the country.

But first, I have to meet Ron at the Mandeville property with his landscaping guy, Rico. I'd tried to talk him out of it—*the election is four weeks away; focus on winning*—because every trip to the property is a risk. The listing agent would be very surprised to find us there.

I'd given Ron the inspection report, obtained from the company who'd performed the inspection on the property a year ago, tweaking dates and adding details to match our needs—appliances that need to be replaced, new gutters on one of the outbuildings. I deleted some of the bigger issues that caused the prior buyer to drop out—a deteriorating roof, an outdated HVAC system, and dry rot. As far as Ron knows, the property is in good shape.

But today we're going to discuss the idea of regrading the back hillside. Ron had noticed a potential for mudslides and wanted his expert to take a look. We park our cars in a cluster in the front courtyard and slip around the side of the house, walking toward the back.

It's quiet, the sound of nearby traffic on Sunset completely vanished. Just the wind, passing through the trees and down into the canyon. A hawk flies in a slow circle above us, and I try to imagine what it would be like to live here. How peaceful and removed you'd feel, as if you were living in another era.

Ron is excited, likely imagining himself as a twenty-first-century Reagan, all the way down to the checkered shirt and cowboy hat he'll wear on weekends. I try to picture how devastated he'll be to learn that nothing he believed was real.

I chose this property carefully, sidestepping Kat and doing my own research. It took me a month of looking at properties—discarding ones too close to town, ones that were likely to find buyers able or willing to rehab them—before I found Mandeville. What makes it so perfect is its checked-out listing agent and all the invisible issues the house has wrong with it. The ones you can't see, no matter how many times you walk through it.

As Ron and Rico discuss grading and native-plant landscaping, I notice a car entering the property and parking near mine. The sound of their doors slamming catches Ron's attention. "Are you expecting someone?"

No one has visited this property in weeks. I spent hours sitting in the driveway, ready with a story that would explain my presence. *Just pulled in to make a quick call!* Not once did anyone show up. Not the owners, or the caretakers, or the listing agent. Not even a car looking to make a U-turn.

But now, fourteen days before my deadline—the one I set for myself back in Pennsylvania, when I'd dreamed not only of taking Ron's money but of snatching the election from him as well—someone's here to look at a house I'd believed had been all but forgotten.

My mind flies ahead, trying to figure out how to get rid of whoever this is and how to explain their presence to Ron. Backup buyers? People who've made a wrong turn? I click through possibilities, discarding them.

"It's probably Sheila," I finally say. "Another agent who said she'd be in the area with some buying clients and could drop off a set of keys for me. I'll be right back."

Ron nods and turns back to Rico, and I hurry toward the visitors, hoping to waylay them.

As I round the corner of the house, I see a woman I recognize from open houses fiddling with the lockbox while her clients wait. "Hi there," I say. "Can I help you?"

She turns to me and says, "Just taking a look. Don't worry—we'll stay out of your way."

"Can I speak to you for a moment?" I ask her.

We walk a few paces away before I say, "Look, my client is really particular about his privacy." My expression is tense and anxious. "I promised him that we would have the place to ourselves while he brought his contractor over to check out that back hillside."

The agent looks sympathetic. In Los Angeles, the demand for privacy is common among a certain demographic, and agents are used to accommodating their requests.

"We're almost done," I tell her. "Perhaps I could treat you all to lunch, and you could return this afternoon?"

She looks toward her clients, who are peering in the windows and whispering on the porch. "Tell you what," she says. "We have two other properties to see in the area today, so why don't we go look at those and return in an hour. Will that be enough time?"

I nearly hug her, my relief genuine. "Thank you," I breathe. "I owe you. And seriously," I say pulling out my wallet and handing her $200. "Lunch is on me."

She plucks the cash from my hand, not even hesitating, before striding back to her clients and conferring with them. Then they head back to their car. "Thank you so much for understanding," I call out.

Soon, they're driving back down the driveway and turning right, toward Sunset. I breathe out hard, leaning against the side of the house, trying not to imagine what would have happened if she'd refused. If her clients had been on a tighter schedule. If we had arrived a little later and already found them walking a property Ron believes is his.

I push off the wall and head back toward Ron and Rico. "All set?" I ask, desperate to be done and gone.

Ron shakes his head. "Not yet. I want to show Rico the creek, where I'm thinking I'd like to expand the bank on the eastern side."

I follow them, my nerves jangling, watching the time slip by, wondering if we can actually get out of here in an hour unscathed. But after forty-five minutes, we're back in our cars, though I don't relax until we've exited the property and are heading back toward town.

# MEG

October
Two Weeks before the Election

It's time to go.

Kat sits across from me, plates littering the table between us as the restaurant empties. She doesn't know it, but this is our last lunch. Tomorrow, I'll be gone, and Kat will be left to piece together what I've done.

"Any new clients on the horizon?" Kat asks. Still digging. Still hoping to figure it out. She's so much closer than she thinks.

I play with my napkin before telling her a partial truth. "I'm thinking of taking a break from real estate," I say, looking through the window toward the street, where shoppers pass by with bags from expensive boutiques. "Maybe take a vacation. I've been doing this for so long, and it's the same picky clients, the same escrow snafus, the same sellers, trying not to disclose a leak in the basement or noise from the airport.

It's exhausting and it's nonstop. I thought moving home would be the change of scenery I was looking for, but I just can't shake the feeling that I need something different."

Kat studies me, and I wonder if she's finally going to break, asking questions I know she's dying to ask. *How do you do it? Who do you target? What's your plan with Ron?*

But the moment passes.

"You're one of those people who can't ever settle," Kat says instead. "The ones who move around, always looking for home and never finding it."

What a gift it's been, to know that Kat sees me as I really am. "Home disappeared for me the day my mother died. And ever since, I've been chasing the ghost of a feeling. Looking for a reset that would put my life back in order. But at some point, a person has to stop chasing something that doesn't exist and just move on."

I wonder if she can hear what lives between my words. I'm done with the lies, ready to find a place—a community where I can build something for myself—and I wish for just one moment of honesty between the two of us. That I could start from the beginning and tell her all of it. Go back to that rainy afternoon in the internet café when I saw a familiar face and an opportunity.

Before I say something I'll regret, I turn the conversation back to her. "Any updates? Have you heard from Scott?"

Her gaze cuts sideways. "No, and I'm relieved, to be honest."

I take a sip of my lemon water and watch her fiddle with her cutlery, looking everywhere but at me. She's lying. But it doesn't matter. After tomorrow, this will all be over.

I have just a few things left to do—pack, book my flight, make sure everything is set so that tomorrow, I'll be ready to act.

In the morning, Ron's business manager, Steve, will get directions to wire the rest of the money, never suspecting that the smooth sale of

Canyon Drive set this one up so perfectly. It isn't a phishing scam if the person on the other end is expecting the link.

Earlier this week, I posed as Ron's assistant and made several phone calls. Confirming details. Setting the timeline. Drafting a press release, Ron's words from that long ago outing with Kat coming back to haunt him. *Once the media gets ahold of something, it's impossible to walk it back.*

I feel as if I'm a dancer onstage, giving her final performance. My body aches, and I yearn for days where I won't have to twist myself into knots. I've tried on enough identities to know exactly who I want to be. Who I want to remain.

But I'm proud of the work I've done. The creative thinking that has allowed me to get to this moment. It takes a village to raise a first-rate grifter, and the world has no shortage of teachers willing to help me build my skills. To learn how to lie convincingly. To manipulate and obfuscate. To use the power of reflecting their best selves back to them, using their egos as vehicles to take back what they've stolen from others.

Kat throws her napkin on top of her plate and stands. "I'd better get going. I need to run a few errands this afternoon. Buy a new toaster oven, since Scott took ours with him."

I look up, my mind crowded with all the things I cannot say, making it difficult for me to think. My eyes fill with tears, and I quickly drop my sunglasses from the top of my head to hide them.

Kat rummages in her purse for her keys, and when she finds them, she gives me a quick look and says, "Talk tomorrow?"

"Sure thing," I say. I keep my eyes on her as she weaves through the empty tables, and then she's gone. "Goodbye," I say, to no one. The way it always goes. The way it always has to be.

# KAT

October

Meg texts me just after lunch. Can you come over? I need your help with a new transaction I have open with Ron. Another text follows with her address.

I set my half-eaten yogurt on the counter, still in my pajamas even though it's after noon. I'd come home from seeing Scott at the beach the other day and looked up properties in Mandeville Canyon, but nothing popped out at me, and nothing's gone under contract in the area since then.

I can be there in an hour, I text back, but she doesn't respond.

I scramble to throw on clean clothes, forgoing the shower I've been putting off, grab my keys and purse, and am in my car within fifteen minutes.

———

Sun casts the facade of Meg's house almost golden as I approach the front door. This is the first time I've been here, and I'm wondering if

I can break away from our conversation to use the bathroom or get a drink of water, just to take a quick look around.

I knock, but there's no sound of footsteps, so I ring the doorbell and wait.

Still nothing.

I try the knob, which is unlocked, and step into a bright and airy living room filled with a white sectional couch, a low glass and chrome coffee table, and a beautiful ceramic-tiled fireplace. "Meg," I call, but my voice echoes back to me.

I wander into the kitchen, the counters bare and sparkling, and open the fridge, only to see its shelves scrubbed clean, a lone bottle of water in the very back. It's as if I've stepped into a model home, staged to appear as if people live there, but the cupboards and closets are empty.

"Meg?" I peek into the backyard, but there's no sign of her.

Where are you? I text.

In the dining room there's a table with eight chairs tucked around it. In the center is a stack of about twenty spiral-bound notebooks, and on top, an envelope with my name on it.

Inside is a letter and a cashier's check made out to Citibank for $31,125. I stare at it for at least a minute, dumbfounded, before starting to read.

*K—*

*A good story can be seductive. Most people are inclined to believe one rather than examine the evidence piling up in front of them. But what they don't know is that no one is a reliable narrator. Reliable narrators don't exist.*

*Have you ever thought about your name? Kat—a predator stalking her prey, waiting for the right moment to strike. Is that how you thought of yourself, spinning a story about an inheritance, a newly rich woman looking for a way to fill her days?*

I look up from the letter, stunned. Scott had been right after all. Of course Meg wasn't going to fall for my story about a big inheritance— she was the con artist spinning big stories, not me.

*I don't mind that you lied to me. One of the hardest things about doing what I do is the burden of always carrying other people's trust. That I didn't have to carry yours was a gift. But even though you expected my lies, I still regret telling them, and I still regret having to leave this way. But this is how it always ends: me disappearing before anyone is ready to say goodbye. Even me.*

*At times, it's been hard to accept that I would never live a normal life. I would never have a normal relationship or a normal family. But I had something bigger. A life that spanned a continent, meeting people I never would have met otherwise. Of course, I left a lot of confusion and questions in my wake, the people I'd befriended often wondering what—if anything— about our friendship had been real. But each one of them has left an indelible mark on me. I love the movie Casablanca because of Diane in Phoenix. I prefer my sandwich bread toasted thanks to Natasha in Monterey. Coworkers and neighbors who have, for a time, become my community. Who kept me from living in isolation. And among them, I've found some good friends. Perhaps not ones I can stay in touch with, but that doesn't keep me from carrying their kindnesses with me.*

*The lies I tell serve a purpose, tipping karma in the right direction. Returning power to those who have lost it. The difference between justice and revenge comes down to who's telling the story.*

*The notebooks will give you a sense of what I've done and why, because context matters.*

*The men I target—corrupt, selfish, and sometimes dangerous—are everywhere. In every town, in every industry, doing what they do best, taking advantage of others. I no sooner dealt with one when another would crop up, somewhere else. I can see now the price I paid, the cost to my own soul. Because proximity to corruption and greed is like living on top of a nuclear waste site. Eventually it'll seep into your blood and poison you as well.*

*There is more I wish I could tell you, but time is up for me here. So know these three things: First, my affection for you was real. I valued our friendship, and I will carry it with me always. Second, you deserve loyalty from the people you love. Third, and maybe most important—if you know a man's weaknesses, it's easy to press them and get the result you want.*

*Be well, and write this story—or a novel, or whatever the hell you want—with my blessing.*

The notebooks aren't arranged in any particular order. The one on top is from several years ago, and when I open it, the pages are dated at the top, filled with Meg's handwriting. Some entries are lists of things she needed to get done. *Call phone company and get internet set up.* Others are facts about towns, locations, and people. *Marco's car was repossessed last year, start with him. Flagstaff is too small, it's not going to work.* Some entries appear to be more personal—memories of her mother, rationalizations for decisions she made along the way. Impressions of the people she met, the men she dated and what she was able to take from them: $50,000 from a man in Fresno, who'd stolen that money from his dying uncle; $100,000 from another man in Houston, running a Ponzi scheme. The list wasn't nearly as long as I'd imagined it would be, because Meg took the time to research first. To make sure the men she targeted deserved it.

I scan the pages, details jumping out at me. Strategies for how to approach a target. How to gain someone's trust. She even outlines what to do if someone catches on to what she's doing—*Pull them close. Distract them with other things.* I look up, thinking about her mystery buyers, who will likely turn out to be no one special at all. Every lead I followed, every theory I had, was curated and handed to me by Meg.

The next notebook in the stack is her first one, dated over ten years ago. *I was born to be a grifter, though I didn't see it until after I'd been one for some time.* I find an early entry about Ron Ashton, the heartache and anger so vivid on the page, I marvel at how she could have spent so much time with him over the past few months. How much that must have cost her. I hope the payoff is worth it.

My question from a few weeks ago comes back to me: *What does success look like for Meg?* The answer is buried in one of these notebooks.

I dig around until I find the most recent one and read about her return to Los Angeles, positioning herself to meet Veronica. The *killer deal* she and David got on their house was nothing more than an illusion created and executed by Meg, her sole purpose to polish her reputation and be exactly who Ron needed her to be.

Canyon Drive was a legitimate sale, a setup for what would come next—Mandeville Canyon—and a DBA for a company called Orange Coast Escrow. I read a draft of an email to Ron's business manager: Congratulations on your new home! Orange Coast Escrow is excited to work with you. Included in this email is your secure link to escrow and wiring instructions.

I pull out my phone and type in the web address jotted at the top of the page, pulling up a website for Orange Coast Escrow. It has all the usual links—Tools and Resources, Services, and one titled Wire Fraud Warning. Criminals often try to steal your money by pretending to be us. Please call before you wire any funds! Then it lists a phone number.

In a new window, I Google *Orange Coast Escrow*. Two links pop up: the one I just looked at and a second one. I toggle back and forth between them, but they're identical, all the way down to the wire fraud warning. Then I see it—an extra underscore at the very end of the web address I entered from Meg's notebook. And a different phone number. When I dial it, a woman's voice says, "You've reached Orange Coast Escrow. Please press one to speak to an escrow officer." When I press it, my call gets disconnected. I try again, with the same outcome.

Next, I look up the listing agent for the Mandeville Canyon property. "Hi," I say when she answers her phone. "This is Kat, Meg Williams's assistant at Apex Beverly Hills. We were wondering when the Mandeville property went into escrow."

The woman on the other end laughs. "God, I wish it was in escrow. Do you guys have a buyer for me?"

I tell her I'll get back to her and hang up, marveling at the level of skill and planning Meg used. She'd known she would never be able to steal a property from Ron, so she tricked him into believing he'd purchased one instead. One escrow successfully closed so the next one wouldn't be questioned.

I return to Meg's notebook, the pages turning faster and faster as Meg's con finally becomes clear. The no-win situation Meg has created for Ron. An imaginary escrow with a fake escrow company. A DBA under the name of Orange Coast Escrow and a bank account with the same name, both of them opened by Meg back in September. The words *campaign donations* underlined three times. Seven million dollars wired into that account—there, and then gone again. And then I read a draft of a press release that, according to Meg's notes, has supposedly just gone public.

"Oh my god," I say into the empty house. Then I start to laugh.

# MEG

The Uber drops me at Terminal 2 at LAX. I'd returned my Range Rover to the dealer yesterday, told them I was moving out of the country and needed to cancel my lease. *So sorry about that bumper!* As the driver pulls my luggage from the trunk, I check my watch, hoping I can get through security quickly and find a TV.

The place is mobbed with late-afternoon commuters. As I wait in line to pass through the X-ray machine, I imagine Kat arriving at my house and finding what I left for her. Then I think about Ron, dealing with the chaos I've created, and let myself relive the moment I told him what I'd done.

———————

It hadn't been hard to find him. He was where he always was at 3:30 in the afternoon on a weekday, jogging through Santa Monica's Palisades Park. Gravel paths winding through stands of trees, with the cliffs dropping down into the ocean beyond, it was well populated with other runners, parents or nannies pushing strollers, and power walkers deep in conversation. But I knew Ron would come. He tended his figure with the committed energy of an insecure woman creeping up on middle age, using the lull between lunch meetings and cocktail hour to do it.

I steadied myself, having imagined this moment for most of my adult life. For many years, I'd fantasized about Ron in handcuffs, the police raiding his company and closing it down. Ron being prosecuted for fraud. But then I grew up and realized there were two different legal systems in this country—one for wealthy white men like Ron Ashton and another one for everyone else.

I pretended to stretch against a tree until I saw him in the distance, then pushed off and began my slow jog toward him. His eyes lit up with recognition. "Meg," he said as I pulled to a stop. "Just the person I want to talk to. Did you get any of my messages?" he asked. "I need the keys to the Mandeville house. My contractors need to get started if we want it to be ready by election night."

I swiped my forehead and said, "That's not possible."

He looked confused. "Has something happened on the seller's end?"

In all the years I'd been doing this, I never got to stick around and see the instant when realization hits. When misperceptions and assumptions about me crumbled. "There is no house," I told him. "No escrow. The money is gone."

He looked confused, but not panicked yet. "What the hell are you talking about?"

"You didn't buy the Mandeville Canyon house. If you look it up, it's still for sale. If you call the listing agent, she'll tell you they haven't had an offer on it in over a year."

I could see him trying to make sense of my words. "How is that possible?" he asked. "The money was wired to Orange Coast Escrow this morning. Steve confirmed it."

"The money was wired to an account I control, and from there, it was transferred to the Los Angeles Homeless Cooperative. They're a wonderful organization running shelters, providing counseling and medical care. They even hold job fairs." I squinted into the late afternoon sun. "As a major donor, you should consider participating in one."

There was a breath—a moment—when everything hung in the air between us. One second, then two, and then it clicked into place. "That's impossible," he whispered.

I checked my watch. "In about twenty minutes, the story is going to hit. The press release has already been sent to all the major outlets. 'State Senate Hopeful Ron Ashton Donates $7 Million for the Homeless.'" I lowered my voice. "Though we both know not all of it was your money. A good chunk of it belonged to your donors."

People were beginning to recognize Ron. One young man had his cell phone out, and I gestured toward him, saying, "Careful. You're being recorded."

"How could you—"

"You might be asking yourself 'Why the homeless?'" I interrupted. "I'm sure your base will be wondering." I took a breath, cementing the details of this moment in my mind—the afternoon air with just a hint of salt in it. The distant sound of waves crashing on the beach below. "Do you remember a woman named Rosie Williams? You dated her about fifteen years ago."

He looked confused.

"Rosie was my mother," I continued. "In 2004 you lied your way onto the deed of our house—the one I just sold for you. She was terminally

ill, and yet you kicked us out. Do you remember what you told her?"
When he didn't answer, I delivered the words from so long ago. "'There
are winners and losers in life. You're the loser here. Take the loss and be
smarter next time.'"

Ron looked around, suddenly realizing we had an audience as more
people gathered. "That's a lie," he said. "That never happened."

"I think evicting people from your properties is a critical part of your
business model."

I lifted my phone and hit play on the voice memo I had ready.
Ron's voice floated into the air around us. *My dream scenario is to
find something in need of repair—I'm a developer and contractor at
heart—evict the welfare queens and drug addicts, do a quick and cheap
rehab, double the rents, and rent to college students too dumb or drunk
to know better.*

I stopped the recording and said, "The major outlets should be
reporting on your surprise announcement very soon. Your statement
is excellent. 'Many years ago, I took advantage of a family's trust,'" I
recited from memory. "'My actions then have always haunted me, and
I've regretted them for years. My donation to the Los Angeles Homeless
Cooperative is my way of repairing that mistake.'"

Ron's face twisted into a sneer. "What you've done is illegal. You stole
my money."

I gave a tiny shrug. "The problem is, you stole it first. Which puts
you in a real bind," I said. "If you let the donation stand, you'll lose
your base and, likely, the election. I suppose you could report the
money as stolen, claim that it was given to the homeless against your
wishes, but how will you explain your business manager transferring
campaign money into an escrow account?" I decided to give him one
final nudge. "When police investigate someone, I imagine they'll
want to look at all their financials. Personal and business. Probably
going back many years." I stepped back, signaling the end of our

conversation. "It's been a pleasure working with you," I said. "Best of luck on the election."

I turned and began jogging up a side street. A glance over my shoulder showed Ron, standing there in his bright white running shoes and overpriced track suit, soft and sagging around the edges.

I sent the text to Kat right after I ordered an Uber to the airport. Can you come over? I need your help with a new transaction I have open with Ron.

Before she could respond, I turned my phone off. I knew she'd come.

―――――――――

Once I'm through security, I pull my carry-on behind me and pass gates for Las Vegas and Nashville. I see two women seated next to each other in the airport bar, heads bent together, and I wonder who they are to each other. What plan they're cooking up. One of my mother's rules pops into my head at the sight of them.

*Two women working together are a force to be reckoned with.*

I locate my gate—a flight to Houston, connecting from there to Costa Rica—and find a place to sit. Across from me, an old woman knits, her yarn spooling out of a bag at her feet. I watch as her needles click, her fingers deftly winding and tucking, the length of whatever she's making growing, row by row.

But then she ties a knot. Slips the needles out, the square piece complete, and she tucks it all away. I think about the last ten years—row after row, city after city, mark after mark. Ron was the knot, and now it's time to put that part of my life away.

I have a rental house waiting for me—a small bungalow on a hill overlooking the beach. I imagine warm sun, soft sand, and sea salt drying on my skin. Maybe I'll learn to surf, or work in a bar selling drinks to tourists. Or maybe I'll spend my time reading on my porch.

Perhaps one day, I'll read a novel about a female con artist traveling the country, dreaming of the day when she will finally mend her mother's greatest heartache.

# KAT

**October**

By the following morning, every local news outlet is reporting on Ron's enormous and unexpected donation to the Los Angeles Homeless Cooperative. I woke up early, just so I could see newscasters puzzling over it at the top of every hour. I look up from Meg's notebooks to catch the latest update.

"With only two weeks until the election, it's an odd choice for a candidate whose tough position on the homeless was so well publicized," Kent Buckley, *Channel Five Morning News* anchor says.

"I can't imagine his base is very happy about it," his female co-anchor responds. "What do you make of the statement Mr. Ashton made? Any information on the family he's referring to? Has anyone come forward?"

"Nothing as of yet. Mr. Ashton's campaign has declined to comment, and Mr. Ashton himself couldn't be reached." Kent shifts to a different camera, ending the segment. "Stay with News Five for this developing story. Now let's check in with Kristy and the weather."

I lower the volume and turn back to Meg's notebooks. I spent most of the night going through them, reading about cons in cities all across the United States, more detailed than my own missing notes ever could have been. I've got names, locations, old websites that no longer exist. The few calls I've made have been to people happy to discuss Meg, Megan, Melody, or Maggie, depending on where she was and what she was calling herself at the time. I'm so engrossed in what I'm learning that I jump when my phone buzzes with a text from Veronica.

Have you heard from Meg? Do you know where she is?

I think about what must be happening inside Ron's campaign. Three million dollars, donations from supporters all over the state, gone. The chaos when they discovered along with the rest of the world where it landed.

Another text. Let me know ASAP if you hear from her.

A line from Meg's letter comes back to me. *One of the hardest things about what I do is the burden of always carrying other people's trust.* I feel sorry for Veronica, who never had any idea how Meg had manipulated and used her. Who will probably always wonder what happened to her friend.

I don't know where she is, I text back. I went to her house yesterday, but it was empty. She's gone.

Then I pull another notebook from Meg's stack and keep reading.

———————

Two hours later, my mother calls. "Tell me you're writing about this."

I set aside the notebook I've been reading, grateful for a break, though I've been dreading this call. "I'm writing about it," I parrot.

"Was Meg involved? Surely Ron Ashton wouldn't make that donation on his own. Was he coerced? Blackmailed? You have a unique angle here. No one else can write from the perspective you've got."

It's always this way with my mother, her insistence on dragging me along, chasing her dreams instead of my own. "She doesn't appear to have had anything to do with it," I tell her. "All the reports I'm seeing point to some kind of restitution for something that happened a long time ago. But Ron Ashton's not talking to anyone."

"Now's the time to tell her who you are and what you want. You have a relationship with her. Promise to protect her identity in exchange for full access. A story like this will open every door for you."

I look at the notebooks containing everything Meg could possibly tell me. "Meg's gone," I say. "I don't know where she went."

My mother exhales, a sharp sound that carries so much with it—blame, disappointment, impatience—familiar criticisms I've grown to expect. "All that time," she says. "Wasted."

"It wasn't wasted." I think about what Meg gave me. Not just the notebooks, not just the money to cover Scott's debt, but clarity.

I found the pages that outlined her exit from Cory Dempsey's life. An idea, jotted at the bottom of a page. *Call Times re: Nate's involvement.* She couldn't have known that the young reporter who'd answered the phone would do something so foolish. *Context matters.*

Blaming Meg for the lie that put me in Nate's path was just a circumstance of chance, no more useful than blaming a lightning storm for a forest fire. Everything burned to a black pile of ash, until new growth can begin to emerge.

"Now that Scott's not keeping you in Los Angeles, you can relocate. My friend Michael told me he heard about a fact-checker position at the *San Francisco Chronicle.* Work hard and in six months you might finally get back to where you left off all those years ago."

My mother will never change. Never stop yearning for what she lost. But it's not my responsibility to give that to her. "I have to go," I tell her, "but I'll consider it."

After I hang up, I think back to the fundraiser nearly five months ago and what I thought I wanted. *You only get one life—how do you want to live it?*

I have some ideas.

# EPILOGUE—KAT

**December**

I take a final lap around my apartment, now empty. All my furniture has been either sold or donated, my remaining belongings packed in my car. Clothes, photos, laptop, and Meg's notebooks.

When I first started investigating Meg, I thought I knew who I was looking for—a master manipulator, an accomplished liar and chameleon. All the research I've done about con artists depict people with an innate ability to trick and obfuscate to their own advantage.

Meg Williams was all of these things. But she was also so much more.

Unlike most con artists, Meg wasn't a sociopath. She was just another woman exhausted by the way the system seems to always fail us. She targeted corrupt men, skipping over smaller marks, refusing to take advantage of opportunities that might have been an easy win for her. Instead, she focused on people like the professor who plagiarized the work of his female colleague. A nephew stealing his aunt's retirement.

A high school principal and former math teacher who preyed on young girls. An ex-husband who didn't know how to share.

Of course, Meg had choices and options. She could have saved her money and gone to community college, as her friend Cal had wanted her to do. I found Cal, living in Morro Bay with his partner, Robert. When I asked him if he had any words for Meg, he simply said, "I hope she knows how much she was loved."

This seems to be the refrain from most of the people Meg encountered. Not the people she stole from, but the people she befriended along the way, the people who gave her access to her targets. I can't tell you how unusual this is for a con artist. Typically, grifters are nothing more than empty shells, lying and manipulating their way toward whatever end goal they have in mind, leaving friends and neighbors hurt and angry if they're lucky, destitute if they're not. But Meg was different.

"She paid my last semester's tuition," says someone who knew her as Maggie Littleton. This woman, who has asked not to be named, told me a story of how Meg—or Maggie—befriended her at a community college in Spokane, where the two were taking a web design course. Meg worked hard to keep her skills sharp, always learning, always growing. The effort paid off with fake websites, photoshopped magazine features, and photographs. "Maggie used to babysit my kids for free. She knew I was struggling to save enough money for my last semester. When I went to the financial aid office to beg for an extension on my tuition, they told me it had already been paid. Maggie paid it in full, right before she left town. Everything I have—my business, my home—I have because of her."

This is the mark of a true con artist, when the people she leaves behind can know what she's done and still want the best for her.

I seriously considered writing the story. I had no doubt I could pitch it to any major outlet and they'd jump on it—a five-part series, a podcast, a feature—but I couldn't do it. I knew the male gaze would quickly simplify a story about a female con artist down to its most basic parts. As if the most notable thing about Meg was her X chromosomes and not her sharp mind, her incredible wit, her cool-as-steel nerves when boxed into a corner.

I couldn't stop reading her notebooks. Studying them like a map. Seeing something new, some small notation in the margin I'd missed the first time. The more I read, the more I learned. How to relocate and remain mostly off the grid. How to alter your name and create a believable backstory that would stand up to scrutiny. And her Facebook profile and password, printed on the inside cover of journal number three, automatic entry into the many private groups she used to find her targets.

What I held in my hands was an instruction manual for how to do what she did—and how to do it well. Meg Williams, the person I spent ten years dreaming of finding, will still change my life. Just not in the way I thought.

Jenna connected me with a literary agent she knows, and I spoke with her last week. "Your early pages are great! Finish the novel and I'm certain I can sell it," she'd told me.

I stand in the doorway to the office I once shared with Scott, remembering the way we used to work in companionable silence. I worried I'd regret letting him off the hook. But I also didn't want to be the one to ruin his life, even though what he'd done could have ruined mine. Scott isn't like the men Meg targeted. He's not greedy or corrupt; he's just an addict, doing what addicts do. A man who needs help, not revenge. I hear he's doing well in an outpatient treatment center in Nevada, working security at a bank.

Ron Ashton lost the election by a landslide, and when it was revealed that nearly half his contribution to the homeless came from campaign donations, his base abandoned him and the FEC stepped in.

As for Meg, I imagine her somewhere warm. A lush property with a lot of space and even more privacy. The freedom to discover her own heart. Her own dreams.

I spend a lot of time wondering what Meg would think if she knew what I was about to do. Whether that was her intention all along.

*The difference between justice and revenge comes down to who's telling the story.*

I lock the door and slip the keys into a padded envelope addressed to my landlord, dropping it in the outgoing mail tray on my way out.

––––––––––––

It took me less than an hour to find him, living in Portland and working as a regional sales manager of a software company. It'll take me about two days to drive there. I'm sure he meets a lot of people—faces and names blending together, making it difficult for him to remember mine from one night, ten years ago. I've already set up a place to live, utilities included, of course. Through Meg's Facebook profile I've identified several people who might overlap with Nate's new circle of friends.

Thanks to Meg, he'll never see me coming.

READ ON FOR A LOOK AT ANOTHER
NOVEL BY JULIE CLARK

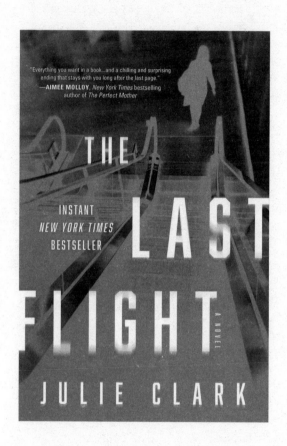

AVAILABLE NOW FROM
SOURCEBOOKS LANDMARK

John F. Kennedy Airport, New York

Tuesday, February 22
The Day of the Crash

*Terminal 4 swarms with people, the smell of wet wool and jet fuel thick around me. I wait for her, just inside the sliding glass doors, the frigid winter wind slamming into me whenever they open, and instead force myself to visualize a balmy Puerto Rican breeze, laced with the scent of hibiscus and sea salt. The soft, accented Spanish swirling around me like a warm bath, blotting out the person I was before.*

*The air outside rumbles as planes lift into the sky, while inside garbled announcements blare over the loudspeaker. Somewhere behind me, an older woman speaks in sharp, staccato Italian. But I don't look away from the curb, my eyes trained on the crowded sidewalk outside the terminal, searching for her, anchoring my belief—and my entire future—on the fact that she will come.*

*I know only three things about her: her name, what she looks like, and that her flight departs this morning. My advantage—she doesn't know anything about me. I fight down panic that I might have missed her somehow.*

*That she might already be gone, and with her, the opportunity for me to slip out of this life and into a new one.*

*People disappear every day. The man standing in line at Starbucks, buying his last cup of coffee before he gets into his car and drives into a new life, leaving behind a family who will always wonder what happened. Or the woman sitting in the last row of a Greyhound bus, staring out the window as the wind blows strands of hair across her face, wiping away a history too heavy to carry. You might be shoulder to shoulder with someone living their last moments as themselves and never know it.*

*But very few people actually stop to consider how difficult it is to truly vanish. The level of detail needed to eliminate even the tiniest trace. Because there's always something. A small thread, a seed of truth, a mistake. It only takes a tiny pinprick of circumstance to unravel it all. A phone call at the moment of departure. A fender bender three blocks before the freeway on-ramp. A canceled flight.*

*A last-minute change of itinerary.*

*Through the plate glass window, fogged with condensation, I see a black town car glide to the curb and I know it's her, even before the door opens and she steps out. When she does, she doesn't say goodbye to whoever is in the back seat with her. Instead, she scurries across the pavement and through the sliding doors, so close her pink cashmere sweater brushes against my arm, soft and inviting. Her shoulders are hunched, as if waiting for the next blow, the next attack. This is a woman who knows how easily a $50,000 rug can shred the skin from her cheek. I let her pass and take a deep breath, exhaling my tension. She's here. I can begin.*

*I lift the strap of my bag over my shoulder and follow, slipping into the security line directly in front of her, knowing that people on the run only look behind them, never ahead. I listen, and wait for my opening.*

*She doesn't know it yet, but soon, she will become one of the vanished. And I will fade, like a wisp of smoke into the sky, and disappear.*

# READING GROUP GUIDE

1. One of the most powerful tools in Meg's arsenal is a familiarity with social media. What do you think she could learn about you from your online presence?

2. Since they both know the other woman is lying about her identity, Meg and Kat also know they shouldn't trust each other. How does their friendship grow despite this?

3. Discuss the role of ego in Meg's cons. How do her targets create openings for her with their own bad behavior?

4. At first, Kat blames Meg for what happened with Nate. When do you think she stopped feeling that way?

5. The greatest downside of Meg's career is the loneliness. Do you think she could have kept in touch with her friends when she

started scamming Cory? How would you feel in her position, moving cross-country every few years and not making any permanent connections?

6.  Meg believes that scamming Phillip to return Celia's cottage was a turning point in her career. How was that job different from the others she had run?

7.  Why does it take Kat so long to recognize that Scott has relapsed? Where would you draw the line between supporting a partner who is trying to overcome an addiction and protecting yourself?

8.  Kat doesn't trust that Scott will be investigated by his colleagues. Is there incentive for police departments to investigate their officers and detectives? What motivations do they have to sweep corruption and violence under the rug?

9.  Meg posits, "The difference between justice and revenge comes down to who's telling the story." What does she mean, and do you agree with her?

10. What's next for Kat and Meg? Do you think Kat will succeed in her new quest? Will Meg really retire from cons?

# A CONVERSATION WITH THE AUTHOR

**What inspired you to write *The Lies I Tell*?**

I'm obsessed with true crime podcasts, and a few years ago, I came across one about a con artist who went to elaborate lengths to lure in his victims, gain their trust, and then steal everything they owned. That particular con artist was a man, but I remember thinking, *What about female con artists? Would people be more inclined to trust them?* From there, my imagination took over.

Like with *The Last Flight*, I didn't want to write a female character who was a true sociopath, so I spent a lot of time trying to figure out a way to write a female con artist with a conscience. A woman who used her intellect and wits to do some good in a world where women often get the short end of the stick.

**Meg and Kat don't trust each other, even as they get closer and closer. What was the most challenging part of writing their relationship?**

The most challenging part was making sure the relationship evolved naturally, while also keeping the timeline relatively short. Kat has the heavy load of her own trauma that keeps her from seeing Meg clearly at first, and I needed her to slowly begin to embrace Meg, despite who she believed Meg to be. The other challenging part was making sure Meg was simmering with her own pent-up rage, while at the same time keeping her sympathetic to the reader. A lot of plates to keep balanced!

**Kat's relationship with Scott is heavily influenced by his gambling addiction. What did you want readers to take from this conflict?**

I want readers to see the complexity and heartache of loving an addict. That they are more than the worst thing they've done. I also want readers to remember that our instincts are almost always right. When something seems off, we don't need to know why; we only need to trust the feeling.

**Meg's philosophy evolves throughout the book from punishment to restoration. Why was it important for you to show this growth?**

All characters need growth, even con artists! I don't really believe that real-world con artists are anything like Meg; however, I don't really view Meg as a true con artist. She's a vigilante, exacting her own brand of justice in a world where too many people have the ability to evade it. It's that quality, I think, that allows us to root for her.

**Meg's greatest disappointment is the transience of her friendships. How do you think you would handle a nomadic and secretive life like hers?**

I'm a homebody at heart, so moving every couple years would be really difficult for me. I like my structures and routines, though I admit a part of it might be thrilling—to relocate and completely reinvent your-self, however many times it takes to get it right. I'd be terrible at the secret-keeping though. I'm pretty sure, very early on, I'd let something slip and the game would be over.

# ACKNOWLEDGMENTS

Publishing a book requires a team of talented, smart people, and I am lucky to have one of the best teams behind me. Dominique Raccah, publisher extraordinaire, everything you do for authors and readers is a gift to the world, and I am forever grateful for your passion and dedication. Shana Drehs, your keen editing eye makes my books so much better. I can't think of a better partner in bringing Meg and Kat to life. Thank you for the many Zoom conversations where we plotted out how to scam people.

My agent, Mollie Glick, is the absolute best champion to have in my corner. Thank you for always having my back—our early morning phone chats are some of my favorite things. The entire team at CAA—Kate Childs, Lola Bellier, Emily Westcott, Gabrielle Fetters—thank you for always being just a phone call or email away. A HUGE thank-you to my film agents, Berni Barta and Jiah Shin, for your enthusiasm and sharp negotiating skills. I'm excited to see what's next!

Thank you to the Sourcebooks marketing and publicity team—Valerie

Pierce, Molly Waxman, Cristina Arreola, Lizzie Lewandowski, Caitlin Lawler, Ashlyn Keil, and Madeleine Brown—for working so hard to sing my praises across the country. And thank you to the formidable sales team—Chris Bauerle, Sean Murray, Brian Grogan, and Margaret Coffee—your vision and talent delivers my books into the hands of booksellers and readers. The creative team of Michelle Mayhall, Kelly Lawler, and Heather VenHuizen made the book sparkle. Much gratitude also goes to Heather Hall and her team for their precision work to polish this book into its final form. Sorry about all those commas.

Thank you to superstar publicist Gretchen Koss. Having you in my corner is like having a secret publicity weapon. Not only are you great at your job; you're a great friend too. And a special thank-you to Gretchen's friend, Annie Bayne, for being willing to read so quickly and offering such important feedback.

Thank you to Nancy Rawlinson, one of the best developmental editors out there. Your early work on this book helped me see things clearly, which made all the difference with such a tight timeline.

Thank you to my foreign team at ILA for selling my books around the world and for being such champions of my work.

Thank you to my writing community, who read *The Lies I Tell* and offered critical feedback: Liz Kay, Aimee Molloy, Kimmery Martin, Amy Mason Doan, Laura Dave, Kimberly McCreight, Amy Meyerson—all of you left your fingerprints on this book, and it is a better book because of you.

I relied on many experts to help me write this book. Thank you to investigative journalist Jessica Luther for helping me flesh out Kat's career and making sure I used all the right terminology. A special thank-you to Claudia Gomez for talking me through the banking side of DBAs. Thank you to Todd Kusserow for his help with DBAs, as well as answering my random questions about fraud detectives, white-collar crime, and general police department details. A huge thank-you to Allison

Gold for all things real estate and for reading an early version to make sure I didn't write myself into a corner. And finally, thank you to Juliet Kingsbury for her eleventh-hour help in nailing down some key DBA rules and regulations. Any errors/deviations from how things really work in California are mine alone.

Thank you to the many booksellers who have been so integral in hand-selling my books! A special shout-out to my two local bookstores—Diesel Brentwood and {Pages}: A Bookstore—your dedication matters so much. Thank you to Pamela Klinger-Horn of Valley Bookseller for your early support (and a special thank-you to Joan Klinger for her sharp eye and witty Post-it reviews). A huge shout-out to Sparta Books in New Jersey for your support and passion for my books!

Thank you to Carol Fitzgerald of *The Book Reporter*—your support and friendship means so much to me.

To all the book influencers on both Facebook and Instagram... There are too many to name you all, but the important work you do to support authors is unparalleled. I am so honored to live inside your universe and interact with you on a daily basis.

Thank you to all the book clubs and readers who have reached out to me—talking to you is the greatest joy of this job. Thank you also to Southwest Florida Reading Festival raffle winner Guy Cincinelli for loaning me your name for one of my characters.

To my family—Mom, Bob, Alex, and Ben—this journey wouldn't be nearly as fun without you. I love you.

# ABOUT THE AUTHOR

Julie Clark is the *New York Times* bestselling author of *The Ones We Choose* and *The Last Flight*, which was also a #1 international bestseller and has been translated into more than twenty languages. She lives in Los Angeles with her family and a goldendoodle with poor impulse control. Visit her online at facebook.com/julieclarkbooks, on Twitter @jclarkab, and on Instagram @julieclarkauthor.

# THE LAST FLIGHT

Two women. Two flights. One last chance to disappear.

You might know a husband like Claire's. Ambitious, admired, with deep pockets. But behind closed doors, he has a temper that burns as bright as his promising political career, and he's not above using his staff to track Claire's every move. What he doesn't know is that Claire has worked for months on a plan to vanish.

A chance meeting in an airport brings her together with a woman who seems equally desperate to flee her life. Together they make a last-minute decision to switch tickets—Claire taking Eva's flight to Oakland, and Eva traveling to Puerto Rico as Claire. But when the Puerto Rico airplane crashes, Claire's options narrow to one impossible choice: assume Eva's identity, and along with it, the secrets Eva fought so hard to keep hidden.

With your back against a wall, would you be brave enough to take the chance you're given?

"You won't be able to put it down."
—People.com

For more Julie Clark, visit:
**sourcebooks.com**